THE HASHTAG KILLER

A. S. FRENCH

NEONOIR BOOKS

1 DOWN IN THE PARK

E van Ripley hated himself.

Apart from that, the things he disliked the most were early starts and physical exercise, yet here he was doing both. But it would be worth it. The sweat dribbled from his forehead, down past the scar on his cheek and settled into the dimple on his chin. When he was a child, all the girls loved that dimple, but nobody had looked at him like that in an age. Evan hated one other thing, and that was being alone. But that wouldn't be for long, not after today.

Dark clouds approached in a group; the smell of electricity in the air as a murmuration of birds swooped low over the park. As a gang of disinterested squirrels stared at him from the tree opposite, he understood why his life had come to this. Twenty years of excessive alcohol, junk food, no exercise, and the occasional dalliance with drugs had led to the doctor's latest warning. If he didn't shape up soon, he wouldn't be doing too much of anything, let alone stumbling through the trees before sensible people had crawled from their beds.

Evan's heart beat faster than he could handle, the blood

pumping through it and filling him to the brim. He placed his fingers on his chest to calm it. He'd been fortunate to get this chance; he couldn't blow it now. Not after what happened before.

'Stay in control,' he whispered to the leaves which hid his bulk. It was lucky he'd got away last time and even greater fortune he'd overheard two of his colleagues talking about the website at the bank where he worked.

'It's called Fit Followers, so it's not for you, chubby.' They laughed at him as they walked away. But at least it was a reaction, an interaction with others which had been missing for most of his life. He'd turned up at work last month with a black eye, and no one had said a word.

Fit Followers. Just the name excited him. He wanted to check it out on his phone but for once was worried his invisibility would vanish and he'd be caught looking at things he shouldn't. So he stayed patient, did his job, and left on time.

The first thing he did when he got home was scrutinise the web pages. It wasn't anything he hadn't seen before, but at least they separated the people into categories: swimming, jogging, tennis, athletics and many others. He'd only been on the site fifteen minutes when the pop-up appeared.

Would you like to know where she is?

He reached for the cross to close the message when it changed.

I can tell you which park she jogs in and when.

A picture accompanied the text, the stunning-looking brunette whose photos he'd downloaded earlier. He hesitated and gazed at the image. A new notification appeared.

Create an account now for free.

Evan's fingers wavered over the mouse, his sweat dripping onto the keyboard. His hand trembled, an itch creeping up his leg and over his chest. The scent of yesterday's pizza wafted out of the kitchen and across the computer screen.

Your anonymity is guaranteed. Your account and personal data cannot be traced.

He dug his fingers into the side of the mouse.

Create an account now for free.

He entered his details and signed up for a month. He wouldn't need longer than that. Evan spent a week going over her information, gazing at the photos, making his plan for when he would meet her; and for what he would do.

And here he was at six-thirty in the morning, legs trembling and heart pounding. She stood only a few feet away. All he had to do was make conversation; they could talk about jogging and fitness. He might ask her for advice. It would be perfect.

As long as he didn't lose control again.

Evan stepped forward, his lips curling up. Then the hands stretched out, fingers clutching at the neck, digging into the throat. He didn't know whether to feel joy or pain.

The nails were neither long nor short, recently manicured and sharp. Blood sprang from the skin and congealed under them; it was warm to the touch. More flowed as the pressure increased. Evan's heart turned into a steam train thundering down a black and white track. He tipped his head up, eyes popping at the sight of the birds swooping and swaying above him. At first, he thought hundreds of starlings performed this dance in the air, but now, as the bouquet of blood overwhelmed his senses, he knew there must be thousands of them, all to observe the apotheosis of his life.

The throat contracted as energy and air disappeared from the flesh. The legs and arms struggled against the pressure, the tongue fighting against the inside of the mouth to shout out, to scream; to call for help which wasn't there. The climax was so close; it was as if Evan floated outside his body, rising to join the birds and peer down at the violent jig below.

Some starlings swooped to the ground, their feet digging into the mud. He thought they were joining him in the dance, but all they did was drag worms up from the dirt. Maggots wriggled around in front of him, fighting against teeth and jaws but failing.

The blood flowed like a river when the clouds broke, and the heavens spat upon the two people writhing and grasping inside the trees. When the body dropped, the birds and the squirrels scattered to the four corners of the park.

There was a smile on Evan's face as nature peppered him and the air hummed and cracked above the branches.

2 FLOWERS IN THE RAIN

If you walk into a room with a fresh lick of paint, then the smell is unavoidable; it's the same at a murder scene: the aroma of death is everywhere. It's as if the soul of the dead occupies that space, the whole of a life lingering behind and stinking of rotting flesh. The rain made it worse, catching the death bouquet in its liquid grasp and showering the aroma far and wide; and the forensic evidence would be washed away. It was my first irritation of the day.

I headed through the uniformed officers protecting the area. Moisture slipped into my eyes as I stared at DI Jack Monroe standing over the corpse. It was a large body, but even from this distance I saw something off about it: the shape was all wrong. Jack gripped onto his stomach in a way I knew his Irritable Bowel Syndrome had kicked in again. I pushed damp strands of hair from my forehead, expecting the cheap black dye to come apart in my hands.

'You don't tie it back in weather like this, Jen? You'll still be beautiful.' He grimaced as he spoke.

The second annoyance of the day: when people call me beautiful. My mother always told me I was pretty, but beautiful was for movie stars, celebrities and models. And my mother was a professional liar.

'Probably the same reason you eat curries when you know they'll wreck your guts.' The nicotine gum stuck to my teeth. I was ready to kill for a cigarette. What was wrong with that body?

Jack tried to frown and smile at the same time. 'It's our shared stubbornness.'

He coughed like an asthmatic volcano. I waited for my partner to empty the contents of his problematic stomach all over the victim. There would be no point in trying to get anything useful out of him when he was in this state. He refused to go to the doctors, and I wouldn't stop harassing him about it. A nervous-looking constable stood two feet away. She had a tattoo of a small bird fluttering on her neck, which I half expected to fly off as I strode towards her. I wondered if standards in the force had declined or increased.

'Are there any witnesses to this?' I raised my voice over Jack's pneumatic coughing. The PC's hand shook as she brought out her notebook. If I could have smiled to ease her fragility, I would have, but my muscle memory didn't go back that far.

'There was a jogger here when it happened, name of Mazz Coe.' The PC pointed to a spot over my shoulder. I turned to see a woman around the same age as me, mid-thirties, but who might have come from another planet. Our witness had a face like a supermodel, all sculpted cheekbones, luxurious dark hair and blue eyes so deep you could swim in them. Her body was to match, though she appeared to be wearing shorts and a top two sizes too small for her Amazonian frame. Jack regained control of his misbehaving lungs and gazed at her.

'I won't tell the wife if you don't, Jack.'

He coughed into his hand and returned his focus to me. I'd never understood what it was with blokes who couldn't take their eyes off any woman they thought good-looking. My father and ex-husband were the same: all incapable of self-control. Was this nature or nurture? Even looks didn't come into it most of the time: it was just women and girls they wouldn't stop leering at. I needed to have that conversation with Abs. That and all the motherly ones I'd forgotten to give her over the years.

Jack gave me one of those expressions which wanted to be a smile but ended up looking like it constipated him. His stomach rumbled like an out-of-control freight train.

'Thanks for nothing, my little flower.' His flower joke became my third hate of a rapidly irritating morning. 'The victim's name is Evan Ripley. It appears to be death by near decapitation.'

We bent down in stereo to inspect the head hanging on by a thread. That's why the body didn't look right. Mr Ripley's face pointed in a direction it shouldn't have. I had a sudden image of the head breaking away, growing a pair of spidery legs and scuttling into the trees. I shook that from my mind and scrutinised the wound.

'This must have been painful.'

'No sign of a murder weapon yet but it might have been an axe or a machete.' Jack clutched onto his stomach as he spoke. It had stopped raining a while ago, but the cold wind continued to float in from the river. And the stink from the water was potent and repugnant.

My legs creaked as I rose. 'It was a garrotte. He was lurking in the bushes when somebody came up behind him, probably with high-tensile wire, and wrapped it around his neck.'

Jack peered at me and shook his head. 'Go on, then, amaze me.'

'This one's simple, Jack, even for you.' I loved to tease him, but he just shrugged his shoulders as I pointed at the victim's clothes. 'Those rose petals between his shirt and shorts came from those bushes behind us.' I nodded at them. 'He was in those when the attack happened and in the struggle tumbled over here to his death.'

Jack bent over the body again, slipped on a crime scene glove and pulled at Ripley's clothes. 'How the hell did all these rose petals get down there?'

It was time to talk to the supermodel in the tight outfit.

'I'd wager our vic was stalking her with his hands down his shorts when he met his grizzly end.' The young PC with the bird tattooed on her neck gave an involuntary guffaw and looked suitably embarrassed. I introduced myself to the witness as she applied the brightest lipstick I'd seen outside of a cabaret.

'Can you tell us what you saw?'

Mazz Coe gathered her emotions and calmed her shaking hands before trailing red across the bottom half of her face. 'I was doing my warm-up before the run when I heard rustling coming from those bushes.' She pointed towards the roses. 'I thought it might be a bird or a squirrel until this fa...' she stopped herself and started again. 'Until this large bloke stumbled from them. He was quite overexcited.'

'What do you mean by that?' I had a good idea but needed her to say it. The PC scribbled down the words as our witness dragged the memory from the safe place she'd stored it.

'He was, you know, in his shorts.' Jack stifled a grin while the tattooed PC's face turned redder than the sun.

'What happened next?'

'Well, he staggered towards me.' Her eyes dripped sadness like a lost puppy or a kid who'd just discovered her friends didn't like her. 'I was about to smack him in the face when something pulled him back into the bushes.'

'Something or someone grabbed him?' Jack asked. The jogger shook her head.

'I never saw who or what it was. I heard some gurgling for about a minute before he stumbled forward and hit the ground. His nut was half hanging from his shoulders. That's when I thought I should ring you people.' It impressed me how detached she appeared. It can't be every day some pervert runs towards you with his head falling off.

'Thank you. A constable will take your statement now.' I focused my attention on our location. A crowd had built up and the rest of the uniforms were keeping them from the crime scene.

Maybe a gang killed him? He was a big bloke, so you'd need somebody with some considerable strength to do this, or there was more than one of them. I waited for the head to roll away.

A woman with a shock of red hair started taking photos, which became the signal for others to follow suit. The crowd had grown to such a size, its over-excited members pushed the constables closer to the body. Somebody caught sight of the head before the uniforms covered Ripley. The screams shook the birds from the trees and prompted digital devices to come to life. The excessive number of cameras and phones flickering into existence added an illumination of fake light, which made Evan Ripley's face look like a poorly constructed Halloween pumpkin. I winced at the thought of this being all over the internet before we even got back to the station. I raised my eyes at Jack.

'Let's have a look at those roses.' Scene of crime officers checked the body and the surrounding ground. I walked to the bushes and peered inside.

'I don't see any footprints, just scuffed up bits of mud.' Jack sounded disappointed.

'They covered their tracks.' The voice was young and female. I turned to see a familiar face wielding a camera spotted with drops of rain.

'What's Cybercrime doing here, Alice? Does our victim have a laptop stuffed up their jumper?'

She snapped a photo of me, and the flash hurt my eyes. 'They're short of crime scene photographers this morning, so I volunteered.' She shook the camera at Jack, my partner's obvious confusion making me smile. 'It's not every day I get to use specialist equipment like this.'

Jack held his hand out to her. 'DI Jack Monroe.'

I grabbed his arm and pulled him towards the roses. 'That's Alice Voss, and we need to concentrate on the ground.'

He wriggled from my grip as Alice's camera snapped away behind us.

'Why here when he died over there?'

'Our killer may have left some fibres on one of these bushes, but I doubt it. This wasn't some chance attack on Ripley. It was planned and premeditated, which means they targeted him.' Not a good sign. Most killers were chaotic, but there was a precision about this which worried me. To be this clean in a public place showed intelligence and forward planning. I preferred the sloppy opportunist murderers.

'What have we got on him?'

Jack checked through the details on his phone. My partner is your classic unflappable copper, so it surprised me when he arched his eyebrows in amazement. 'This is weird.'

'Let me guess. He has a record?'

Jack whistled slowly. 'Yes and no.' He handed me the mobile to read through the information.

'He had web pages about him removed?'

Jack nodded. I called over to Alice.

'Can you check on something for me and access the computers at work?'

Alice hung the camera over her shoulder and got out her phone. 'In the right hands, modern technology can do almost anything.'

'What can you find on Evan Ripley, especially regarding the removal of web pages about him?'

It took her less than a minute to complete the search. 'Well, this is curiouser and curiouser.' She handed me the phone.

Jack stared at me. 'What was our vic trying to hide from the world?'

I gazed at Evan Ripley as he was zipped away. It took two goes before the SOCOs got his head in. Perhaps they should have yanked it off and slipped it into a smaller bag.

'Five years ago he was charged with rape, but the CPS dropped the case.'

Jack let out another long whistle. 'This might not be random, then; it could be revenge?'

A shiver of apprehension crisped my skin as Ripley's body disappeared from the scene. Crimes of passion, or greed, or spontaneous bursts of anger; those I could deal with because the perp would make a mistake eventually. Those actions were never thought through or planned, but with this one, it was calculated in its execution.

A soundless breeze little more than a whisper split the air between us.

'Life is never random, Jack. And neither is murder.'

We left the park together, my mind fixed on one thought.

Evan Ripley had to die so somebody else could live.

3 RUBY

I had a puppy crush on the new girl in the all-night McDonald's. It was the only reason I was lingering near the park so early in the morning. It was the first time in my life unrequited romantic attention had any benefits at all. And what benefits they were. The chance to see a murder victim before the coppers did.

My good fortune was down to the social media app I'd created which collected keywords about crime. It ran across different web platforms and sorted them into categories depending upon importance. Then the results rolled onto the screen according to relevance, frequency and location. I'd considered selling it through the Google or Apple stores, but came up with a better idea. Modern crime reporters didn't need years of training or stupid qualifications, only the ability to get to the scene before anyone else, and then put it into the most compelling words possible. I may have had a shit time at school, but I was always creative. I could write. I just needed a story to spark my career.

And here it was.

The Facebook post got me to the park, and then I used

the location tracker to get me to the right spot. I hated running, but had no choice. The rain was a nuisance, spitting into my face as I ran. As soon as I got through the gates, the police sirens cut through the air. My legs moved, but not how I wanted them to. I was always embarrassed about doing any exercise in public. My body wasn't designed to go at a pace where my feet travelled faster than my brain; after a hundred yards, my lungs felt like they'd been transplanted from a chimney. I grabbed the nearest bench and slumped into the wood. As I did so, the uniforms approached from the opposite direction.

'Fuck!' I wouldn't waste this opportunity. I could still get there before the media did. I controlled my breathing and jogged across the grass. The police secured the area as I got there. Apart from the coppers, all I saw was a woman in the tightest shorts created by man, and they had to have been designed by a bloke, and a strange shape on the floor.

And amongst the blue uniforms stood someone I recognised. My luck was still in.

The smell of jasmine and death hung in the air. The rain stopped as I pulled the hood on my jacket down. I grabbed the pills in my pocket as my contact walked towards me.

'What are you doing here, Ruby?' I loved how the bird tattoo on Grace's neck fluttered when she got flustered. I also loved how Grace looked in her uniform. I preferred her half in and half out of it, but this was good. She appeared authoritative and nervous at the same time, a vulnerability hard to resist.

'What happened here?' I brushed my fingers against Grace's hand and smiled at her.

'I can't tell you anything, Ruby; I could lose my job.' Grace glanced anxiously around. The rest of the police were dealing with the scene, waiting for the detectives to arrive.

'I need one little thing, Grace. It'll help me in my work, and nobody will know it came from you, I promise.' My hand lingered on hers. 'And I'll make it up to you later.'

When I turned fourteen, my mother, in one of her frequent drunken stupors, instructed me in the best ways to attract men. Most of them were crude and useless to me since I had no interest in the opposite sex, but I used one of those techniques now, curling my top lip while running my tongue across it. It always felt funny but got the required results.

Grace leant over the taped area and whispered to me.

'The victim's name is Evan Ripley; that's all I know.'

'What happened to him?' Unknown to Grace, I was recording the conversation on my phone. If I wanted to be an internet journalist, I needed to keep a record of my sources.

Grace's face turned into an unhealthy-looking cabbage colour.

'Somebody nearly chopped his head off,' she said before walking away.

I couldn't believe my good fortune. Outside of disastrous attempts at home cooking, there was only one reason people got their heads severed.

Perhaps it was a terrorist attack. What a story that would make. Extremism strikes in a local park, only yards from a children's play area. I scanned the space. There was no playground, but that didn't matter. Heightened factualisation, that's what I called it.

More coppers arrived, the forensic people and the brains who would try to solve the crime, some dour-looking woman and a smartly dressed bloke grabbing at his stomach.

And the public had appeared in droves. They pushed against me as the uniforms tried to move us back. I removed my phone for some photos. I wasn't close enough to get pictures of the fatality, but I got what I needed to illustrate the post I'd write. I had the hook to the story: possible terrorist attack in Adams Park. Now to get something about the victim.

I started the internet search on the phone as I left the park. The Google request for the removal of pages popped up as I stepped into the underground and lost the signal. I hated travelling on the Tube at the best of times, but it was even worse during rush hour. People pushing up against me, mainly men, and it was obvious some of them tried to grab a feel. If there were more room, I'd cause a fuss, but it was always too crowded. So I put up with it and channelled my anger into my work. Apart from that one time I scratched a bloke's nose, and he bawled like a baby.

This morning it was like sardines in a lift, with bony arms squashed against my ribs and the stink of sweat and halitosis everywhere. It was only three stops, but I was so stressed by the end of it I didn't recheck my phone until I got in the house. My mother would be safely ensconced in the betting shop, which meant I'd missed her daily rant about how useless I was. But I understood how it would go. Experience had taught me well.

'If you leave school with no qualifications and no friends, you'll get nowhere in life.' The irony of my mother's words, a barely literate woman who alienated everyone she met, was lost on her 'You're just like your father, Ruby.'

I had no idea what he was like since he buggered off before I was born. If only he'd taken my mother with him. I put the kettle on as I went back to my search for everything about Evan Ripley.

'What did you want to hide from the world?'

I'd find the removed pages eventually, once I activated the hacking tools on the laptop. Nothing stayed secret on the internet, even deleted files. I found the app I needed and set it running in the background. The Google search had finished by then, showing a new result at the top of the list, and it annoyed me.

'Fuck! Have the police released the details already?'

No, it was too soon for that. Perhaps some other journalist was at the scene this morning. I kicked myself for taking the Tube and not finding a café close by and uploading the post there and then. But there was no story, really, just another dead bloke in a London park; something about as common as coke-headed D-list celebs cheating on their partners. The terrorist thing was a stretch.

The new link had two hashtags in it.

#justiceforall #evanripley

That was it. Posted sixty seconds ago by somebody called Justice For All. The hacked search finished as I pondered what it meant. I scanned the web pages Evan Ripley was desperate to erase from history. They made for interesting reading. Not only did I know the story to write, but I coined a name for the killer. I uploaded it within thirty minutes and a smile crept across my face as I fell asleep.

A SWEET DREAM about Emily Watson had me in its thrall when thick fingers shook me awake. Bloodshot eyes and the stink of booze hovered over me.

'Did you have a blackout again?' The voice sounded like nails scratching against glass. Mother peered at me like an emaciated vampire dredged up from some black and white horror movie; the only colour in her face being those fiery red pupils. I slapped her hand from my shoulder, my twitching fingers rubbing the sleep from my eyes. The computer hummed a lullaby and warmed my lap. I closed the lid; I didn't want her seeing what I'd written.

'I haven't had an episode for ages. Everything's been fine since I got those pills.' The illegal medication I purchased off the internet. Well, not illegal, but not supposed to be used for my symptoms and diagnosis.

Isabel Vasquez sneered at me and lit a cigarette. If I thought of her as someone sharing my surname and not my mother, I hoped it would make me feel better. But it rarely did.

'You must still be dreaming, child; you had one earlier.'

'What?' My hand slipped from the keyboard.

'You flaked out at two o'clock this morning.' The woman who'd spent twenty years masquerading as a parent was enjoying herself. My pain was one of the few things in life which gave her pleasure. I knew this because she liked to remind me of it daily. I could never fathom out why she enjoyed tormenting me so much.

'I left you to it; didn't want you attacking me again in your madness.' She let that insult sink in. I blacked out sometimes because of stress; there was nothing else to it. 'When I came home at four, you'd gone.' We glared at each other like mirror images separated by three decades.

I couldn't remember anything between going to bed at midnight and getting to the fast-food joint, with no memory of how I got there.

'I can't have blacked out; I took my pills.' I removed the bottle from my pocket and gazed at it. Did I take them before falling asleep?

'Maybe you're just like me after all, kid.' Mother let out

a low, annoying laugh. 'You never know what you're doing or why.' The yellow of her teeth shone thick with an aroma of sulphur.

'Go away, Mother.' I dug my nails into my palms.

'You know why there's something wrong with you, don't ya?' Her hoot made my guts hurt. I didn't want to hear this again, not now.

'I don't care, Mother.'

She coughed phlegm onto the floor. 'You don't care what he did to me; what your father did to you?' I'd heard this a thousand times before, and it got worse on each hearing. 'You're not bothered he punched me in the stomach when I was six months pregnant. That's why you're not right in the head.'

'I don't care, Mother.' I wanted to shut it all out, to have a life without this constant hammering about a past I had no control over. All that mattered was what I did now.

'You would if I told you about what he did; things much worse than punching a pregnant woman in the belly.' She moved from the bed, her lopsided body dangling near the door like a marionette hanging in the air: if only I could pull those strings away from me. An angry, ringing bell banged against the insides of my skull.

'Leave me alone, Mother.'

That would have been too easy for her. She was on a roll now, here in a rare lucid moment between last night's drink and the next one.

'You've always been trouble, Ruby Vasquez.' She hated the surname her errant husband had foisted upon her. I liked it; it was the only thing about my family I did. 'I nearly died giving birth to you, and you've caused me nothing but pain ever since.'

I refused to get angry in front of her. 'Go away.'

'You scared all my friends away, with that temper of yours and your fits.' The old woman raised her painfully thin arms to continue her chastisement as I closed my ears and mind to her. I had to escape from this house and live somewhere else.

'You're trying to wind me up again.' I leapt from the bed, my hand on her raggedy shoulder, and pushed my mother out of the room. I slammed the door shut. My heart thumped against my chest as if something was desperate to burst through my ribcage.

'Forget this and focus on your work.'

I returned to the computer and the blog I'd posted earlier. My jaw hit the floor as my eyeballs screwed up to the ceiling. The responses were amazing, hits and reposts in the hundreds.

Glad he died.

Dirty rapist.

He got what he deserved.

On and on they went. The occasional poster lamented the callousness of the others, but they were mainly happy Evan Ripley was dead.

And the name I'd given the murderer was all over social media and the mainstream news.

The Hashtag Killer would make me famous.

4 JUSTICE

When the phone rang, I was staring at the computer, plotting the deaths of many people. Imagine my surprise when I answered it, and the caller tried to sell me insurance.

'Go on,' I said down the line. They rambled on, but I didn't listen. It fuelled my anger, ready for Ripley. 'I know where you live.' I put the phone down.

I was ready then.

Evan Ripley, a slug in a meat suit. My fingers trembled a little as I imagined the events to come. How strange and capricious our minds are; how deluded we must be to purport to be in control of them, to think we have evolved past the fear. But it was the fear of failure which drove me now.

My thoughts kept me awake all night. Hunger gnawed at my insides, and at two in the morning, I slipped away from the computer and headed into the kitchen. I opened the fridge and stared at the multi-cultural array inside: chicken shawarma and falafel pita sharing the shelf with Nigerian tomato stew, while around them were German pumper-

nickel, lupini beans, Italian speck and pancetta, halloumi, and feta. If the country were as well behaved and integrated as the regular contents of my stomach, we'd all be living in a haze of peace and prosperity instead of the divided dystopian shit imposed upon us by a minority of ideological ignoramuses. I dropped some cheese into the stew and washed it down with a cheap bottle of white wine from Tesco.

I prefer not to use any of the mainstream supermarkets; you meet the most uncouth people in those places. Only yesterday a woman wearing a one-piece pyjama suit looking like Frosty the Tiger sidled up to me at the fruit and vegetable section. She caressed some ripe bananas wholly inappropriately as I scuttled off with my trolley in the opposite direction.

From an early age, I'd had the belief instilled in me by my parents it was our sacred duty to support our local businesses, and I'd tried to do that ever since. Globalisation was only useful if it encouraged the creation of independent commercial enterprises. Giant multinational corporations who paid less tax than me were a blight on the world.

Once my local convenience store closed down, I had no choice but to shop in such pantheons to capitalism run riot. A lovely Pakistani couple had owned it for the last ten years, but a declining economy and rising intolerance had driven them away. If my workload wasn't already too large to handle, I'd considered adding vocal bigots to my to-do list. It warmed my soul as I sipped at the soup. The broth pushed against my chest and ignited the sparks in my brain. It also meant I had no chance of getting any sleep.

Ripley, Ripley, Ripley. I tried not to focus on him too much. It could prove too distracting at the most significant point. Instead, I switched my attention to two hours of Seinfeld episodes, fifty pages of the latest Dan Brown novel and another listen to that Lou Reed album everyone hated. I spent the last hour before the countdown using the gym I'd built in the house. I hate exercise, but it's a necessity. Just like most things.

I did one last check on his messages, then made the preparations for the park. My lack of nerves surprised me. There'd been plenty of them during my years of planning, but now, on the brink of a new beginning, nothing worried me.

A FLOOD of euphoria washed over me after the event. The disconnect I'd felt with the world had vanished. Looking back at me in the mirror was me. This had rarely happened for most of my life. I don't remember at what age it started, but there came the point when I disappeared from my existence. I was a ghost, or a vampire, a doppelgänger, a simulacrum, a replicant, even a golem.

But not now; now I was alive again. Ripley's life had fled from him and into me. It was like recharging a car battery. I'd had no sleep for twenty-four hours, but the tiredness had evaporated like milk left out in the sun. I went back to the fridge and devoured half of its bare contents. I had to be at work in an hour, but it didn't matter.

It's a thin line between life and death. Many people who end up on the autopsy table thought it would be just another day. Evan Ripley woke up with terrible ideas scrolling through his skull, but he never would have guessed he wouldn't make it till lunchtime.

I fell into the photographs again, washing my mind in the sight of his head about to pop from his shoulders. We're programmed to fear death, but there are worse things in life than the idea we'll never wake again. The image of the skin hanging from his neck made me hungry once more. It was a curious sensation, to peer at a photo of rotting human flesh and get a craving for food.

I stuffed the chicken shawarma into my face and turned the TV on. It was too early for Ripley to be on the news. It was annoying, but expected. Patience was a virtue, and now more than ever I needed to be virtuous. The grease stuck to my fingers, adding warmth to my skin. I wiped them on my legs and reached for the laptop. It didn't matter it hadn't hit the news yet; there was one last thing to do on the internet.

I rerouted the connection and found the right account. Social media was a hive of activity at every time of the day. It was the great progress of modern living that its digital tentacles reached across the whole of the globe and into every nook and cranny of humanity. The hashtags slipped from the keys with ease.

#justiceforall #evanripley

I watched them do their work before heading into the shower.

By the time I left the house, it was a brand new world we lived in.

A world of justice.

5 JEN

Detective Chief Inspector Merson was the senior investigating officer on the case. She put together a Murder Investigation Team in the main briefing room. Sandra Merson was not an easy person to get along with. She prowled every place as if there was a big sign around her neck with the words FUCK OFF scrawled on it. It made constructive interactions with her underlings somewhat challenging. DCI Merson was also twelve months away from retirement, meaning she was uninterested in any work which came her way. Which is why she'd handed this presentation over to me.

'At around six-thirty this morning, May 2nd, thirty-five-year-old Evan Ripley was murdered in Adams Park. Forensics tell me the murder weapon, still to be found, was likely steel wire. This was used as a garrotte which severed seventy-five per cent of the victim's head from the torso.' The crime scene photos were laid out in neat rows on the screen behind me.

'You'll find copies of these on the table and in the shared case file on the computer. We're still waiting on the autopsy report. Five years ago, Evan Ripley was charged with raping one of his colleagues in Newcastle. The CPS dropped the case because of evidence not released to the defence by the prosecution.

'Ten minutes ago, more information came to light about the murder.' I changed the display again. 'This was posted online less than an hour after the discovery of the body.'

Hashtag killer strikes in London park.

'You can read the whole thing later, but this internet journalist, Ruby Vasquez, has our victim's name and personal history, including the rape allegations, with photos of him and images from the park. She also has a link to a tweet from this morning with Ripley's name and the hashtag #justiceforall. Miss Vasquez is claiming we have a vigilante killer on our hands.'

The term vigilante brought an audible moan around the room.

'We need to contact Newcastle police and arrange an interview with the alleged rape victim. I need Cybercrime to go through Ripley's electronic devices and find out what you can about that tweet and who posted it. Uniforms should speak with Ruby Vasquez. Officers are still canvassing the area and checking for any CCTV footage. We'll come back here in three hours for an update.'

DCI Merson nodded at me. That was her work done; now it was down to Jack and me to get this solved as soon as possible.

My partner and I returned to our desks. I searched through the documents on the computer and found the taped interviews with Ripley. He'd put on weight in the last five years, but even then he was a big bloke. He smiled all the way through, confident it was only his word against hers. But she had bruises on her head and the rest of her body. And the witnesses who'd said she was in no state to give consent. It should have been enough to take it to trial, but then the defence discovered the text message the police had withheld from the case files. I switched the video off. Fifteen years of experience as a copper told me he was guilty, but he'd walked away and ruined Debbie Swift's life. I glanced over at Jack.

'Have you gone through the Newcastle file?'

'Yes. It makes for grim but familiar reading.'

'Do you think somebody close to Debbie Swift waited five years to get revenge; a family member or friend?'

'It's possible. Perhaps she did it. I wouldn't blame her.' Jack came from the old school of justice, where it was an eye for an eye. 'You've read about her brother?'

Not long after the case collapsed, Kyle Swift posted vague threats about retribution on Facebook.

'Can you arrange for Newcastle to interview her again and see if they know what the brother's been up to?'

Jack reached for the phone while I focused on the bit of evidence which had taken us all by surprise: the internet post. I logged into my personal Twitter account and searched for the hashtag #justiceforall. Someone only posted it a few hours ago, but already it headed the top trending tweets on the social media platform. Thirty thousand retweets, fifty thousand likes. Some comments and replies made for ugly reading, with so many gloating at Ripley's death and cheering on the person now known as the Hashtag Killer.

I hated it when the media gave them headline-friendly names. It only encouraged them more.

'Newcastle are following through with our requests.' Jack put the phone down as I browsed Twitter. I clicked on the original poster's account, finding no personal information or other tweets. Cybercrime might discover something, but it seemed unlikely. Whoever had planned it was too methodical to make such a silly mistake as leaving an online trail leading right back to them.

I closed the web browser. 'Have you seen the shit storm this has created on the internet?'

'Aye, it looks like our killer is the toast of the digital world. Can't say I'm surprised.' Jack threw a piece of gum into his mouth and chewed on it as if it was his first meal of the day. As soon as I thought of food, my stomach groaned. I ignored it and turned to the website which had broken the story, *Ruby Vasquez Investigates*. The blog page had as many comments, likes and links as the #justiceforall hashtag. And the remarks followed a similar pattern: unbridled joy at Evan Ripley's murder.

'This so-called internet journalist, Ruby Vasquez, had our victim's name not long after we did. Then she dug up Ripley's web history, including the rape allegations, before stitching them all together into this story. She even has some blurry photographs from the crime scene.' I didn't have much time for traditional journalists, but these online kids pretending to be investigators were ridiculous.

'It's increased her popularity,' Jack replied. I searched through the rest of the site.

'She's only posted two other pieces since the blog went live, both of them about harassment on the Tube and how it's overrun with perverts.'

'She's got a point,' Jack said. 'I'm sure most of the blokes using the underground only use it to glare at women.'

'You glare with your eyes, Jack, not your hands.'

I skimmed the rest of the pages, looking for information about the owner. All I found was an email address. I opened a new browser and started a search for Ruby Vasquez, settling on a YouTube account for *Ruby V Rant*. A young woman slid into view and talked calmly and assuredly about toxic masculinity. I paused the clip and turned to Jack.

'Have the uniforms gone to Ruby Vasquez's house?'

Jack nodded. 'They should be there now; why?'

'Tell them to bring her in for questioning. I think Ms Vasquez may know more about this morning's murder than she let on in her blog piece.' I moved the screen around. Jack stared at the frozen image of the young woman with a shock of red hair.

'She got to the park before we did. That's some coincidence.'

I believed in coincidences much like I believed in unicorns, ghosts and the inherent generosity of the wealthy and privileged. I combed through the police database for any records for Ruby Vasquez. The only ones we had were from twenty years ago. Domestic violence recorded at the same address Ruby lived at. 'She doesn't live near the park, so why was she there today?'

I waited for Jack to get the same information on his screen. 'Maybe she went there for a jog.'

'More likely she was going to work.'

'Work?' Jack arched his eyebrows in mock surprise.

'Like the early bird, journalists need to be out before their competitors if they want to catch the worm. Perhaps she killed him so she could write this story?'

Jack's sneer was unattractive. 'People have done a lot worse for fame and fortune.'

Ruby Vasquez didn't look tall enough or strong enough to decapitate someone the size of Evan Ripley, but I wasn't ruling anything out. I moved past the Vasquez information and opened the personal documents we had on Ripley.

'Thirty-five at the time of death, only one living relative: his eighty-six-year-old mother who's been in a care home since he put her there last year. What's the likelihood a woman in her eighties paid for somebody to kill her son?'

Jack leant back in his chair and considered the question.

'There was that pensioner who shot her kid because he was sending her into residential care. Shot him with his illegal firearm no less.'

'It's not quite the same as squeezing someone's head from their shoulders, is it?' The grumbling in my gut got worse and interfered with my ability to think. As I considered what to eat for lunch, my phone vibrated on the table. I picked it up and grimaced when I recognised the number.

Abigail was in trouble again.

'Detective Inspector Flowers,' I said into the screen.

'Ms Flowers, this is Doreen, the Receptionist from Abigail's school.'

I froze, unable to contemplate what might have happened. 'What's wrong?'

Frost travelled down the line and into my cheek. 'Abigail hasn't attended her classes today, and we wondered if she was ill. You should have informed the school if that was the case.' She had enough ice in her voice to sink the *Titanic*.

'No, Doreen; Abigail seemed fine when I left this morning.' A hollow sensation nothing to do with hunger spun around inside me. Was Abs okay when I rushed from the house to go to the park? Was she even out of bed? I'd been in too much of a hurry to check behind that locked door.

'I'm sure I don't need to tell you, Ms Flowers, as an Officer of the Law how important it is for children to have regular attendance at school.' She stretched out the word law, so it sounded longer than the rest of the sentence.

'I'm sure I don't need to tell you, Doreen, how important it is for children to feel safe at school.' I spat the words out, wishing I could reach down the line and throttle the annoying woman. The sight of Evan Ripley's corpse on the computer screen brought me back to my senses. Doreen appeared not to have noticed the invective.

'Abigail has had too many unexplained absences this year, Ms Flowers, so we have no choice but to pursue a course of action. I'll be in touch within the next twenty-four hours to arrange a meeting with the school welfare officer at your earliest convenience. You and Abigail will both be expected to attend. Good day.' With that, the line went dead. How I wished for the days before mobile phones, when there were only landlines, and you could smash the cheap plastic against the wall when you were pissed off. Jack must have noticed my annoyance.

'Problems?'

I didn't want to talk about it, but he was the closest thing I had to a friend and the only one I'd spoken to about Abigail's situation.

'Abigail missed school today. Again.'

Jack left his desk and walked over to me.

'They never found out who sent her those messages?'

I gritted my teeth and let the anger simmer.

'I don't think they even tried. None of it was in school time so it could have been anybody doing it.'

'How do you know it's some of our children?' Doreen, the Ice Queen, had said when I'd told the school about the bullying which had escalated into taunts for Abs to kill herself.

'Because my daughter told me so.' I'd screamed the information so loud in the school office some other parents stared at me when I left. So Abigail had become a virtual recluse for the last month, not only avoiding school but hardly leaving the house. And considering how much time I spent working, the two of us were like ships passing in the night.

'I'm sure you've been a big comfort to her,' Jack said. I wasn't sure I had, wasn't sure I'd taken the whole thing as seriously as I should have. After all, it was only emails and online posts. I'd told Abs to ignore them and keep off the internet.

'They're only words', that's what I'd said to my impressionable teenage daughter. I scrolled through the files on the computer screen again, finding the documents from Newcastle. I read the statements Debbie Swift had given after the attack, pausing halfway down the first one, my eyes settling on the middle paragraph.

When we were on our own in the office, he'd always leer at me and make crude comments, sexual suggestions, that sort of thing. I knew it was a waste of time reporting them because nobody would take me seriously. They were only words.'

I checked the time and got my coat from the chair.

'Jack, can you collate everything for me and push the briefing back an hour? I need to go home and speak to Abigail.'

'Of course, Jen. Do you want someone to come with you?'

'Thanks, but I'll be okay.'

Serial killers, terrorists, and rapists didn't worry me; but the things hidden inside a thirteen-year-old girl's mind did.

6 RUBY'S HEALTH

I stared at the bottle of pills in my hand. The drugs rattled around inside the plastic container like the thoughts bouncing through my skull. My last encounter at the doctors wasn't one to inspire confidence in the medical profession.

The doctor didn't look up from the computer screen, an infrequent wave of his finger being the only sign he knew I was sitting there. While I waited, I studied those fingers, those bony appendages covered with too much hair and dirt around the nails. They seemed far too unclean to belong to a health service professional. In that white overall, he might have been a confused baker who'd wandered into the wrong building. There was an aroma in the room of fresh bread and croissants. Or perhaps it existed only in my head. I sighed like a locomotive to attract his attention. He pushed the screen to one side and gazed at me as if I was disturbing his sleep.

'My colleagues diagnosed you as suffering from the occasional psychogenic blackout.'

It sounded like an accusation, not a statement of

empathy.

'Initially, they thought I was epileptic, but that changed once I left school. My last doctor said the blackouts would probably stop then because I would be in a stress-free environment.'

Stress-free living with my mother and trying to find work.

'But they didn't?'

'No. I need something to control them. Do you have that?'

He didn't. Instead, he lectured me on my alcohol intake, even though I told him I was teetotal. The whiff of booze on my clothes must have made him think otherwise.

So I bought some Zarontin online and had used it for the last couple of years. I shook the tube again.

'Did I take you last night? Did we have a date?' I should count them, really, and keep a record of what I'm taking and when. But I didn't want to study the condition that much. It seemed best to ignore it and concentrate on my life.

I peered at my reflection in the computer screen. Mirrors were my mortal enemy, always reflecting a part of me which made me unhappy. The digital display glowed dark enough for me to imagine someone prettier staring back. Did people ever stare into the mirror, I wondered, and desire to be anybody other than who they were? Did they gaze at the many visual examples in the world which told us this is what perfection is, told us this is what beauty means, and then despair when they didn't measure up? Would it matter when the one person who raised you spent every day hammering into you how ugly you are? Did that ugliness come because something was wrong inside me? Enjoying the death of another was surely a prime example of internal ugliness.

'Malice makes the woman,' I'd whisper to Mother once she finished her daily rant at me. I could shout it at her, it would make no difference.

There were times growing up when I felt I would die of isolation. Mother would always die for a fag or a pint, my teachers were dying not to be teachers, and the kids at school were dying to be adults. But twenty years of loneliness meant I was dying not to wake up. I thought it would go away with my first relationship, but that human contact only provided a brief fluttering of the heart and the sporadic electrical surge of sexual pleasure.

What was the point of me? Mother said I was a blight on human existence, especially her own. In twenty years, I'd contributed nothing to the world apart from a few notes in the mountainous files of the NHS describing how I liked to fall asleep when I wasn't tired. Maybe liked wasn't the proper description. If I disappeared from the planet, would anyone notice? Before Ripley's death, I would have said no.

But now, as I stared at the flickering pixels of the computer screen, I felt connected to all those commenting on my post. The reporting of Ripley's murder on the mainstream news was brief. It was on social media where it had taken off. And I appeared to be a big part of that. Was it right to be this happy at another's death? Was it right to benefit from the loss of human life? The more I read through Ripley's behaviour in Newcastle, the more I agreed with what most put online. He got what he deserved.

I pushed his details to one side on the screen. I was more interested in the Hashtag Killer. The name had been splashed over several other blogs since I'd posted my story, added as an actual hashtag all over the internet, so much so I wondered if I should have copyrighted it. Ripley's killer had to be a person he knew, someone he'd wronged. His victim from Newcastle wasn't named, but looking through the deep hacking search I'd used, I found links to Ripley on Facebook around the time of his arrest. All I had to do was click on them and then follow the trail.

My fingers hovered over the keyboard. Was it right to peer into the victim's private life for a story? I glanced away from the computer and towards the TV. The *Snow White* animated movie played in the background, and I turned the sound up. The witch gave the confused girl the apple as the vultures watched gleefully. Taking unwashed fruit from an old woman dressed in black must have been the cartoon equivalent of accepting a drink from a stranger in today's dating landscape. I switched the TV off and returned to Twitter.

As I scanned through the tweets, it became clear the majority displayed little sympathy for Ripley, but every once in a while some irate poster went off on a rant about Men's Rights and how Ripley was a victim of a murderous social justice warrior. I had to restrain myself from replying to those posts.

I was basking in my sudden popularity when the bell rang downstairs. When it continued to shriek for two minutes, I knew Mother was out in either body or mind. The noise annoyed me so much, I stomped down the stairs and dragged the door open. A morose-looking woman peered at me.

'Ruby Vasquez? I'm Sigourney Moon, from Artemis.' She shoved an identity card in my face and her foot in the door. If I'd wanted to close it, I couldn't because of her size ten.

'Artemis?' All I could think about was the ancient Greek myth. Had my blog post angered the gods? Wasn't

Artemis the goddess who protected young girls? She was a few years too late for me.

'It's the housing association your mother rents this property from.'

'Oh.' It seemed a wholly inappropriate response when inside I screamed fuckety fuck fuck. I wanted to get away from my mother and this place, but only when I was ready. Being thrown onto the streets to join the growing homeless population of the nation wasn't in my immediate plans.

'What's she done now?'

Moon pushed her way into our house, though technically I suppose she had more ownership of it than me since she worked for the landlords. Do people still use the term landlord? Landladies should run a company called Artemis. Or perhaps it's landpeople?

'There's been another complaint from your neighbours. What's happened to your head?'

Before I answered, she started writing in a notebook. I raised my hand above my eyes, touching a bruise I hadn't noticed earlier. That wasn't there last night.

'New cat,' I said as Moon lingered in the corridor. She looked in her thirties, flustered and ready to drop.

'I hate pets.' Sigourney Moon peered nervously around to find my fictitious feline.

'It's okay; I've locked Buffy in the dungeon.'

Her face turned blank, eyes wide open and glued to me. It took her a minute to work out that Buffy was the name of the cat and I was joking about the dungeon. I was sure there were plenty of people on the estate who liked to partake in some less than savoury activities, but it would be challenging to create such a space in this dump.

'Is your mother here?' She moved close enough to me, I smelt her perfume of fresh lemon. It was that, or she'd fallen into a bucket of toilet cleaner. I try to avoid wearing scent. The cosmetic companies' history of experimenting on animals left me hesitant towards drenching myself in liquid derived from the death of another living creature. If someone could design a fragrance reminiscent of the joy created by positive Twitter comments, I'd happily take a bath in that.

'No. I don't know what time she'll be back.' It would be whenever they kicked her out of the bookmakers, or she ran out of free drinks in the boozer. Sigourney Moon ignored my gesture for her to leave. She headed down the corridor and towards the kitchen. She pushed the door open.

'Have you had any interaction with your neighbours?'

Pots and pans stood piled up in the sink and along the worktop. I rarely ate at home so wondered how my mother had accumulated so much dirty cutlery and porcelain. Moon had all the personality of a paper cup and scowled at the surrounding tip.

'Look at this.' I moved the tattered kitchen curtains to the side and showed her the outside. The back had a patch of green surrounded by burnt grass and broken stones. Clothes flapped on the line between the house and a pole at the end of the garden. Pushing each other through the billowing pairs of pants and shabby shirts stood two twenty-something men. 'That's Bob and Terry, ex-students, once of Newcastle and now independent pharmaceutical dispensers for this area. In about five minutes they'll be arguing over the washing-up.'

She leant forward and stared at their unkempt hipster beards moving in the wind.

'Whatever argument they've had with my mother will have been about drink or drugs. I can write a blog piece about it.'

'A blog piece?'

I took out my phone and showed her my webpage about the Ripley murder. 'It's catching fire on social media now. Look at all the followers I have; they'll be fascinated by an article connecting Artemis housing association and the local distribution of illegal narcotics.'

Her face hit the floor like a shooting star. 'What... no, no, there's no need for anything like that.' She shoved her notebook away. 'I'm sure we can put this down to a minor argument between neighbours.' She skirted past me and out of the kitchen. Before I could say another word, she stepped through the front door and out of the house.

I waved at Bob and Terry through the window. They'd been married for five years, and their only connection to pharmaceuticals was occasionally buying me some extra painkillers from the shops. I grabbed a glass of water and made my way back upstairs.

My sudden celebrity had demonstrated its benefits to me. I bathed in the neon glow of the laptop on one side and my mobile phone on the other. But how long would it last? The concentration span of the modern person appeared slightly shorter than the life cycle of a butterfly, but not as pretty. My previous failed attempts at viral fame had proved an invaluable lesson in needing to stockpile material ready to post daily: make it exciting and keep it moving.

The door slammed downstairs. There was a heavy thump as, I assumed, Mother fell into the living room. Her obscene rants did not affect me. I returned to my blog and reread all the positive posts, ignoring the odd negative one.

The Hashtag Killer had brought happiness back into my life.

Now I had to figure out how to keep it going.

7 ABIGAIL

I kept the blue light flashing for most of the way, only turning it off as the car approached the house. I saw no need for the neighbours to know what was happening. The tyres screeched as I barely missed Abigail's cat sitting on the kerb. It hissed at me as I climbed out.

I strode towards the house, curtains twitching in next door's window. A thousand and one terrible thoughts had possessed my mind on the journey from the station, images of the things Abigail might have done to herself. If your kid's getting bullied online, shouldn't you take it more seriously than shouting at the school receptionist? I'd read the texts, and what had my response been to them? I'd treated my daughter's situation as if it was something unimportant and trivial.

'When I was at school, bullies hit you over the head and kicked you when you were on the floor. Being called names online is nothing, Abs. Words can't hurt you.' I thought she'd sulk or shout, but all she did was turn away and go to her room. I'd gone to work and pushed it from my mind. I had to give the kid her space; that's what I told myself. My parents were smothering and controlling. I'd promised I'd never be like that, but perhaps I'd gone too far in the other direction.

The key fumbled in the lock as I opened the door.

'Abs, are you here?' I tossed the car keys onto the corridor table and barged into the living room. Rufus, the cat, followed me in and jumped into the middle of the sofa. I didn't have the energy to shout him down. There was no sign of Abigail. I checked the kitchen and the back room with the same results.

'Are you upstairs, Abigail?' The silence embraced the cold of the house, the sound of nothing creating a cacophonous ringing in my head.

I bounded upstairs; the bathroom door stood open at the top, and it was empty. I turned right and strode towards Abigail's bedroom, ignoring the keep out sign on the door and barging in. I hoped to see her curled up in bed, was ready to chastise her for staying off school again while desperate to throw my arms around her.

There was nothing there but a mountain of clothes scattered over the floor. Every single piece, from short socks to thick jumpers, was devoid of colour. It was like peering into the heart of a black hole. I waited to be sucked into it, hoping to find some light on the other side. The sideboard was covered with bits of food and dirty plates.

Rufus slipped into the room and nibbled at the cake stuck to the carpet, and I had to restrain myself from shouting at him. The lack of a regular nicotine intake was making it harder to control the anger.

I cursed under my breath and went to my bedroom. It was also empty, the bed unmade since I'd left this morning. I felt twice my age, sinking my weary legs into the duvet and rechecking my phone. There was no reply to all the texts and voicemails I'd left for Abigail in the last half an hour. There were two messages from Jack. The first asked me if Abigail was okay, the second was to remind me of the meeting this afternoon. In my mind, Evan Ripley's head fell from his shoulders and Abigail caught it as a giant Facebook logo dragged her under a sea of dark jackets.

Black was Abigail's invisibility shield. Wrapped in those clothes, she could slip into the shadows and avoid the harsh light shining on her. It was no way to live. I had to do better.

'Where are you, Abs?'

My eyes scanned the room. I didn't search for Abigail, but for evidence my daughter existed in my life. There were no photos, no souvenirs, no little pieces of things she may have created or done at school. I was a ghost in my child's existence. I was worse than my mother. At least she never pretended to care for me. But I wasn't acting; I just wasn't doing a very good job.

I lifted off the bed and returned to Abigail's room. Posters of pop stars and TV celebs I didn't recognise covered the walls. I needed to stop thinking like a parent and return to being a copper. I stepped over the mass of darkness on the floor and headed for the chest of drawers. Rufus looked at me quizzically, its eyes peering deep into my soul and finding me wanting.

I rifled through her possessions. Lipstick and jewellery lay in the first drawer, scarves in the second, and underwear in the last one. My knees trembled as I bent down and checked under the bed. Something hairy with many legs scampered from my vision as I sneezed through the pile of dust gathered there amongst more dirty outfits and unwashed plates.

'Where's your laptop, Abs?'

I searched through the wardrobe like a burglar, looking

for the most prized possessions they could find. I marvelled at how my daughter had got so many clothes into one small space. As I closed the door, something rattled on top of it. I lifted upwards, perched on my toes and saw the computer. I brought it down with more dust swirling in the air and sneezed again. I sat on Abigail's bed and opened the lid. The machine gave out a low hum as it started, the power warming my legs. There wasn't much time before I'd have to leave to make the briefing. Even though Jack was there, it wouldn't look good if I turned up late.

I looked for excuses for why she wasn't in the house or at her classes. I imagined Abigail might be out with friends. But Abigail didn't have any friends, or so she said. Everyone at school hated her because she was a copper's daughter, that's what she'd told me.

Perhaps that's why the bullying started, because of me. Did a bunch of kids taunt Abigail to kill herself because I was a copper? Or was it something else altogether? Not everything had to be about me.

Maybe I hadn't taken the messages seriously because I didn't believe her. Or was this all about me rarely being in this house, or not being in her life? My professional experience was about seeking answers to difficult questions, but I couldn't think of any for the problems consuming my personal life.

The screen kicked into existence as I contemplated the thought Abigail might have done this to get my attention. Maybe I'd ignored her so much, she invented the bullying to force me to take notice of her. I shook such a terrible idea from my head as I stared at the computer. It was a shock to see what Abigail had as the desktop wallpaper. The two of us grinning into a camera from a concert we went to last year.

Something alien and long-forgotten crossed my face as I peered into the millions of dots which made up the image of my daughter and me enjoying each other's company. It was a genuine smile, not forced like when I'm at work or talking to other people. This came from the heart.

Abigail may want more of my time, but she wouldn't make something like this up to get it. This was serious, and I had to take it seriously: she took priority over the search for a killer.

We'd only drifted apart when the bullying started. A pang of guilt struck me; not for letting Abigail down about those vile messages, but the fact I sat in her room, spying on her. My hand hovered over the lid to close the laptop when the bedroom door slammed behind me.

'Is this what you do when I'm not here, go through all my stuff?'

I dropped the machine and ignored the resentment in my daughter's face, standing to throw my arms around her. The emotions surprised me.

'What's wrong, Mum?' Abigail pulled away to stare at me, her anger replaced with concern.

'The school rang to say you weren't there. I thought something might have happened to you.'

Abigail threw a magazine and a packet of crisps onto the bed.

'I nipped out to the shops for a bit.' Guilt covered her face. 'I couldn't go to school, Mum, not after what's happened.' I hugged her again. There would be no more mistakes on my part.

'Don't worry, love; I only wanted to see you were okay. I promise I'll get this sorted with the school soon.' If I could put gangsters, killers, rapists, and abusers behind bars, I was damn sure I'd find a few teenage bullies. Abigail's complexion seemed grave. She looked older than her thirteen years, and it aged me as well at that moment. Obsession with my work meant I'd missed so much of her childhood. Now she stood on the cusp of adulthood, I couldn't lose any more.

'There's been more of them, Mum.'

'More of what, love?'

'Messages and threats.'

Sickness flowed through me. I had to steady my hand on the bed, my head awash with terrible thoughts and images. Jesus, what a terrible mother I'd been to let it go on like this.

'Texts to your phone?' It seemed a dreadful thing to think, but I hoped so. They'd be easier to trace through a mobile number than some anonymous web pages. Abigail took out her phone and showed it to me.

'No; on my social media.'

'Oh, Abs; you promised not to use those sites again.' I tried not to sound disappointed as I took the phone. There was an Instagram page with a fake image of Abigail's head pasted onto a nude female murder victim. *This will be you soon* was typed underneath. I pushed the anger down and flicked the image away; to replace it with a real photo of Abigail Photoshopped next to a group of naked men leering at her. I wanted to throw up. Demonic fingers clawed at my guts and my heart. Rage mixed in with fear inside my blood. I could kill the people who'd done this. My legs shuddered and my hands shook. I couldn't let Abigail see me like this; I gave her the mobile and forced the bile back into my stomach.

'Are there any more like this?' I tried to section my mind, to switch off the bits as a mother and focus on the detective parts. Instead of dismissing the posts and photos, I'd treat them as evidence, like I should have done.

'There's five,' Abigail replied. 'They were all posted this morning.'

I took out my phone as I received a text, expecting it to be from Jack, but it came from the school Ice Queen confirming the meeting. I kissed Abigail on the cheek.

'We've got a meeting with the welfare officer tomorrow at four. I promise you we'll get it all sorted then. You stay inside, and I'll see you tonight.'

'Won't you be at work then? I saw the news about a vigilante killer.' The expectation in her voice, the desperation in her eyes, killed me in slow motion. This is what I'd done to my daughter. I gripped her arm.

'No, love; I promise you we'll both be at that school tomorrow, and this will be sorted.'

The corners of Abigail's mouth curled up slightly as I let go of her. I closed the bedroom door, moving down the stairs with two invisible weights sitting on my shoulders.

Find a killer and protect my daughter.

No. Protect my daughter, then find a killer.

8 DOWN AT THE DOCTORS'

T he man before me turned up for his appointment with a black eye and a broken arm. When he left, it looked like he'd been crying and you could hardly blame him. It was written all over his face. I thought about that while I waited and went through the images of Evan Ripley in my mind.

The one where he stares up just before his head comes away is particularly engaging. I'd been tempted to post some online, but worried it might turn some of my new fans against me. In my experience, many people are okay with violence as long as they don't have to look at it. Tell them hundreds had died in a faraway place and they likely wouldn't bat an eyelid. Stick a photograph of an emaciated dog under their nose, and they'd shake like a baby.

When I'd arrived at the surgery, I was greeted by a callow harridan with the most unpleasant attitude. Training in communication and people skills was not a requirement in this practice. The woman wore a shiny white uniform regardless of the fact she was devoid of any medical expertise or knowledge. It left me feeling somewhat untrusting of this place. My previous charlatan had retired to Papua New Guinea and had recommended this therapist.

Sprawled on the table in front of me lay a smorgasbord of downmarket magazines and adverts for insurance companies. I glanced at the other unfortunates waiting to have their brains prodded and poked. I knew what my issues were, but still, I came to places like this. I'd begun to believe I saw it as a challenge and not as an exercise in searching out clarity and insight.

While I waited, I checked my phone for news on Ripley's death. Behind the surly receptionist's head was a large poster declaring no mobile phone usage, but I ignored it. The timid bloke on my right shrank so far back into his pew, I thought they were in a symbiotic relationship.

A tall man looking like a lumberjack, with a baggy checked shirt and a beard you could grow apples in, burst into the room and headed straight for the seat to my left. When he plonked his shabby jeans in the chair, I got a potent whiff of cooking oil and grease. There were burn marks across the tips of his fingers and the middle of his palms. I guessed he was a pyromaniac. The mouse next to me seemed neurotic. I harboured a theory that the receptionist was psychotic. This must have all been a wonderful bus woman's holiday for her.

And what about me? Well, that's what I was there for. I'd been collecting alienists like London collects Russian oligarchs. And I'd never told the truth to one of them.

The red light above the desk flickered into life, and the receptionist beckoned me forward. I slipped the phone into my pocket. I knew exactly what ailed me, always had done: this was all for research.

As I entered the room, I wondered how many people would miss me when I was gone.

INITIAL INTERVIEW WITH DR MAL.

   Him: Tell me what you did this weekend.

   Me: You don't want to hear about my childhood?

   He rifled through his papers, pretending to stare at the notes I'd accumulated from several professionals over the years. It's all a façade; I know everything is stored digitally nowadays. Even his face was a smokescreen. Glasses big enough to store footballs hid his eyes; teeth so white they sparkled like bleach. A tumultuous beard covered the rest of his head. His hair appeared dyed black, shining like the centre of an exploding sun underneath the light of the room. He had the hands of a delicate porcelain doll and resembled a hastily packed sleeping bag.

   Believe nothing you see.

   Him: Let's focus on the present.

   Me: I encountered a woman who'd been deceived by her husband. Not the usual run-of-the-mill lies, but something special, a grand whopper of deceit. When they met, he told her he had incurable cancer. They got married and he carried on telling her that for five years until she found out. She was in the pub celebrating with friends her release from this villainous Cyrano, but I don't think it was a celebration for her. I saw the emptiness behind her eyes. He'd destroyed her ability to trust ever again. Imagine having someone do that to you.

   Him: And how did you feel about that?

   At that moment, with that question, I knew this latest alienist would be no help to me. I suppose I always did.

   Me: I drank to her excellent health and the whole pub drowned our sorrows together.

   Him: Do you think you've been deceived?

The thick glasses had somehow slid down his nose, so he pushed them back up with what I noticed were long finger-nails for a man. Not that I was judgemental or anything, but these weren't Cabaret style lovely nails, more like Nosferatu on a bad night. The sight of them made me trust him even less, if that was possible.

Me: From birth to death, we're all deceived, Doctor. Parents, teachers, co-workers, managers, leaders, family, friends, lovers and strangers – it's all just one continuous trail of secrets and lies. It's how we deal with the trickery which defines us.

Him: Are you lying to me now?

Me: Does it matter?

Him: Everything we say and do matters.

I pondered his question, contemplating if he was trying to catch me out or whether he was stretching out the hour to get his thirty pieces of silver.

Me: Are you a believer, Dr Mal? Do you follow the teachings of Mohammed, Jesus, Buddha or even L Ron Hubbard?

Him: This session isn't about me.

We went around in circles for another forty minutes before I left. The morose receptionist had been replaced by someone perkier with fake eyelashes and braces on the teeth. She tried to get me to arrange another appointment, but I made my excuses and said I'd email them.

It was time for the next stage in my grand opus.

9 JACK

I returned to the station as everyone shuffled into the briefing room. Jack seemed cheerful, whistling some god-awful pop tune from the charts. We'd worked together for five years, since my transfer from Leeds, and no matter how I'd tried, I'd never been able to improve his musical tastes. Surely there was something wrong with a grown man humming Taylor Swift tunes?

'The pace down here will be too quick for a Northerner,' he'd joked on our first meeting. I smoked twenty a day then so kept a semblance of humour.

He was a year older than me, happily married to Jean, a doctor, with teenage twins, Tom and Jack Junior. Until you got to know him, he could appear to be unassuming. The thing which made him stand out from the rest of our colleagues was his dress sense. Most coppers tried to base their style on contemporary police television shows, all grim in tone and appearance, switching between a *Broadchurch* beard and a *Happy Valley* hangdog expression. Jack Monroe was having none of that; for him, out went the long dark coats which wouldn't have looked out of place on Burke and

Hare. He turned up for work in pale blue tweed coats, and mustard-coloured leather jackets or asymmetric wool over-coats, underneath which could be vibrantly decorated shirts by Hugo Boss or Jack and Jones. He also had more shoes than anyone I'd ever met. Tan leather and navy suede brogues, and more Chelsea boots than you could shake a stick at. I felt casual every time I stood next to him.

He was an expert analyst, always happiest when ploughing through data and evidence. I was more a people and location person. I had a knack of spotting the devious games others play when dealing with the police. I was also quick at recognising the dynamics of a crime scene.

'You'll like some of this,' Jack said as we took our places at the top of the room. My mind was full of thoughts about Abigail and how I'd let her down. I pushed them to one side and focused on the team. There was something I needed to tell them before Jack got things underway.

'I'd like to thank you all for the hard work you've done today. Every little helps, no matter how trivial or inconsequential it may seem at first. Remember, we'll only solve this case as a team.' Unlike most of the senior officers I'd worked under in fifteen years on the force, I didn't believe intimidation and negativity were good motivating factors for the job. I could be strict when needed, but had always found the carrot was better than the stick.

I handed over to Jack.

'We have the CCTV footage of our victim leaving home this morning at five o'clock. It took him forty-five minutes to drive to the park. From the first look at that video, it doesn't appear that he was followed from his house. This means our suspect waited for him there, or it was a spontaneous random attack.' He let that information sink in for a minute, even though I was sure nobody in the room believed there was anything casual about this crime. It appeared too clinical, too precise, and too clean.

'Ripley waited in his car for ten minutes. Five minutes after he got there, our jogger, Mazz Coe, parked next to him. We also have video footage of her journey there, and nothing on it looks suspicious as of now. She gets out of the car and enters the park. He waits five minutes, and then follows her.' Jack played the two short clips on the screen behind him. He was a born public speaker, the gift of the gab wrapped up inside the face of a 1940s movie star. I always pictured him in monochrome and a Raymond Chandler hat.

'All the CCTV material has been checked for three hours before this and five minutes before the attack. We have some other joggers entering the park at that time. Uniforms are trying to identify those people. I'll say now that I don't think any of them is our suspect.' He didn't explain why. 'Unfortunately, there are no working cameras in that location, so we have no other video evidence from the morning.'

He cleared the clips from the screen.

'Eyewitness accounts have Miss Coe walking into the grounds just after six am, stopping next to a fountain to start her warm-up. We have no sighting of Ripley, so it's safe to assume he hid inside the rose bushes. Forensics found material from his shorts on some thorns. There's no evidence of anybody else behind him while he was there. This means whoever killed him came prepared with forensic countermeasures or cleaned up after.'

Jack didn't let that disappointing news linger for too long.

'However, the pathologist's initial autopsy report has provided two important details. First, she's positive Ripley was strangled with a garotte made of a material like this one.' He held up the wire, so everyone saw it. 'The pathologist is also sure our murderer is at least six foot four. This gave them the angle and leverage to pull on Ripley's considerable weight.' Jack took a drink of water. As he slurped, I thought about the strength needed to drag Ripley's bulk back and then tilt his head up. Instinct would have kicked in; he should have struggled. But there'd been no signs of that in the ground around the bushes.

Jack rubbed at his stomach and I grimaced at the pain he must have felt.

'The pathologist recorded the time of death at six twenty this morning. We received the first call from Miss Coe at six twenty-five. However, when checking Coe's phone, Cybercrime found a post from her to Facebook at six twenty-three.' A hushed chatter went around the room as Jack displayed the Facebook post on the screen.

OMG! Just seen somebody attacked in the park. I think his head's fallen off!!

'This wasn't mentioned in Mazz Coe's original statement. We need to re-interview her and double-check to see if there are any links between her and Evan Ripley. I'll be sending out job details when this is over.'

People tapped into their screens as he spoke, whether it was their phone, a tablet or a laptop. I'd made sure all the team could access relevant information through a shared digital folder. It also made it easier to keep DCI Merson updated, not that she would bother too much with the data she received.

'The first officers arrived on the scene at six forty; DI Flowers and I were there ten minutes later. At seven-thirty, the following tweet appeared on Twitter from an account called Justice For All.'

There is no escape for the guilty. #evanripley #justiceforall

'It gathered more traction when it was linked to a blog post about the crime. I will hand over to Alice Voss from Cybercrime to update you on these.'

Alice Voss dragged herself to the head of the room. I hadn't expected Alice to put herself in the spotlight. It must have been Jack's charm which convinced her to address the team since the two of them were whispering together when I entered the station this morning. She cleared her throat and nerves, pushed her thick black glasses up her nose, and tugged at the sleeves on her shirt. She looked like she wanted to be anywhere other than in front of the rest of us.

'The tweet and the account it came from were relayed through several proxy servers and dummy accounts, but I traced it to a server in Russia.' Deathly silence engulfed the room at that news. Alice brought her hands up to her face, then dropped them. I wondered if anybody else had noticed how the cybercrime analyst's fingernails had been bitten down to the bone.

Everybody knew what the Russian connection meant, but Alice stated it anyway. 'This means it's untraceable. The original tweet has had remarkable coverage and inter-action since the link to the post naming the victim and his connection to an allegation of rape in Newcastle five years ago. This blog was easier to identify as the author, Ruby Vasquez, was happy to take credit for her work. She's been posting online as an internet journalist for six months. Before that, she spent two years unsuccessfully trying to become a YouTube celebrity. That's all there is to her public life.'

Vasquez was a lead, but I wasn't sure where it would

take us yet. I asked Alice about Ripley's computers and phone. The glasses were at the end of her nose now.

'We've found little of interest on his mobile.' She reached into the beige coloured file she'd brought with her. 'He had half a dozen contacts on it, mainly taxi firms or food deliveries, but no family or even work colleagues. There are links to pornographic websites on his laptop, but nothing illegal or,' she cleared her throat, 'bizarre or extreme.' There was a slight blush to her cheeks. I guessed the definition of bizarre or extreme was down to personal taste and not an official police classification.

'Just the same as any bloke's computer then,' some wag from the back of the room shouted.

'We'll continue to search through the hard disk and let you know if we find anything significant.'

Alice finished and returned to her seat. Jack resumed his duties.

'And finally, we have this information from our Newcastle colleagues regarding the allegation of rape against our victim five years ago. All the information is in the shared drive so I won't take up time with the terrible details now, but one important piece of material relates to Debbie Swift's brother, Kyle. Two years older than her, he recently left the military where he was in the parachute regiment. He completed three terms in Iraq and one in Afghanistan, which is where he was when the alleged attack on Debbie took place. The local bobbies in Newcastle tell me he turned apoplectic when he returned home and found out what happened. He's also six foot four in his bare feet and built like a brick shit house. Newcastle is arranging to speak to him and his sister.'

Jack completed the briefing. 'We'll meet again once

everyone has followed up on their tasks. We have Ruby Vasquez in an interview room downstairs.'

I nodded my thanks. 'Excellent work, Jack; I owe you one.'

'Think nothing of it, Jen. Here's Ruby Vasquez's file.' He handed me a fat folder full of papers. Before I could look inside, Alice Voss approached me.

'Do you want me to ask Twitter to close down the Justice For All account?'

I'd considered it. 'Not for now; it might prove to be a useful lead.'

Alice nodded. 'There's something about our internet journalist you won't find in her records.'

Jack raised his eyebrows. 'That sounds juicy.'

'It could be. She has a juvenile file I can't get into.'

I dismissed it. 'Curious,' Jack said as we left the briefing and headed for the interview room. I thanked Alice as she went in the opposite direction. Watching her leave gave me an idea of how to solve the problem of Abigail's online threats. I grabbed hold of Jack's arm as we reached the lift.

'Let's take the stairs. Miss Vasquez can stew for a little longer.' We turned down the corridor and he pushed open the door. I pulled a cigarette packet from my coat.

'I thought you'd given up?' Disappointment sprang from his lips.

I lifted the pack to his face. He winced at the photo of a mouth infected with cancer. Brown blistered lips and rotten teeth smiled at him.

'I have. I use this to remind me what I'm missing when the temptation becomes too much.'

He turned from it and changed the subject. 'How were things with Abigail?' We stepped into the cold stairwell and

I allowed myself a second to forget about our killer and concentrate on my problems.

'She's had more of those obscene messages online, even worse than the other ones.' I pushed my back into the wall, hoping the concrete would transfer its strength to me.

'Christ, Jen, I'm sorry. Can't the school do anything about it?'

I shook my head. 'They're just as useless as they were last time. We have an appointment with the school, but I can cancel it if we get some movement on this investigation tonight.' As I listened to my voice, I wondered why I was looking for ways to abandon my parental responsibilities again; to let down my daughter once more. I needed to go to the school tomorrow, regardless of what was happening in this case.

'No, Jen. Everyone knows how brilliant you are, but we'll survive a few hours without you for one day.'

I was thankful he was a friend and my partner. I pulled away and opened the Vasquez file.

'Give me two minutes to scan this, and then we can ask Miss Vasquez how she got Evan Ripley's name before anyone else.'

I stared at a hard copy of her blog. The number of people happy at Ripley's murder was worrying.

'Do you believe the killer posted on here?'

'I could go through all the comments?'

'Let's speak to the author first.'

I gathered the questions in my head, but all I could think about were those terrible fake images of Abigail. What would my justice be for those who sent them?

10 RUBY'S INTERVIEW

I was scrolling through the comments on the article when somebody rang the bell downstairs. Mother wouldn't answer it; she'd be in the backroom for the rest of the day with her fags and booze, only coming out when she needed food. The bell buzzed again. I sighed and headed down. Maybe it was someone after an interview, or Sigourney Moon had returned.

I bounced down the stairs, feeling more alive than I had for an age. Whether I'd taken my medication didn't matter; I'd written something people liked. And that made me like me again.

All of that positivity vanished when I opened the door and saw the blue uniforms.

And now here I sat, waiting in this dour room to be interviewed by the police. The place was bare apart from a table and three chairs, plus the uniformed copper pretending not to stare at me. I guessed it was the tussle of red hair which did it.

'You get it from your father.' Mother meant it as an insult. 'You should change the colour or shave it all off.

Then you wouldn't remind me of him every time I look at you.'

I ignored her advice.

My earliest memories were of adults commenting on that hair.

'I bet she's fiery,' some of them would say as they patted my head. The kids at school always teased me for it, calling me Carrot Top or Ginger Nuts. As I got older, Mother's many boyfriends would stare and leave their fingers on my shoulders for too long. That all stopped when I stabbed one of them in his grubby hands with a kitchen knife.

I gained a reputation as crazy and emotional, but I didn't care. It kept the predators away, and the other kids backed off. The only person desperate for confrontation was the one who should have been looking after me. Nothing could deter the old bat's hatred for her only child.

I was wondering why I was reminiscing like this when the copper caught my attention again. He coughed nervously and turned his face away. I smiled and was thinking of Grace when the door opened, and two plain-clothes plods walked in. I recognised them from the Ripley crime scene; the woman introduced herself as DI Flowers and the man as DI Monroe. Flowers appeared stressed, with too many crease lines on her cheeks and forehead. A dollop of Botox would sort that out in a jiffy. She was pretty if you liked that type, but she seemed worried about something. He was the opposite of what I'd expect a bloke detective to look like, decked out in an Armani suit and stylish shoes. His hair was greased back like a young Elvis before he joined the army and lost all sense of danger.

'Do I need a lawyer?' I'd watched enough crime shows and movies to know I shouldn't be talking to the police on my own. But I'd done nothing wrong, so there was zero to worry about. I'd panicked a little when the uniforms turned up at the house, hands shaking and forcing the stutter to the back of my throat. Even before they spoke, I'd recognised it would be an excellent opportunity for a follow-up blog about the Hashtag Killer.

'Do you think you need a lawyer?' the bloke said. I'd already forgotten his name.

'Perhaps you should tell me what this is about before I decide.' I knew what it was about. It had to be because of the article about Evan Ripley and his killer.

The woman didn't look at me, peering inside a sizeable brown folder stuffed with papers. That can't be real. Most of it must be blank paper to make me think it's all about me. That's an old cliché. I wonder if she's the bad cop, and he's the good one. Do they still do things like that, or is it just a trope of lousy crime fiction?

Ideas flowed through my head.

I took out a notebook and pen and placed them on the table.

'Do you mind if I take some notes for myself?'

I watched him hesitate, needing to seek confirmation from the woman but not wanting to break this little act they'd contrived.

'This is an informal interview, but if you publish anything else which may harm our investigation, you'll face a charge of perverting the course of justice.' The woman's voice was emotionless, like a talking clock.

'What do you mean by anything else?'

Flowers never looked at me, handing her partner a piece of paper from the file. He pushed it toward my hands.

'Did you write this?'

I did. And I was proud of it. 'That's my name on it.'

The woman finished with the file, leaving it open and

deciding to give me her attention. He continued with the questions.

'What were you doing in Adams Park so early this morning?'

How much of the truth should I tell them?

'Is it a crime to have been there?'

Flowers stared at me as if I was pulling strings at a puppet show. 'A crime was committed then.'

I didn't see the point in messing about. 'I wrote a computer program which trawls internet posts as they happen and identifies keywords relating to crime. The government has something similar, involving terrorism. It highlighted a Facebook post about an assault in the park. I was only around the corner, so I thought I'd have a look.'

'We've checked your school records, Ruby.' I started to tell him off for using my first name without permission, but he continued. 'You left with no qualifications and haven't had a proper job since. How could you create something like that?'

My fingers curled tightly around the pen. In my mind, I saw my hand crushing his windpipe. I controlled my breathing. Anger could bring on stress, and the stress could cause a blackout. And I didn't have my pills with me. The corners of my lips wanted to fall and reveal my true self, but I forced them up through sheer mental strength. I had to thank my mother for all practice I'd had at creating a fake smile.

'There's more to intelligence than grades on a piece of paper. The rigid education structure this country forces onto its children can do more harm than good. It's no coincidence most prisoners in the British penal system don't even have basic reading and writing skills. I was lucky enough to teach myself what I needed to know.'

'But why did you write this?' He pointed to the paper.

'I'm an internet journalist specialising in crime stories.'

The woman wanted to laugh; I could see it in her face. He didn't hide the contempt in his voice.

'You have no experience or qualifications in journalism, Ms Vasquez; what makes you think you're capable of doing something like this?'

I rolled my eyes. 'People are sick of experts and those who speak through privileged tongues. They want to hear authentic voices from the marginalised and the overlooked. So-called real journalists look down on me because I'm not one of them. The world is changing and is passing people like you by.' I leant back into the chair, heart thumping against my chest, fingers trembling under the desk. I didn't know where that came from, but it sent an electric buzz along my skin.

Flowers reached into the folder and pushed an A4 colour photograph at me. I peered into the lifeless eyes of Ripley, fixated on the dangling piece of flesh keeping his head connected to the neck. I flinched at the image, but it was a fake reaction, giving them what they expected. I felt nothing. I'd seen dead bodies before; this was just another one.

'How did you know about the victim, Evan Ripley?' When the woman spoke, her voice sounded like the low rumbling of a train in the distance. If you waited around for too long, it would eventually overrun you.

'I'm not at liberty to reveal my sources.'

The policeman laughed in my face. 'So you share some characteristics with proper journalists?'

Flowers pushed a second piece of paper at me. This one contained the hashtag #justiceforall. 'What do you know about this tweet?'

'It came up when I searched for Ripley's name. I added

it to what I had and the photos and put out my piece. And that's all I know.' I reached for the notebook and scribbled down some notes in shorthand; descriptions of these two coppers and how I could incorporate them into the follow-up story. The only decision to make was whether to post it tonight or tomorrow. The modern news was fast moving, so perhaps I shouldn't wait.

'What did you say your names are?'

The man repeated them with a deep sigh in his voice.

'That tweet and your linked post have taken on lives of their own. Are you surprised by that?' DI Flowers said.

She's analysing my reactions, trying to spot any deceit. But I had a lifetime of hiding my true feelings to fall back on.

'You mean the lack of sympathy for his death?' I pointed at the photo of Ripley's near decapitated head. 'People want to see justice for criminals who use a failing legal system to evade the law.'

'Evan Ripley wasn't convicted of any crime.'

I was surprised at the policewoman's words. I thought it would be the man who'd defend the rapist. I stared into DI Flowers's unwavering blue eyes.

'Do you think he was innocent?'

Flowers never hesitated with her response.

'No. I believe he was guilty, just as you're guilty of with-holding information. Two wrongs don't make a right. This isn't a vigilante system where revenge overrides the law.'

'Thousands would appear to disagree with you, DI Flowers, according to the replies to that tweet. There's even a call to bring back the death penalty.'

'People are always calling for the return of the death penalty,' Flowers said. 'Are you willing to sacrifice one inno-cent person to punish the guilty?'

I hadn't given it much thought before, but decided it would make a good subject for another blog post. The ideas were piling up and I jotted them down in the notebook.

'Can I go now?' The sooner I got back, the sooner I could start on the next piece. DI Flowers looked right through me.

'When was the last time you saw your father, Ms Vasquez?'

That train arrived and knocked me sideways. I dropped the pen onto the floor, my eyelashes flickering and a lump in my throat.

'What did you say?' I bent to pick up the pen, my guts boiling like mincemeat in a frying pan. I was unsure why I felt queasy. The thought of my father was annoying, but I wasn't afraid of him. He was probably dead by now.

DI Flowers waited until I raised my head above the table.

'When was the last time you saw your father?'

'I... I... I've never met him. He scarpered before I was born.' I tried to close my mind to the image of my mother going on and on about him again. The noise rattled around in my brain so much, I missed what Flowers said next. 'What did you say?'

'I said it's probably a good thing he left home when he did, for your sake.' Flowers pulled more papers from the file. 'He has a long list of charges against him: armed robbery, assault and battery, GBH, domestic violence. Rape.'

Something clawed against the insides of my chest. I imagined a creature from the movie *Aliens* bursting out of me at any second. When I was a kid, I wanted one of them as a pet.

'I want nothing to do with my father.' I got up to leave. Flowers closed the file.

'He was released from prison a year ago, and then disappeared. Do you think he's in touch with your mother?'

I pushed past the woman and headed for the exit, shaking my head and struggling to keep my emotions under control. I staggered out the door and clung to the wall. Was this another blackout coming on? A hand rested on my shoulder and I turned to face a uniformed policewoman.

'Come on, let's get you a nice cup of tea.' Her voice calmed my nerves.

I found my strength. If they were dredging up my father, they were clueless to who had murdered Ripley. And that meant there was plenty of time to build my momentum and get another blog post out linked to the Hashtag Killer.

And this little interview had given me the perfect subject to write about.

11 EVIDENCE

'You might have gone easy on her at the end,' Jack said as I opened the file and studied the murder scene again. The space around Ripley's body wasn't disturbed; the leaves were lying near his lifeless husk. He'd died in that spot, but the attack hadn't started there.

'Vasquez is hiding something from us.' I knew it in my heart.

'Yeah, like where she got Ripley's name from. I'm not sure I believe her story about creating a program she claims scans the internet for keywords. If she's that clever, she should work for the secret service.'

'Don't be blinded by her youth and poor school record. She's intelligent enough to perform how she thought we wanted her to. It was all an act, how she reacted to our questions. She'd tried being an actress online, and now we gave her the biggest stage possible. And she got Ripley's name from one of the constables at the scene. It's amazing what a little flirtation will get you when you aim it in the right direction.'

'How do you figure that?' He didn't sound convinced.

'I remember seeing her in the park. It's hard not to notice that flame-red hair. She lurked near the barriers when the uniforms were keeping the public away. That's probably when she got his name and her photos.'

'Or she set him up.' Jack removed a piece of fluff from his jacket as if it was a stain on his character. 'She doesn't appear to have the strength to have killed him without help, but she might have lured him there, and then a partner finished him off. If she's good enough to create that computer program, then she's capable of setting up a Twitter account from a Russian server.'

'I suppose it's possible, but what's her motive?' It was conceivable, but I didn't believe it. Vasquez hadn't killed Ripley, but she knew something and was keeping it from us. She had that attitude which thought to speak to the police was tantamount to slitting your grandmother's throat.

'It's like you said earlier, Jen, she might have set the whole thing up to write that blog post and promote her journalistic career. What better than having the scoop on a new vigilante killer stalking the city? Maybe she killed him as well?'

My facial expression must have been one of absolute disdain.

'She's perhaps five foot four in high heels. She'd have had to stand on a chair to strangle Ripley. And even if she's stronger than she looks, she couldn't have lifted him on her own.'

'It's possible she has a partner who killed Ripley, someone strong enough to do it, while she got the photos and wrote the story. Then they added the Twitter post and hashtags, and she coined the name for the killer.'

Jack liked the idea, but I didn't. 'However Vasquez is

involved, we need to dig more into her past; investigate her home life and what happened to her missing father.'

His phone rang while I was studying the information in the file one more time. There was something I'd missed about the scene, but I couldn't figure out what. My mind was too busy with thoughts of Abigail, the school meeting, and those messages I hadn't taken seriously enough.

'That was Newcastle.' Jack slipped the phone into his pocket.

'Not good news, from the look on your face.' I pulled out the photos of the rose bushes in the park.

Gloom seeped from Jack's eyes. 'Debbie Swift was admitted to the hospital two days ago for an attempted suicide. She's in a coma.'

'Shit.'

'Her brother found her in the house. When the para-medics removed her, he went wild, smashing up the house and attacking the neighbours who tried to calm him down. He wanted to strangle one of them. It took four people to drag him away.'

I got out of the chair and peered at the photo. What was I missing?

'Is he locked up?'

'Kyle Swift got a train here an hour after nearly killing his neighbour. Nobody has seen him since.' As that informa-tion penetrated my brain, a lightbulb went off in my head. I realised what I'd missed. How could I have been so stupid?

'Is the scene still closed in the park?'

'I think so, why?'

I grabbed the photo and stuffed it into my jacket. 'Ring ahead and tell Forensics not to leave yet. We're going back there.'

Jack spoke on the phone as we took the lift down. I

checked my mobile for messages from Abigail. There were none, so I texted her.

Hope you're okay, love. The pizzas are on me tonight.

I pulled the car out of the garage while he finished the call.

No matter how many times he asked on the way over, I wouldn't tell him what I'd discovered. While I drove, he updated the team about the latest developments with Debbie Swift and her brother. Irritation rippled through his words as we got stuck at another set of traffic lights.

'Kyle Swift was in the city for at least twenty-four hours before Ripley's murder.'

And we had no idea where he was now.

The lights changed to green and I put my foot down. 'He has the motivation and the physique to be our killer, but would he be capable of setting up a Twitter account in Russia? Do we know anything about his background with his work in the military?'

'His regiment wasn't forthcoming with the details. The woman from the Ministry of Defence I spoke to on the phone kept referring to the Official Secrets Act.'

I pushed thoughts of the brother to one side and focused on his sister. 'Do we know why Debbie Swift attempted suicide?' I weaved past an errant cyclist and headed towards the park.

'I didn't get any details on why she did it, only that it wasn't her first attempt since she claimed Ripley attacked her.'

'You don't believe her?'

Jack pulled at his seatbelt as I turned a corner sharply. 'I watched her interviews, read her statements; I believe her. That doesn't mean Ripley deserved to die, or I agree with those who are lapping up his murder.'

'Does it make me a bad person if I'm struggling to find any sympathy for him?' I asked of myself as much as him.

'No, of course not. Your empathy with Debbie Swift's terrible ordeal makes it difficult to feel anything for Evan Ripley.'

The entrance to the park lay ahead. The crowds had disappeared. I pulled into the first available space.

'Make sure the Geordie Bobbies don't bother her while she's in hospital. We'll put out a search for her brother once we've finished here.' We stepped out of the car. I strode towards the taped-off area and the handful of coppers lingering there.

'Are you going to tell me what this is about now?' Jack picked up his steps as we headed to the bushes where Evan Ripley had met his end. I looked over to where Ruby Vasquez had taken her photos. Could she be part of a plot to kill Ripley as a ploy to become famous on the internet? Plenty of people had killed for stranger reasons.

My colleagues from forensics hung around like worker ants. I signalled for the one I recognised to join us.

'We were about to finish up when we got your call, Jennifer.' Athena Temple had been on the force for as long as me and was well aware I hated being called Jennifer. She strode towards me as if she was the most important person in the park.

'This won't take forever, Tena.'

Temple grimaced at the shortening of her name. 'It's already taking too long because I'm stuck here talking to you.'

'Jack, have another look at where they found the body and tell me what you see.' I pointed at the ground, which still held the considerable indentation of Evan Ripley. Jack brushed through the bushes, careful not to contaminate any spots even though it appeared Forensics had completed their work. This morning's damp had been absorbed into the earth and dissipated from the trees. He peered into the murder spot, scrunching his face and scratching at his neck. Jack was a hardworking, diligent copper and a great partner, but spontaneous bursts of inspiration were not his thing. He liked to batter a case into submission.

'What am I searching for, Jen? I see nothing different from this morning.'

I put my hand on his shoulder and eased him back a little. 'Do you remember how we said our perp probably covered their trail behind them?' He nodded. 'I got fixated on how difficult that must have been and never considered the alternatives.' I still couldn't believe how I'd missed it. I tried not to blame Abigail's situation at school, but the longer the day had gone on, the more I realised how much I'd been off my game after the panic I'd felt when I thought she was missing

'What alternatives?' Athena and Jack said in stereo.

'Tena, can you get one of your people to bring a ladder over?' Temple seemed peeved at not being back in her warm office, but put the request in over the radio. Jack looked baffled.

'We were so busy focusing on the ground, we never thought to look upwards.' I pointed above their heads.

'You think it was divine retribution?' Jack said sarcastically. I shifted my gaze above the bushes to what surrounded us.

'What if our killer isn't some six-foot-four giant lurking over Ripley, but was hanging around up there?' I stared at the tree overhead. 'They might have been sat in that branch, leant down with the garrotte, slipped it over his head and pulled backwards. Ripley would have been on his tiptoes as they strangled the life from him.' I pictured it in my mind. It wasn't a pretty sight.

'Ingenious,' Athena said as one of her people brought over the ladder. I wasn't sure if she meant my theory or, if it was true, the killer's dexterity. 'It would still have taken a pair of good, strong arms to lift him to cause that amount of damage to his neck and head.'

I pushed the image away but guessed how it could have worked. 'He wouldn't need to be off the ground too much, just high enough for the wire to cut through his throat. And there might have been more than one person in those trees.'

'Jenkins, check those branches for evidence.' Temple pointed into the greenery. Her colleague pushed the ladder against the tree.

Jack looked concerned. 'Shouldn't somebody hold that while he climbs up? You know, because of health and safety and everything.'

Athena Temple shook her head. 'Jenkins knows I'll catch him if he falls.' There was a glint in her face which told me something was going on between her and the bloke up the ladder. I turned a blind eye to whatever it was. Office relationships were frowned upon in the force. Intimate interactions with your subordinates were off-limits if you wanted to keep your job.

'Let me know if you find anything as soon as possible, Tena.' I left the bushes and headed to the car. All I required now was to spend some time with Abigail. We needed to prepare for the meeting at school. I couldn't stand in front of the welfare officer without a plan of action for Abigail's future, no matter how extreme it might be. I had to treat it like a case, examine the evidence and put forward a solution to the problem.

Jack caught up with me.

'If that's how the killer did it, it might have been Kyle Swift or Ruby Vasquez up there.'

'It could have been anybody, Jack. We still don't know how they knew Ripley would be in the park then, or what it's got to do with the post on Twitter.' I pushed each piece of the puzzle to different parts of my brain. Now was the time to concentrate on fixing the problem of Abigail's anonymous tormentors.

It was more important for me to find them than to discover who the Hashtag Killer was. I had one foot in the car when my phone rang. Jack's went as well, and I knew it wasn't good news.

12 FREEDOM OF SPEECH

Bobby Thomas sat in the back room of his flat and contemplated his next move. Lavish furnishings adorned his residence, paid for with the help of his internet admirers and those who believed he was a bastion of free speech in this oppressed and wavering country. On the wall behind him, the flag of Saint George fluttered in the draught wandering in from the open window. It was unusually warm for an English summer.

It's not known if Bobby knew that legend stated Saint George was a Roman soldier of Greek origin, or that the red cross on a white background dated back to Philip II of France in the twelfth century. Considering Bobby Thomas had been born one Robert Lewellyn-Graves and had previously used the pseudonyms, James Grimshaw and Albert Wiggins, the lack of authenticity in the room was unsurprising.

He read the message on the phone once more. Anger flowed through his red and white and blue veins. The organisation he'd founded wanted to kick him out. His continued presence in the media and the courts was, according to them, bringing the English Martyrs into disrepute. He spat his Guinness onto the floor and considered his options.

Bobby reached for the remote and turned the music up; there was nothing like a bit of 77 punk to make him happy. If it hadn't been for the raucous sound of laced-up boots and corduroys blaring around the flat, he might well have heard the intruder crawling through the window.

But nothing could have prepared him for the blow to the back of his head. Or for the many which followed. There was much red on white in the room that night.

POSTED AT 8 PM: What is Justice? by Ruby Vasquez

Yesterday the whole of the country was shocked/engrossed (delete where applicable) by the murder of Evan Ripley and the subsequent tweet #justiceforall which claimed Mr Ripley was a rapist who'd escaped justice. It was this site which first ran the story linking Ripley's death with an apparent vigilante killer - #thehashtagkiller.

Hundreds are murdered every year, so why did this one catch hold of the public's attention in a spectacular way? The original tweet has been the top trending post for twenty-four hours. Most people not only appear to be celebrating what happened to the alleged rapist, but are calling for similar types of justice to be carried out on others. There has even been a widespread call for the return of the death penalty.

Is this because we've become a nation desensitised to violence, where we switch the news over when another genocide is mentioned to focus on fictionalised crime and tragedy? Why do so many people want to watch fantasy stories where women and children are raped and murdered while ignoring the same things happening in their communities?

There's a disconnect between the world we live in and the world we want to live in. Society has progressed rapidly in the last fifty years to where it has outstretched some people's ability to accept the planet doesn't only belong to them.

What does justice mean to us all? What does it mean to you?

Evan Ripley was charged with rape. The police told me he did it and they had the evidence for it. But the case was dropped because of one jokey text the victim sent him. Never mind the physical scars he left all over her body. A single message was enough to drop the case. Never mind the emotional scars she has to live with for the rest of her life. Never mind the wounds to her family and friends.

Does that sound like justice to you?

Detectives interviewed me yesterday, and all because of my post detailing Ripley's behaviour. Those two officers were old beyond their years, worn down by a legal system which works against them and a Government which doesn't value the police.

Does that sound like justice to you?

The authorities set Evan Ripley free five years ago. He was going to attack another woman in that park, do not doubt that. He was only stopped because justice found him.

So do not shed any tears for Evan Ripley and those like him. Cry instead for all the victims who will never find real justice in this world.

BROKEN ORNAMENTS and upturned furniture littered the floor as I entered. Abigail replied to my text when I said I'd be late home. She was used to these disruptions in our family life, but I'd hoped they'd be less frequent starting from now.

'I'm missing dinner with my daughter to stare at the cracked skull of an extremist.' And the nicotine craving had returned with a bang.

'I once knew a man who tried to steal the London Eye.' Jack held his arm out to me, a bloody statue of Big Ben inside his gloved fingers.

'He must have had huge hands.' I'd taken Abs onto the Eye once and she'd hated it. That's when I discovered she loathed heights. She was ten and I didn't know she had vertigo.

'He was so drunk, he thought he was Hercules. He'd wrapped his belt over part of the Eye and tried to drag it across the river. When I got there, his trousers had dropped around his ankles, and he was projectile vomiting like the kid from the *Exorcist*.'

'Is that the murder weapon?' I pointed at little Ben and the red liquid sliding down it.

'Someone bashed in Bobby's head with this. It bonged at least half a dozen times.'

'This is our killer again?' The MO was so different, I couldn't see what the connection was. Apart from both victims being complete bastards.

'According to the internet, yes.' Jack handed the figurine to someone from the crime lab, pulled off his gloves and took out his phone. I moved closer to stare at the post.

#justiceforall

#englandforeveryone

#thehashtagkiller

Underneath was a photo of Bobby Thomas's lifeless face.

'Some of the original replies condemned the crime. Until our killer posted more images from the flat, including these.'

The next photos were more unpleasant than the sight of the cracked skull near my feet. I'd seen some horrendous child pornography in my time with the force, but these were vile.

'These magazines are in here?' I glanced around the place.

'In his bedroom. There are hundreds of them. God knows what we'll find on his computers.' As Jack spoke, Forensics carried a laptop and digital tablet from the flat.

'I'm surprised he kept this secret for so long.'

Jack slipped the phone into his pocket. 'A contact from the press tipped me off about a story which will break tomorrow about Thomas and his hobby. Someone from that group he founded, the English Martyrs, leaked the details to the media.'

'Do you think our killer could be a member of that organisation, maybe with a grudge against him?' My eyes drifted down to the red stain creeping across the wooden floor. First Ripley and now Thomas. How determined did I feel in trying to find the person who'd committed these crimes?

'Why leak the story to the press and then kill him?'

'Let's check to see if there's a connection between him and Evan Ripley.' I moved from the lounge and into the bedroom; the pornographic magazines were scattered over the floor and the bed. Jack followed me into the room.

'Did we do this?' I pointed at the publications.

'Nope; they were like that when we got here. I think

whoever killed him wanted to make sure we didn't miss this stuff.'

'Well, that's one connection: their love for pornography.'

Jack shook his head. 'As someone joked earlier, that's going to connect to a lot of people.'

I walked over to the filing cabinet in the corner. Neo-Nazi paraphernalia and papers connected to other far-right groups filled the drawers, including publicity material for when Thomas stood for parliament in the last General Election. He'd failed miserably and lost his deposit.

'Are there any witnesses?' Could we get that lucky? Apparently not.

'Nope.' Jack shook his head. 'And there are no CCTV cameras in this area. It's a crime as meticulously planned as Evan Ripley's murder. But without those tweets, there's no connection between the two so far.'

'Apart from the heads.' I returned to the body.

'What about them?' Jack appeared perplexed.

I knelt to peer into our victim's haunted orbs. 'Well, both victims were attacked around the head. I think our murderer tried to decapitate Ripley but, for whatever reason, couldn't complete that action.' I pointed at Thomas's blood-covered skull. 'Apart from the eyes peeking through the red, his face is virtually gone, obliterated by all those blows. Our killer wanted to destroy Bobby Thomas until he was unrecognisable. They had to remove Evan Ripley's head so nobody would know who he was. Our killer doesn't just need these people dead; they want their image removed from the world.'

Jack nodded towards the door. 'Athena's here.'

I rose and watched Temple scrutinise the scene like a general on a hill marshalling their troops below. 'We should check unsolved murders where the victim suffered maximum damage to the head or face. I find it hard to believe this is our killer's first rodeo. There's too much violence involved in these.'

Athena wore a glamorous ball-gown underneath her work clothes. Her down-turned lips and pained eyes informed me she wasn't happy.

'The first time I get to visit the opera in six months, and this happens; it's not every day you get to see *Lucrezia Borgia* on the stage.' She zipped up the top of her overall and looked ready to land on the moon. 'And it's our same killer?'

'It would appear so.' Fatigue seeped through me, but I hoped it didn't show.

'I'm afraid the initial analysis isn't so good, Jennifer, from what I've just been told.'

Great, more bad news. I wasn't in the mood to play games with her. 'Tell us, then.'

She looked over the room as her people continued their work. 'This place has had many visitors recently; so far, we've collected over two dozen fingerprints and fibres from the same number of clothes and shoes.'

'As long as you get the details to my team as soon as possible, Athena.' I headed to the door.

'Anything for you, Jennifer, you know that.'

Temple started singing something in Italian as we left. The night drifted in and I was annoyed at being away from Abs. Jack must have noticed my irritated look.

'Are you going to spend time with Abbey when you get home?'

'Well, I can guarantee she won't be in bed; it's far too early for that. I need to make sure we're both on the same page when we go to the meeting with the school tomorrow.'

He hesitated before stretching out and placing his hand on my arm. I'd describe neither of us as tactile, but I appreciated his effort to comfort me.

'She's lucky to have you, Jen.'

Not for one second did I believe that. In my desperate efforts not to repeat the same mistakes of my parents and their obsessive attempts at controlling every single point of my life, I'd stood back too far and left my child to fend for herself when she needed my support the most. I'd always put the job before her. And here I was doing it again.

'When Abigail was about six years old, she kept quizzing me about my work, worried about the bad folks I met daily. To calm her nerves, I told her this life was full of kind people. I'd have hated to have to prove it to her, but I said it anyway.'

A pain gripped me on the right side of my chest as if someone had sliced open my ribs and dropped half a pound of lead in there. If you've ever had a cramp in your leg, it was like that but ten times worse.

'Are you okay, Jen?'

My feet stood frozen to the ground, my nails digging into the palms of my hand. Was this a panic attack? Is this how it feels to be spiralling out of control? It was difficult to breathe, as if every cigarette I'd ever smoked was marching through my lungs to squeeze the breath from my heart.

'Jen, what's wrong?' Jack's grip strengthened to shock me back into the world. The pain didn't dissipate, lingering in my chest, but eased sufficiently for me to pull away from my partner.

'It's fine, Jack. I think I need some rest.'

Rest was the last thing I wanted or needed. The agony vanished and I was real again. It wasn't quite euphoria I felt, but I could control my breathing once more.

'Why don't you have tomorrow off? There are plenty of people in the MIT to take care of this and Ripley. You could spend more time with Abigail and be refreshed when you go to the school.'

It sounded tempting, but I couldn't do it. Whatever had just happened to my body, I wouldn't let it beat me.

'You know me, Jack, I have to keep the brain busy. Six hours sleep and some fat-infused pizza will have me right as rain tomorrow.'

I ignored the thunder inside my head and wondered when this Hashtag Killer would strike again.

13   VOX POPULI

I t surprised me how well the second one went. I shouldn't have been, considering how much planning and training had gone into it. Staying awake all night was a bit of a pain, but I had to be sure Thomas would be at home. Finding his details was child's play, same for getting into his emails and social media accounts. You would have thought a prospective politician would implement greater security around himself. The amount of Russian troll bots I found attached to his Twitter and Instagram posts was remarkable.

Darkness had descended upon the city and a fine drizzle murmured in the ether. Hustlers and pimps drifted in and out of the shadows, sometimes attempting to approach me but slinking away once I scowled at them. During the day, I could exhibit the most unassuming of identities, but at night an invisible barrier surrounded me which fellow travellers in the dark-life recognised.

It may have been late, but unwanted kids and runaway animals still littered the streets. Just outside the Diablo dive bar, a bunch of these urchins stood laughing and pointing as a small black and white dog attempted to have sex with a *much larger member of its species. I walked past them and pushed the front door of the tavern open as the smaller beast fell to the floor panting, its seed extinguished, its mouth salivating.*

The bar was the zenith of low-life drinking establishments, full of Bukowski wannabes, failed Hollywood princesses, and kings and queens of the night. Plastered across the walls were wrinkled posters advertising faded musical combos, gaudy strip shows and numerous acts of magic.

A bottle of cold Mexican beer set me on my way. The bartender poured a whiskey into a plastic glass. I scowled at his audacity to decency and the rules of civilised living. He shrugged his shoulders as if to say it was all beyond his control. When we can't use glass for fear of safety, and we can't use plastic for fear of the environment, what will we have left?

I scooped up the drink and clasped it to me like lost treasure, taking it to a table in the shadows. I swept the spit and sawdust from the top with my arm and sank into a chair. The TV blared neon in the corner. Thomas had been pushed from the news feeds, replaced by some Z-list celebrity who'd choked on a frozen Mars Bar.

My mind invented new ways to kill using only sweets: clubbed to death with a Toblerone; blinded by a Twix; throat sliced with an After Eight Mint; conked on the back of the head with a Terry's Chocolate Orange. I finished the rest of the beer and suffered a sudden craving for an Easter egg.

I got out my phone and flicked through the media.

The Mystery of the Hashtag Killer was the third story on the news, only topped by the buffoonish American President's regular Twitter rants and warnings of another fall in the Pound. I read the article with glee, noting the links to my original tweets and the blog where Ruby Vasquez promoted my actions. I rechecked Twitter, ecstatic by how much traction the #justiceforall and #thehashtagkiller hashtags were getting. Somebody had added #bringbackthedeathpenalty to my tweets.

The pub filled up around me. People bought their drinks, started an initial conversation, but then it always followed the same pattern. There came a lull in the chatter, or someone went to the bar or the toilet, and then the phones came out and they were all lost in the digital world. Here, in this teeming watering hole, in the most social of places, they sought solitude with something which never ignored them. It was the only connection they craved. Why talk to another person when you could peer into a flickering screen at a grumpy cat or a baby wearing a suit?

I gazed at them tapping their screens, scrolling through the minutiae of the electronic universe, and wondered what the next level of progress would be; if this were progress. For now, it was the perfect tool for what I needed.

But what to do next? My original plan had been for a gradual increase in events, but the response had been far higher than I expected. It would be easy for other things to overtake my spot in the limelight, and my long-term strategy relied on a continued presence in the media.

And it looked like my audience was supportive and hungry for more. There'd been some adverse reaction to Thomas's death, those extremists will stick together, but it had soon withered away with those photographs of his deviant sexual habits.

A woman strode past me, giving me a lingering look unmistakable in its lack of subtlety; she had so much cake on her face, it didn't match the rest of her body. It was tempting, but there was still much for me to do.

Some drunken office buffoons stumbled into my table and staggered towards the bar; their eyes were soulless saucers, dragging their bodies into an eternal limbo of shattered dreams and the realisation every single thing they did was pointless.

The masses were sold a sunken dream, chasing a materialist utopia which was sinking beneath the waves before the first credit check turned up. They were a poorly educated population, gorging on fake news and post-truth, easily diverted by consumerism and celebrity with little concept of decent governance and how the climate will be unliveable for humans in the next fifty years.

I was allowing myself to get distracted. This happens when I spend too much time around other people. There's something good to be said about choosing isolation over social interaction.

I finished my drink and was slipping away from the crowd, heading towards the door when the sight of the most unexpected thing stopped me in my tracks. Two blokes walked to the bar wearing the same design of shirt. Printed on the front were the words I'd remember for the rest of the night and into tomorrow.

The Hashtag Killer 4Ever

This was beyond my wildest dreams. The momentum was with me, and I couldn't let it slip. I had to speed up my plans and move everything up a notch.

When I got home from work, Abigail was slumped on the sofa staring at an old black and white movie. It was one of my daughter's many surprising traits, how she was interested in things most teenagers didn't know existed.

'What are you watching?' I put the kettle on and ignored the cat's vacant stare.

Abigail paused the broadcast.

'It's a Hitchcock classic, *The Wrong Man*.' Henry Fonda had fascinated Abigail ever since she'd seen *Twelve Angry Men*.

I took out my phone. 'Okay then, we'll have a movie night and order some pizza.'

Sometime later, we'd gorged on two pizzas, a bag of chips, and a slice of chocolate cake each while watching *Harvey*. I was stuffed when I sloped off to sleep, but it was the closest I'd been to Abs in a long time. And there had been no mention of school and that problem. The dead eyes of Ripley and Thomas didn't haunt my dreams.

The aroma of fried food woke me the next morning.

'Can I smell cooked bacon down there?' I crawled out of bed and headed to the bathroom.

'It'll be all gone if you don't hurry,' came the reply. I brushed my teeth and forced my face and hair into some form of respectability. When I got downstairs, there was bacon and eggs, a glass of fresh orange and a cup of coffee. I downed the caffeine and ignored the omelette.

'Mum,' Abigail said in mock amusement.

'I need it to wake me up, love.' I covered the meat in brown sauce, determined not to ruin the first time she'd cooked for me. Abigail turned her nose up at the sight of it.

'You're killing all the flavour that way, Mum.'

I laughed and shook my head. 'I'm enhancing the taste of the dead pig, dear daughter.' I was so relaxed, I considered not going to work. As I contemplated such an unlikely option, I received a text from Jack.

Vasquez has posted on her blog again. You should read it.

'What will you do today, love?'

'Just laze around the house I suppose until we go to school.'

I put the phone away and stared at Abs. I didn't like leaving Abigail at home on her own again before getting the bullying problem sorted.

'How would you fancy coming to work with me, and then we'll head to school from there?'

Abigail's face lit up like a Christmas tree. 'Are you sure, Mum? I won't get in the way?'

'Of course you wouldn't, love.' Now I'd mentioned it, I didn't know what Abs would do all day while I worked. She must have read my mind.

'But what will I do while you work? You've got two murders to solve. I don't want to be in your way.'

I finished the food and gulped down the orange juice.

Another message pinged into my phone, this time from Alice Voss in Cybercrime. It gave me an idea.

'Grab your gym gear and stuff it in a bag with a change of clothes. You can use the top-notch facilities we have at the station. You might as well try them since I never get the chance.'

Abigail's face transformed into a crumpled blanket. 'I'm not in the mood for exercise.'

'Spend some time there this morning, then after lunch, try Cybercrime's new training programme.'

I remembered Alice telling me how the unit used to go into schools to explain to the staff and the kids about the dangers of browsing online, from bullying to identity theft. But Cybercrime had become so overwhelmed with cases they'd had to cut down on those visits. Instead, they'd devised an interactive training and awareness programme which would work in a school with minimum police involvement. It sounded great in my head, but I saw the doubt in Abigail's face.

'That sounds like being back at school, Mum.' The thought of it dragged her eyelids so far down, I barely saw her eyes.

'They need beta testers for something new they've devised, and they'll only take the cleverest people for it.' I waited for Abs to protest more, but my charm must have worked on her. She jumped up and hugged me.

'Thanks, Mum; you're the best.'

I'd never got used to how quickly the typical teenager could swap moods. Was I like that at her age? She ran upstairs to find her stuff. A warm glow I hadn't felt in a long time flowed through me.

I let the idea linger in my head for a minute before checking the text messages, starting with the one from

Cybercrime. Alice updated me with the news she'd found no links between Ripley, Vasquez, and Mazz Coe; there was also nothing to link Ripley and Bobby Thomas. I texted my thanks as a reply and asked if Abigail could spend some time using the school programme this afternoon.

Absolutely. I look forward to it, Alice replied. As Abigail bounced around upstairs, I read Ruby Vasquez's new post. I still couldn't work out what her intention was. Was she that desperate for attention she'd sink to the level of promoting a killer? Or commit murder? She'd posted the blog about the same time as Bobby Thomas's death, but I didn't see a connection between the two.

Thirty minutes later, we were at work, and I checked Abigail into the building.

'I'll see you at lunchtime.' I dropped Abigail off at the gym and headed down to see Jack.

He squeezed his SpongeBob Square Pants stress reliever as I grabbed my seat. 'Was Abigail with you?' I explained my plan for the day to him. 'I hope you get everything sorted with the school.' He slammed SpongeBob's plastic head into the desk.

'Thanks. What did you make of Vasquez's latest attempt at journalism?'

He laughed while flicking SpongeBob into the drawer. 'At least she didn't mention our names.'

'It was curious how she referred to Ripley throughout her piece, changing how she addressed him to the point he became less than human.'

Jack was about to reply when the phone vibrated on his desk. He picked it up before it rang again. The news must have been good considering the smile it gave him.

'Thanks,' he said as he finished the call and stood.

'We've had a hit on Kyle Swift's credit card. He's in a

pub, not more than a mile away from Adams Park. We could let the uniforms bring him in and concentrate on Thomas's crushed skull.'

My mouth was drier than the Sahara. I slipped some nicotine gum between my lips.

'No, let's leave that to the team. I need some fresh air and exercise.'

We rushed from the building, and I pushed all thoughts of Abigail to the side. It was painfully easy.

'Tell the uniforms to wait outside the pub. Don't engage with him unless he tries to go,' I said into the radio. Four PC's were waiting for us when we got there.

'What's he doing?' I said to the closest one.

'Sat at the bar on his own, ma'am, drinking heavily by the look of it.'

'Great,' Jack said. 'I guarantee you he's an angry drunk.'

I put my hand on the door. 'I'll go in on my own.'

'No way, Jen.' Jack reached towards me. 'Even if he doesn't have a weapon, he's big enough to knock you out.'

'He won't see me as a threat. You and the uniforms will only anger him. You can watch through the window. Any sign of trouble and you have my permission to run in and bash him on the bonce.' The words made me think of Thomas and those dull eyes peeking between the river of blood covering his face. Was there a connection between the murders of Ripley and Thomas? What if last night was a copycat?

I pushed the door open before Jack protested, surprised to see how busy the pub was so early in the morning. About half a dozen pensioners supped pints and ate breakfast in the corner, while a group of blokes in their mid-thirties gathered around a tatty looking pool table. It was one of those pubs my dad used to frequent after work and at weekends instead of spending any time with his family. It stank of stale beer and desperation.

Kyle Swift stared into a pint glass while sitting at the bar. I pulled up a stool next to him and asked the young girl behind the counter for half a coke. The extra caffeine would keep me on edge. Swift was grasping his phone and flicking through the photos in the gallery. Every one of them was of the same pretty dark-haired, blue-eyed woman: his sister. He gripped the mobile so hard, I thought he'd snap it in two.

'Debbie needs you at home, Kyle.' I kept my words quiet so nobody else would hear. Swift turned towards me, his eyes burning red.

'Fuck off, copper.'

I picked up the drink and sipped at the coke. The volcanic anger in his voice attracted the attention of the others in the bar.

'I can't do that, Kyle, I need you to come with me.'

He had three-quarters of a pint left, pushing it to his mouth and draining it in one go. Then he dropped the glass to the floor where it shattered.

'You fucking coppers ruined Debbie's life, but at least that monster Ripley is dead.' He shouted the words at me, his alcohol-fuelled breath making my eyes water. The blokes from the pool table moved towards us.

'Are you talking about Evan Ripley, mate?' The one who spoke was close enough I smelt his cheap aftershave. Swift stood up and faced the group.

'Ripley raped my sister and I'm glad the cunt is dead. I wish I'd done it sooner.' The bar was quiet for a split second, and then all the other customers got up and started clapping.

'Good for you, son,' the pensioners shouted.

'And these fucking coppers did nothing about it.' Swift

pointed at me while reaching into his jacket. He pulled out a long. dark piece of material, like a shoelace but thicker.

'When I was in Iraq, my squadron had to kill with anything we got our hands on, even stuff like this.'

Before I could react, he had it around my neck and pulled it tight. I fell towards him and clutched at my throat. Blood pumped through my skull as the pool players roared at him to kill the copper. I forced my head into Swift's chest as Jack and the uniforms burst into the pub.

'Police,' Jack shouted unnecessarily as they came under a hail of balls and pool cues. Swift and I crashed to the floor as he pulled harder on the thread and I struggled to get it from his hands. He used his weight to roll me onto my back and leer over my head.

'Why do you care he's dead? I did your job for you.'

I lifted my leg and kneed him in the balls. He fell backwards like a sack of spuds. I tore the material from my throat, spluttering air from my lungs, glad I could breathe again. Swift tried to reach for me again, so I kicked him in the groin one more time.

The cuffs were in my hand as he groaned on the floor. I rolled him onto his stomach and pulled his hands around his back. I slipped the cuffs on as tight as they'd go. I read him his rights as my colleagues dealt with the pool playing hooligans.

'There'll be a nice bruise across your neck in a few hours.' Jack rubbed the top of his head as he came up to me.

'Looks like you'll have the same on your noggin, partner.'

'Aye. One of these twonks caught me with the white ball, and you know how I hate sports.' He grinned at me as a bevvy of blue flashing lights pulled up outside and the hooligans were hauled out into the wagon. I stared at Swift as he cursed at me from the floor.

'Those Geordies certainly can swear,' Jack said as paramedics came up to us.

I glared at Swift. 'We'll be having another chat, soon.' My colleagues dragged him away as a medic checked my throat.

'Ouch.' Cold hands touched my skin. I hoped it wouldn't look too bad when I met up with Abs later. I could imagine what they'd think of me at the school, looking like this. As the medic poked at my weary flesh, I texted Alice to ask if she might take Abigail to lunch before taking her through the training programme.

I turned to Jack. 'The Ripley case may be over.'

'How come?' he replied.

'Because Swift confessed to me.'

I dabbed at the pain in my throat, knowing it was never this easy.

15 RUBY'S FANDOM

COPPERS ATTACK RAPE VICTIM'S BROTHER
I stared at the tweet, always amazed that people in their seventies could use Twitter. Unless he'd lied about his age in his profile, and the photo of a grey-haired old man wasn't him. I direct messaged him, explained who I was and asked for more details. He was a quick typist and replied immediately.

From the description he gave, I guessed the female copper in the bar was DI Flowers. The tweeting pensioner also sent me some photos of the damage done to the pub; some brave justice seekers, including a group of senior citizens, had tried to protect the brother of the woman Evan Ripley attacked when the coppers went to arrest him. Stories kept falling into my lap and I wouldn't waste the opportunity.

I was unconvinced my Hashtag Killer had murdered Bobby Thomas; there were too many differences in the methodology and I'd failed to find a link between him and Ripley, no matter how far I'd dug. It wasn't beyond the realm of possibility a worm like Ripley would share the same warped world view as the horrible human being that used to be Bobby Thomas, but I couldn't see the connection. No, I had to focus on my original plan.

'I wonder if I can name those two detectives in my next blog post?' The legal necessities of such a thing seemed hazy to me.

'Are you peddling filth and lies again?'

My mother's voice was like sandpaper against my cheek. It forced me to snap forward, so I caught my elbow on the sharp corner of the computer.

'Fucking hell, Mother, what have I told you about sneaking up on me?' I glared at the old woman, breathing in the tobacco's stink as pain rippled through my arm. She took another drag on the cigarette and blew smoke at my face. I resisted the urge to punch her teeth in.

'You better take care on the streets with all those criminals if me and my creaking bones can get the drop on you.' She sounded like a gangster's moll from some 1940s film noir. She cackled and grinned as a mushroom cloud of smoke drifted around the room. I steadied my beating heart.

'What do you want, Mother?'

'I've read your stories, your made-up morality tales of murderers and victims.' She slunk toward me. 'You think I can't use a computer, but I took some classes in the library last year, and I know everything about the digital world and the maggots who crawl through it.'

This revelation stunned me. Isabel Vasquez was a dinosaur in every respect, from being a parent to appreciating equality and diversity. When she was sober, she was barely literate, so the thought of her surfing the internet had my brain in tatters.

'You've been reading my articles?' I closed the laptop to shut out Mother's piggish eyes from crawling over my work.

'Articles my arse. They're fairy tales and you're no journo. I've read and seen everything you've done, including those laughable YouTube videos and pathetic attempts at being a pop star.' She stubbed the cigarette out on my bed. 'I've even got more Facebook friends than you.' The cackle returned, the Wicked Witch of the South tormenting me again. A volcano built up inside my mind as I gripped the computer.

'You need to hit me, don't you, Ruby? Go ahead then, you'll be your father's daughter after all.' Her eyes tormented me. I wanted to rip that shrivelled head from its useless body. Instead, I dropped the laptop onto the bed and stormed by her and out of the house.

'Run away, Ruby, just like you've always done.' That yell was an echo which had followed me all my life.

I sprinted, anger burning through me, running aimlessly, pushing past people on the street and avoiding the chattering teeth of hyperactive small dogs. I turned the corner and paused for breath. My heart beat as if I was an arthritic coal miner. I had to find somewhere else to live before one of us killed the other.

My hair billowed behind me in the wind. I had little money of my own, but that would change soon. There'd been two job offers, but I'd turned those down. The first was for the Naked City website. The owners offered me the reporting assignment for where I lived, joining the massive rota of street journalists they had all over the country. The pay was minimum and I'd be just another voice lost amongst hundreds. I needed to be the star of the show. It's why I'd also refused the opportunity of an apprenticeship at the city's leading free newspaper. I wondered what Mother would think of me rejecting such respectable jobs.

And I'd been presented with paid advertising for my blog. I wasn't sure what to do about those offers; they were tempting, but I didn't want to be perceived as a sell-out.

The Kyle Swift article sat in my Cloud account and I needed to get it online as soon as possible. I had to keep the momentum going. The pub was only a couple of Tube stops away, but it meant heading back past the house and the possibility of seeing my mother.

I could walk there in about forty minutes.

The exercise would do me good, and it would clear my mind for the next step. I pushed the hair from my eyes and set off at a brisk pace, devising a plan as I went. At least one article posted per day to keep ahead of the competition. The one this morning had proved popular, and now people clamoured for more. I could take photos at the pub and interview staff and customers.

The sun caressed my face, creating warmth both inside and out. There would be a piece featuring the coppers who'd interviewed me and who were obviously involved in arresting Kyle Swift: DI Flowers and the smartly dressed bloke I couldn't remember the name of. I wouldn't have to name them, just give them nicknames and descriptions. A bit of research online about them would add some background details.

I scanned the messages on my phone. I would do a follow up on the initial tweet, interact with some who supported the vigilante, write an article about the mood of the country. All my mother's negativity vanished from my shoulders as I made my way through the city.

The original Twitter poster fascinated me. Were they the murderer? I'd messaged them through Twitter numerous times with no reply. What about a request for contact through my blog? Sure, I wouldn't know if it was the real Hashtag Killer or not, but I'd still be able to use the replies, just like those fake messages which attracted media attention during the Yorkshire Ripper case and the Dear Boss letters during the granddaddy of them all, Jack the Ripper. I couldn't keep the smile from my face, my mind awash with serial killers and Evan Ripley's head on the verge of decapitation.

My skull throbbed with noise. I tried to blanket it out, but there was another sound right on my periphery. I cleared everything away and focused on it, fearful it might be a trigger for a blackout. Usually, just before an incident, my eyes would blur and the throbbing at the front of my head would explode in intensity. I stopped walking and reached for my tablets. As I placed two in my mouth, I realised what the repetitive clatter was: footsteps behind me. When I threw the drugs between my lips, the steps paused. I wanted to turn around, but didn't. My throat was dry, and the medication scraped against my flesh as the pills struggled their way down into my guts.

It's all in my head. There's no one following me. Why would there be?

I continued walking, about twenty-five minutes from the pub. My mother's words returned to jag at my brain; not only those from this morning, but all the ones from across my life.

'You'll never account for anything.'
'You're useless.'
'No wonder you have no friends.'
'You're a freak.'
'You're just like him.'
'Him. Him. Him. Him.'

My heart pounded and the footsteps resumed, louder and nearer this time. I glanced either side of me, but not behind. I was all alone on the street, apart from those steps. Maybe Mother had followed me to torment me some more? In the middle of all the viciousness, she was right about one thing: I had been directionless in life, drifting aimlessly like everyone else, searching for tiny glimpses of joy amongst the pain and despair. But not now. Now I had something to aim for, had goals to achieve. I would tell the story of the Hashtag Killer and those who championed him.

The noises in my head matched those behind me, increasing in volume until it was a cacophony. I dug my fingers into my palms and was turning to face the din when a giant hand fell onto my shoulder.

'I've been searching for you, Ruby Vasquez.'

Sweat dripped down my arm and from my fingers. His nails were long and yellow and cut into my skin. I tried to pull away, but he had hold of me like one of those games scooping out toys at the seaside.

'Who are you?'

I tensed my muscles and twisted my shoulder, seeing a big man, over six foot and built like a bodybuilder. He dragged me closer, his aftershave an aroma of French cheese. His chin was dotted with cuts as if shaved by Edward Scissorhands.

'I'm your biggest fan, Ruby.'

His mouth had more gaps in it than teeth, with breath which would strip paint from a wall. He let me go and I staggered backwards.

'My biggest fan?'

I couldn't get my thoughts in order, confused about what he wanted from me. My eyes darted to find someone for help, but the street was empty apart from the two of us.

'Of the support you're giving the Hashtag Killer.' His grin made my stomach tremble. 'You're doing the country a great service.'

'I'm not supporting him. I'm only reporting the facts.' I didn't believe my words, but panic consumed me. His eyes shrank and turned grey.

'Don't put yourself down, Ruby. Without your posts, nobody would know who he was.' He held out his arms as I inched away. Was I fast enough to outrun him?

'And there's more coming soon, you'll see; more for you to report.'

I moved back from him. My foot slid off the pavement, my ankle twisting a little as I stepped into the road. Pain jabbed through my toes, but I never took my focus from him.

'What do you mean, there's more coming?'

He crept towards me. 'I've read all the tweets, thousands of them. I've made them into a book. Look.'

He dipped into the plastic bag he carried and pulled out a ream of paper covered in text.

'There's a Movement coming, a Crusade. Others will take up his mantle.'

Fear gripped my throat as I inched off the pavement. He was talking about copycats. Copycat vigilantes dispensing justice on the guilty. Is that what I wanted?

A motorbike whizzed past, barely missing my leg. My admirer moved into the road and towards me; he held the paper out.

'You should read this. I've highlighted all the best bits. You could write about them, mention my name.' I reached for them, pulling back when he let go so they dropped into the road. The pages were loose and scattered everywhere. He screamed and scrambled to pick them up. I took that as my chance, turning and sprinting across the street. Head-lights yelled in my face, brakes shrieking as a car swerved to miss me. A multitude of horns blasted into the air as I made the other side and kept on running. From the corner of my eye I saw he'd gathered up his papers. I moved round the bend, ducked down an alley, and sprinted towards the pub.

If ever I needed a drink, it was now.

16 SCHOOL'S OUT

Kyle Swift rattled the handcuffs connected to the table. Two burly uniformed officers stood behind him, Jack and I sitting opposite. In England and Wales, the criminal law is based on an adversarial system, which means it's the police's goal to get a suspect arrested, charged and convicted, and the defence lawyer's job to prevent this. Swift was a suspect in the Evan Ripley murder; I'd told him this when I returned to the station and watched him gaze at the bruise around my neck. He didn't care, and he didn't want a lawyer, which was fine with me.

Jack switched on the recording device. My throat ached and I resisted the urge to scratch at the wound Swift had made. I hoped his genitals suffered more. 'You have a right to silence. Whatever you say can be used against you in a criminal case in court. If you don't mention something now which you mention later, a court might ask why you didn't mention it at the first opportunity.'

'When did you arrive in London?' Jack asked him.

Swift glared at me. 'How's your throat?'

I peered deep into his angry face.

'Are you still pissing blood?' Jack said. Swift rattled his cuffs again and grimaced. 'Two days ago, where were you at six o'clock in the morning?' Swift stretched his frame to its full height. Even secured to the table, he was still imposing.

'I murdered that cunt, Evan Ripley.'

Jack glanced at me, then back at Swift. 'Is that a confession?'

Swift pointed at his head and grinned.

'I've been murdering him every hour of every day for the last five years.'

I opened the file and pushed the photos towards Swift. 'You deny killing Evan Ripley?'

Swift tried to scratch his face until the cuffs reminded him he couldn't.

'What do you think would happen if I confessed?' He stared at Jack first, and then me. 'No jury would convict me. I'd be a hero to the public.' I held up the photo where Ripley's head hung from a thread.

'We don't live in a lawless society yet; whoever did this will go to prison. We need to eliminate you from our enquiries.' I peered into his eyes and saw deep, vivid pools of guilt. If he had murdered Evan Ripley, I couldn't imagine him feeling guilty about it. No, that remorse must be for something else.

Swift shifted in his chair, examining the mark he'd left around my neck.

'I remember nothing about coming here. I was pissed leaving Newcastle and had a hangover when I arrived.'

I placed the photo back into the file. 'So you have nobody to confirm your location when Evan Ripley was murdered?'

'No,' he replied. 'But it eased my headache when I found out what happened to him.'

Kyle Swift was a difficult man to intimidate. Whether that was to do with his military training, his impressive bulk or something inherent in him, it didn't matter to me. Staring at him, at his body language and the smug grin on his face, I knew he wouldn't tell us anything. Most of his service file was sealed, but what was available was significant: the Taliban had held him in Afghanistan for two weeks. If he could resist their interrogation techniques, there was no chance of him buckling from our attempt. We'd have to wait and see what was discovered at the cheap hotel he'd booked a room at.

'Which side of the political spectrum would you say you stand, Mr Swift?' It was hard to tell which of the two of them seemed more surprised by my question. Jack raised his eyebrows at me. Kyle Swift grunted.

'What are you on about, copper?'

'I always assume the grunts in the military lean towards a far-right worldview, and I wondered if you shared such thoughts?'

He leant back into his chair. 'You're fucking mental.'

'You're not a fan of Bobby Thomas then?'

'I don't know who that is.'

I believed him. I grabbed the file and got up. 'I hope your sister recovers soon.'

Jack scampered after me as I left the room. 'What was that all about at the end? You think he killed Thomas?'

'I've no idea what he's capable of. I only wanted to see what reaction I'd get when I mentioned Thomas's name and his political affiliations. Kyle Swift is feeling guilty about something, but I'm not sure what it is. We better find out where he spent his time since getting off the train at King's Cross.'

A message hit both our phones simultaneously; I

checked it as we walked. It was Forensics saying they'd found no evidence on the branches of the trees where Ripley was murdered.

Jack's stomach groaned. 'Well, that's useful.'

'The only thing Swift is concerned about is his sister. You might rattle him by mentioning her, but I wasn't going to do it. She deserves better than that.' I rubbed at my throat. I didn't want Abigail to see me like this, and God knows what the school would think when we turned up. The meeting was in an hour, so I made my way to pick Abs up from the Cybercrime unit.

Jack pointed at my wound.

'I could lend you a scarf to cover that up.' I considered the offer, but declined.

'Thanks, but I don't want to keep any secrets from Abigail. What will you do while I'm gone?' We reached the lift and I stepped inside.

'I'll let Swift stew for a bit before grilling him again before I finish. I hope everything goes well at the school.'

I got out of the lift three flights up to see Abigail and Alice Voss waiting for me in the middle of the corridor.

'What happened to your neck, Mum?' Abigail's face darkened with worry.

'I'll tell you about it on the way over, love. I need a quick word with Alice. Can you meet me at the lift?' Abigail reluctantly did as I asked.

I smiled at Alice. 'Thanks for looking after her this afternoon; I owe you one.'

'Think nothing of it; it was my pleasure. She's a terrific kid. I'm sorry to hear what she's been going through.'

I pulled a face like a wet frog, surprised Abigail had been so open with a stranger.

'She told you about the messages?'

'It came up as part of the programme she went through today. One unit is about not hiding things which make you uncomfortable online. I think she was glad to talk about it to someone she didn't know. I hope you get everything sorted this afternoon.'

I nodded. 'So do I.' I changed the subject. 'Has Cyber-crime got anything from Bobby Thomas's electronic devices?'

The glint in Alice's eyes dulled a little. Her lips shone deep red and glistened as she spoke, a stray dark hair often dropping to obscure the vision in her right eye before she brushed it away.

'There's a bucket full of incriminating evidence on his phone and laptop, horrible stuff connected to his deviant tastes and extremist views.' The blue of her eyes shimmered in what seemed like anger, but her tone was professional. 'But as yet, we've found nothing hinting at a murder suspect or any connection to the first victim. The team will keep working on it.' The smile returned to her face. 'I'll search through Kyle Swift's mobile this afternoon.'

I thanked her again and joined Abs at the lift. We had a lot to talk about on the way to the school.

IT TOOK a thirty-five-minute drive across the city to get there, plus another twenty minutes wait outside the office while Doreen scowled at me. Then we were welcomed into the seat of power.

When Abbey's school transformed into an academy, a new principal arrived with an attitude that discipline was the priority. Standards would be raised, and student behaviour would be at the heart of everything the academy did. I had no issue with any of that, but the school's lack-adaisical approach to online bullying infuriated me beyond belief.

Abbey checked her makeup in a small mirror. I stared at my thirteen-year-old daughter and, regardless of the severity of what was happening, could only admire her creativity: Abbey's jet black hair was immaculately brushed so it stood up on her head, with strands shooting in different angles. It looked like a perfectly groomed witch's hat. Her lipstick was redder than the heart of the sun and seemed to burn just as bright. Black lace top, black lace gloves, and long, flowing dark dress completed her elegant combination. I couldn't help but smile and was pleased when Abbey smiled back.

'Thank you for coming today, Ms Flowers; I know you're busy with the police force.'

The welfare officer Adam Giles sat behind his desk and ignored the student he was in charge of. He used the term Ms as if it was a crime to be unmarried, especially if you were a parent. He wasted no time on more pleasantries and cut straight to the chase.

'Persistent absence is a serious problem for students. Much of the work children miss when they're off school is never made up, leaving them at a considerable disadvantage.'

He didn't wait for me to construct a reply. Thick glasses slipped down his nose and lingered there like the crashed bus at the end of the *Italian Job*. The original movie, not the rubbish American remake.

'A student defined as a persistent absentee is one who misses ten per cent or more of school. Abigail has lost fifty-seven per cent of her lessons this academic year.' He seemed proud they'd worked the percentage out exactly. He repeated the number just in case I wasn't paying attention. 'Fifty-seven per cent.'

'What?' I didn't know what else to say.

'How do you intend to address this problem, Ms Flowers?' He gave me a little smile as he asked the question. He still hadn't looked at Abbey.

'Have you considered why Abigail has missed so many lessons?' Ice shimmered behind my eyes and in my voice.

'There's nothing we can do about your daughter's out-of-school activities, Ms Flowers.' If my tone had been cold, his was an iceberg. 'Isn't it a police matter to check on things like online bullying and harassment?' He brought his hands together, face sparkling with contempt and desire to dismiss us from this precious school. I'd promised to stay calm, to do everything in my power to help Abigail in this situation, but staring at him, all I saw was my father glaring back at me and telling me to stop crying and stand up for myself. I hadn't thought of him in years, but the image of his crooked grin pierced my eyeballs.

Then my vision blurred and it was Evan Ripley's head slipping from his body and rolling across the floor, where it bumped into a blood-covered Bobby Thomas cradling a red crusted statue of Big Ben. The hands on the clock pushed through the gore and struck at the witching hour. The sound and fury of the end of my world consumed me. Everything I'd been keeping back tumbled from my mouth, with no consideration for what it might do to my daughter or me.

'Supermarket trolleys with wonky wheels are more stable than the leadership of this school, Giles; you're the idiot's idea of a thinking man. God knows what the Principal sees in you, but I can only assume you have a collection of dodgy photos of some of them since you're at your best when you say or do nothing at all.'

'Mum!' Abigail's shout was loud, but not enough to derail my rage. Giles's voice narrowed as he gasped. Abigail clutched at my arm.

'If it takes the rest of my life, I'll make sure I get this school closed down.' I dug deep into my handbag to retrieve a sealed envelope. 'Abigail will be schooled at home from now; this is my letter requesting your permission.' I handed him the envelope as his breathing returned to normal. The bulge in his eyes shrank. Abs appeared gobsmacked.

My whole career could have gone up in smoke at that point, but the little man did nothing but stare at me. Deep inside, I knew my anger was not directed at him but at myself for letting things get this far. I'd pressed the self-destruct button which I thought I'd lost years ago.

Giles opened the envelope using a pretentious ornate silver letter opener. I left him reading the contents as I took Abigail from the office and the school for good.

Abs's face was paralysed with shock as we got into the car. I wasn't sure what had stunned her the most: my verbal attack or the prospect of being taught at home.

'You'll be teaching me?'

'No, my dear daughter; when do you ever listen to me? I can afford tutors, and since you're spending most of your time, fifty-seven per cent of it, away from school and at the house, I thought you might as well be there permanently.' We strode towards the car. 'We just have to work out your timetable now.'

The look on her face gave me more satisfaction than catching any crook had ever done.

17 TEENAGE KICKS

The visit to the pub was a great success. The pint of coke cooled my nerves after the encounter with the loon in the street, and it helped me mix with the regulars. And they were quick to talk about what had happened with Kyle Swift and the coppers.

I took the Tube home, deciding to put up with the crush for once. I didn't want to take the chance of bumping into my strange admirer again. I'd uploaded the pub article before going underground and it was getting favourable responses before the signal disappeared. I avoided eye contact with anybody and everybody and drafted the next piece while travelling.

Mother was out when I got home. I jogged up to my room, much happier than when I left a few hours ago. I pushed a chair up against the door and started the laptop. Once I entered the password, I connected the phone to the computer and transferred the draft over.

I still needed a catchy title. This wouldn't be straight reporting but an editorial on the Hashtag Killer case and its broader effect on society. There had to be a change to the narrative. The text sat open on the screen and I stared at it.

An hour later, I was finished, running it through an app to check spelling and grammar. It would have been handy to run it past someone impartial before publication, to get another set of eyes on it, but I had no one I trusted. I reread it for the umpteenth time, speaking aloud to hear the words in the air.

HERO OR VILLAIN?

The title was okay, but did it need the question mark? I left it in for now.

Somewhere in the City, a police detective, let's call her Rose, is searching for the Hashtag Vigilante.

I pursed my lips at that line. Was it a strong enough opening? At least I got the change of name in early. If the narrative was to move forward, they couldn't be the Hashtag Killer anymore. It was hard to keep justifying support for a murderer.

I've met Rose. She's convinced she's doing the right thing, but is she? The Law tells her the Hashtag Vigilante is wrong and she has to find justice for Evan Ripley. But the public isn't too sure.

#justicefordebbie. Evan Ripley deserved to die.

#justiceforall. The Ripley effect is coming.

And now Bobby Thomas has been added to the list for his crimes against humanity.

#justiceforthekids. Thomas got what was coming to him.

The majority who speak are shouting loud and clear that Evan Ripley and Bobby Thomas had to pay for their crimes.

But the Law says otherwise. So maybe the Law is wrong.

An abuser of children should be brought to justice, wouldn't you agree? Yet those we vote into power regularly

bomb kids, even though the people protest against it. And
when our politicians are not doing that, they sign pieces of
paper which condemn millions of children into poverty, star-
vation and even death. Nearly 4.5 million UK children are
living in poverty today. And we do nothing about it.

A man commits himself to God, but preys on the weak
and the vulnerable. Whose justice is that?

Kyle Swift was arrested yesterday because Rose believes
he murdered Evan Ripley. Kyle Swift, a decorated war hero
who sacrificed so much for his country. Kyle Swift, whose
sister was violently attacked by Evan Ripley. What justice
would you pass on to him if you sat on his jury?

Perhaps a few edits in the language. Keep it short and to
the point. Most people don't want to read a wall of text on
the internet. Add the links to the poverty figures and my
Swift post from earlier, then some images from Thomas's
flat, links to the child porn he had. Rumours were flying
around online it wasn't only magazines he had in his home,
but photos of kids he'd taken himself.

I lay on the bed and gazed at the ceiling. Not even the
sound of my mother slamming the door downstairs would
knock me from my blissful state. For once, everything was
going swimmingly in my life.

'ARE YOU OKAY, MUM?' Abigail's face was a blanket of
fear. Guilt stabbed at me for what I'd put her through in
that room; for what I'd put her through since this whole
thing had started. I put my arms around her as we got to
the car.

'I'm fine, love. I'm probably still a bit shook up from this
morning.' I reached for my throat, but then pulled away. I'd

promised to get this bullying sorted out for Abs, but I'd failed again. As I opened the car door, I got a text from Jack.

'Shit!' A group of parents and teachers scowled at me as we climbed into the car.

'What's wrong, Mum?' Abigail was on the verge of tears. I forced the anger deep into my gut.

'Remember the guy I told you about, Kyle Swift?' I turned the engine on.

'The guy who hurt you?' Abigail pointed at the purple bruising on my neck.

'That's the one.' I pulled the car out of the school with a screech of tyres, missing the Ice Queen only by a few inches. 'He's been released from custody.' I wondered if my day would get any worse. Abigail looked shocked.

'But how could he? He nearly strangled you.'

'There are eyewitnesses from the pub who swear I attacked him first, and he only acted in self-defence.' Lying bastards, I wanted to say. 'So his lawyer got him out.' So much for him not wanting legal representation.

'Oh.' Abigail hung her head. I thought she was about to burst into tears.

'Don't worry, love, I'll sort everything, you'll see.' I hoped it sounded convincing. 'We'll get some burgers and fries like we used to. And a big tub of ice cream for afters.' I wanted to forget all about our problems, just for a little. Junk food and comfort eating would do that. I drove to the McDonald's nearby. It was full of kids when we entered.

'They didn't miss a trick opening this place here.' We headed to the counter. Abigail pulled on my arm.

'Not like that, Mum. It's all modern now. You order from a touchscreen.'

'A what?' We stopped in front of a display bigger than our television. I watched in amazement as Abigail's fingers flicked across the digital screen and ordered our food and drinks.

'Your turn,' Abigail said.

'For what?' I replied. Abigail pointed at the payment option. I shook my head and got out the debit card. Abigail dragged me into the nearest booth once I'd paid.

'They'll bring it over to us, Mum, so you can relax now.'

I only realised my hands were shaking when Abigail took hold of them. 'I'm surprised I didn't put the wrong number into the machine.' My laugh was nervous and hurt the back of my throat. Abigail stared at me.

'Did you mean what you said to the welfare officer about taking me out of school?'

I resisted the urge to scratch the bruise. What I'd said to that moron was fuelled by anger and frustration created before we'd even got to the school. I'd prepared the letter last night, but didn't think I'd have to use it. Looking at Abs, I saw the excitement in her face. Perhaps it wouldn't be such a bad idea.

'Would you like that, being taught at home?'

'It sounds great. But how would it work?'

Our order arrived before I replied.

'That was quick.' I thanked the stressed-out assistant.

'That's why it's called fast food, Mum.' Abigail spoke while eating half her burger, which I found equally disgusting and impressive. We slurped our drinks and dumped the fries into little squares of barbecue dips before returning to the topic of homeschooling. I answered Abs's question.

'I haven't considered all the details yet, Abs, but I'll look into getting you some private tutors for home.' I wiped burger sauce from my lips. I'd forgotten how good junk food tasted. I avoided the number of calories it contained detailed on the wrapper.

'Won't you teach me?'

I nearly choked on a pickle when I heard those words. Abigail frowned as I touched my throat and blamed the bruise for my difficulty in speaking.

'What do you think I can teach you, Abs?' I was curious to hear the answer. Abigail scoffed the rest of her fries and returned to the drink full of sugar.

'You know all kinds of stuff, Mum, and you have a degree in criminology.'

Yes, I can teach you about the criminal mind and what to do when lunatics try to kill you. And how to deal with the jealous stupidity of most of the blokes you'll work with, especially your so-called superiors. The last part was something I would have to explain to her at some point. I'd put off telling her so many things. How could my future with her be an open book if there were still secrets buried in my past?

'That reminds me: how did it go with Alice Voss and the Cybercrime unit this afternoon?' Abigail's eyes perked up and she stole some of my fries.

'It was great and Alice is so interesting. I want to learn more about that kind of stuff.'

I remembered Alice telling me about Abs confiding in her about the online harassment.

'Well, you'll have to work hard at maths and computer technology, but we'll sort that out.' Even after the terrible day I'd had, it felt great to be sharing this time with my daughter. Perhaps there was something to look forward to.

And then Abs clutched at her chest and fear engulfed her face. I thought she was choking on her burger.

'We need to go, Mum.' Abigail grabbed my hand and

she was trembling. Her eyes went over my shoulder and to the noise behind us. I twisted to see a group of kids, four girls and two boys, joking around as teenagers do. Or at least like most do. I wondered what the fuss was about until I noticed the girls laughing in our direction. When I switched back to Abigail, she had her head buried on the table.

'Do you know those kids, Abs?' Abigail's shoulders trembled, and I was concerned she was having a fit. I shifted seats and squeezed up against her. I pressed our heads together. The sniggering transformed into laughter and I realised who these teenagers were. I snapped my head around as fire burnt through my blood and turned my skull into an inferno. That rage was returning. I jumped from the seat, scattering rubbish and plastic cups everywhere.

'Mum, no.' Abigail found her voice. I strode towards the kids and glared at them.

'The queue for pensioners is over there, love,' the tall girl with the pink hair said. They laughed in unison like machine guns. I continued to glare at them, fighting to control the anger. The boy with a ring through his nose sneered at me.

'Maybe she's lost her hearing aid.' He pushed his face up to mine. He stank of cigarettes and teenage hormones. 'Can ya hear me, ya old biddy?' He pulled back, and they shrieked with laughter as one.

'You better leave my daughter alone.' My voice was calm and collected. The pink-haired girl peered over my shoulders.

'Who, Scabby Abbey?' She puffed out her cheeks and flicked her hair to the side. 'Who'd want anything to do with her?' They stumbled forward to the electronic ordering screen as I flexed my arms; Abigail grabbed hold of me before I said something foolish.

'Can we go home, Mum?' Her fingers shivered as I peered into the face of my daughter, pained by the fear and the torment I saw there. If I couldn't protect her at this moment, then when could I?

'Sure, Abs. We'll get some ice cream and watch a movie together.'

'See ya, Grandma,' the teenagers shouted as we left the building. I seethed all the way to the car.

'Those are the kids who've been harassing you online?'

Abigail nodded as the car pulled away.

'And in school?' She nodded again.

We were silent the entire way home. Inside the house, I got us both some ice cream and let Abs choose the movie. We settled in to watch the Marx Brothers in *Duck Soup*.

Two hours later and I'd decided how to help Abigail with those kids just as I received a phone call from Jack. I'd thought things couldn't get any worse.

'There's been another murder,' he said down the line.

18 FAITHLESS

F ather Maxwell slipped into the church and hugged the shadows. He wasn't allowed to be addressed as Father anymore, just like he wasn't supposed to go anywhere near a church again, never mind this one. But old habits die hard and his body was failing fast, so what difference did it make? What could they do to him now?

He lowered his bones into the distressed wood.

The modest church pew, sometimes padded, but more likely not. They were never comfortable, but comforting. An invitation to the weary traveller to sit and hear the Word of God; a simple reminder to follow a humble crucified carpenter; the perfect symbol that all are equal at the foot of the cross. It reassured him to be there. Nobody could deny him this.

He stared at the stained glass on the walls and the magnificent ceiling above. So many years of his life spent in this place. To take it away from him now was surely as big a crime as what they'd accused him of? He welcomed the stale air into his failing lungs and shifted his weary body into the creaking wood.

'You're not supposed to be here, Joe.' Father Abraxas towered over him, all stern eyes and crossed arms. Father Maxwell peered into his accusing gaze.

'Am I not allowed a final confession, Samuel?'

Father Abraxas was unmoving.

'No, not after what you did. And then putting those poor people through it all again in court. If you don't leave, I'll throw you out.'

Father Maxwell had a grin the Devil would be ashamed of. 'I'm not sure you have the strength to lift me, Samuel. Dead men are heavier than broken hearts.'

'What?' Father Abraxas shifted uncomfortably in the presence of the older man.

'It's okay, Samuel; I was only quoting some Chandler.'

In the fading light, Father Maxwell's skin had a yellow sheen to it like a tortoise with jaundice.

'You think if I weren't dying, I'd be behind bars now. That's where you want me, isn't it, Samuel? Removed from the church and away from you.' His laugh was broken glass. 'These defence lawyers earn their money.' His wrinkled fingers grabbed hold of the musty bark of the pew as he pulled himself up and into the face of his old colleague.

'Admit it, Samuel; you'll miss me. You'll miss all our long conversations on many subjects.' The two men were so close there was hardly a gap between their faces. 'Do you remember all those blasphemous things we spoke about?'

Father Abraxas stepped away from the older man. 'I'm not afraid to call the police, Joe.'

Father Maxwell picked wax from his ear and wiped it on the pew. 'I don't doubt that at all, Samuel.'

He walked to the back of the church, turning his head before leaving.

'Did you think to question God's role in all of this,

Samuel?' There was no answer, only cold silence and the whisper of the wind in the rafters. 'Maybe he wanted me to love all those kids in my special way; maybe this was all part of his grand plan.' A withered laugh escaped his mouth as he exited the church. The doors closed behind him, locked for the last time to his presence.

'What shall I do with the rest of my life?' Father Maxwell raised his head into the night sky for inspiration. Would he hear the Voice of the Lord one more time before he left this earthly existence? The doctors had given him six months to live at the maximum, and he intended to enjoy every minute. He still had contacts who would provide him with what he wanted for a price. They did say God loved a sinner.

'Father Maxwell, I have something for you.' The voice startled him, drifting over from the shadows in the alley next to the church. It sounded like a young child. It excited him and he threw all caution to the wind. What could anyone do to hurt him now?

His hand brushed against the damp and dirt of the wall, nails scratching across pale concrete. He stumbled forward, feet kicking through the rubbish and the puddles. A sharp flash of moonlight distracted his view, so much so he tripped over some object and tumbled into the side of the dumpster blocking that enigmatic voice.

Pain shifted through his arm and shoulder, water flowing over his shoes and into his socks; the air stank of human faeces and wet paper. As Father Maxwell pushed away from the large bin, he was amazed to see a stack of cardboard boxes towering over him. From behind them came the mysterious voice again.

'Are you excited, Father?'

The words sounded like glue and glass.

'Do the memories of your crimes thrill you to the bone?'

'Who are you?' Father Maxwell said to the shadow.

'I am justice,' the voice replied before throwing a foul-smelling liquid over Maxwell and the pile of cardboard next to him. The stink of the gasoline rushed up to his nose and dived between his lips. He reached for his mouth, choking through the pungent aroma. He spat onto the ground and coughed violently.

Father Maxwell blinked through the tears, his eyes trembling at the fragment of light flickering before him. He needed to move, wanted to run, but the bones had frozen inside his flesh, his tongue glued to the sides of his mouth, the words stuck to the back of his throat.

Father Maxwell's scream was strangled at birth as the lit match flew through the air, the yellow shimmer glistening against the dark of the night. It landed at his feet and sprang to life in a tremendous glowing surge. The blaze danced over his shoes, ignoring the damp of the leather and sprinting up his legs. It ate through his clothes and devoured his chest, spreading up and over his neck and head.

As the flames gobbled through his body, he finally realised there was something worse than a natural death.

19 FLAMING DESIRE

I was in a foul mood when I stepped from the car and strode towards the alley. It was worrying enough to lose my temper with the welfare officer, but what happened with those teenagers bordered on insanity. My fingers shook as I stepped up to the blue lights and yellow tape. It wouldn't be too hard to get the names of those kids; Abs would tell me if I used the right words. And then what? Find out where they live? Speak to their parents? That wouldn't make any difference. More often than not, the adults behaved worse than the children. A drastic solution lingered at the back of my head and it worried me.

'How did it go at school?' Jack held the tape up so I'd get my frame underneath it. The last thing I wanted was to talk about the events with the welfare officer. My brain focused on what was in front of me.

'Never mind that, what happened here?' The place stank of smoke and cooked flesh, reminding me of a barbecue. Forensics were already on the scene, but the public was being kept outside.

'Father Joseph Maxwell, sixty-five years old and burnt alive less than thirty minutes ago.'

'Christ,' I said as Jack led me to the remains of the body in the alley. I covered my nose. Part of an arm stuck out from the dark mess.

'I should say disgraced Father Maxwell.' Jack pulled away from the body so the crime lab boys and girls could get on with their jobs. I peered at the remains of the skull as a gust of wind forced bits of it to drift over Jack's new shoes.

'Shit,' my partner shouted. An officer covered entirely in a white protective suit glared at him.

Jack scowled back. 'What? It wasn't my fault.' He stood still as the ash was scraped from his feet and into a container. He looked more concerned about the damage to his shoes than the fact the crumpled remains of a human body lay over him.

I ignored his discomfort and returned to his description of the victim. 'Disgraced because he was a paedophile?'

Jack nodded as the SOCO finished cleaning him up.

'The court case lasted three years, one retrial and a change of jury. Sixty-seven victims came forward, though it seems likely there were many more, with the allegations stretching back over three decades. They proclaimed his guilt two weeks ago.'

'So why wasn't he in jail?'

'Terminal lung cancer. Six months to live at the most.'

I stared at Maxwell's remains being shoved into bags and boxes. I felt nothing for the thing which was once a person.

'Less,' I said and turned to Jack. 'Why are we here? We've got our hands full with the Ripley and Thomas murders, someone else can have this.'

Jack moved forward and showed me his phone. It displayed his Twitter account and a new set of hashtags.

#justiceforall

#fatherjosephmaxwell

#justiceforpaedophiles

#thehashtagkiller

#thehashtagvigilante

The photo with it was Maxwell in the alley before he went up in flames.

'Jesus,' I said with no irony at all. This was all I needed.

'You'll burn in hell,' Jack replied.

'What?'

'That's what some of his victims shouted at his trial.'

I strode further into the backstreet, wondering how complicated the case had got. Apart from the stink of burnt flesh, there was an aroma of unwashed humanity and fresh piss. The ground was wet and littered with broken pizza boxes and what looked like used condoms. I turned from them and back to the pile of dust.

'How do we know that's Father Maxwell?'

Jack pointed to the church next door and the flickering light from the window at the top. 'We have an eyewitness.'

Great, a proper lead at last.

I followed Jack away from the heap on the ground which was once a human being. We turned out of the alley and towards the steps into the church. I hesitated at the bottom.

Jack's hand was at the entrance. 'You okay, partner?'

A bitter wind swept across my face, obscuring my vision and taking me back twenty years and to another man leading me into a House of God. I strode up to the door and pushed past Jack to get in.

'It's been a long time since I've been inside one of these.'

I peered at the Christian iconography surrounding us, expecting a sense of comfort but finding nothing but darkened memories best left in a previous lifetime.

'I forgot you're a Catholic.' He bit his lip and I imagined the taste of wine in my mouth.

'Not me. That was my parents.' At the front of the Church, a PC was speaking to a priest.

'There's our witness, Father Abraxas,' Jack said. The holy man glanced at me as we walked forward.

'I remember that crucifix you used to wear when I first met you. Whatever happened to that?'

'I threw it away.'

We reached the priest. The constable left and we made our introductions. 'Can you tell us what you saw, Father?'

In the wavering light of the candles, he appeared drained. Deep lines crisscrossed his face and lethargy filled his eyes. His voice sounded equally weary.

'I was retiring for the night when I heard voices outside.'

'And where was this?' Jack said.

'My room looks out upon the alley.'

I gave him a half-smile. 'Can you show us?'

'Of course. It's this way.' He took us past the altar and through a door at the side. An aroma of incense and ancient rituals seeped into my head. I followed the two men upstairs, running my fingers over the faded wood of the railing. A thought popped into my skull, and it worried me.

Should I tell Abigail about her grandfather when she's older? I promised there'd be no more secrets.

Jack spoke to me, but I didn't hear what he said. I nodded and walked towards the window. Outside, Forensics were still scraping Maxwell into a bag.

'What did you see, Father?' Even with all the police lights in the alley, it was difficult to get a good view of anything through the shadows. The white suits flitted around like fireflies in the gloom.

'I heard the voices first, but I thought it was drunks arguing again. Many vulnerable people come to the church and they sometimes linger in that alley.'

I didn't take my face away from the window. 'Did you hear what they said?'

'No, but I recognised Joe.'

'You saw his face but not that of the killer?' Something about the priest made me suspicious he was telling the truth. Or maybe I was just distrustful of all men of the cloth.

Father Abraxas cleared his throat and looked nervous, his fingers repeatedly scratching at his neck. It reminded me of my bruise.

'No, I couldn't see either of them clearly, but Father Maxwell has a distinctive shape to his head.' He corrected himself. 'He had a distinctive shape to his head.' His hands shook so much I thought they'd fall from his wrists.

'It was horrible to watch that happen to him. Ghastly.'

'And you didn't see who did it?' Jack seemed as doubtful as me. Father Abraxas wiped the sweat from his face and sat on the bed.

'No, I only got an outline as... as...'

'Maxwell burst into flames.' I was in no mood to be gentle. I had nothing against this priest, he may have been a perfectly kind man, but my anger had to find an outlet somehow. I was angry at Giles and those kids. And I was mad at myself.

Abraxas slapped his hands together to stop them shaking.

'I only saw a shape as the flames increased.'

'Could you tell if it was a man or a woman?' At least

that one piece of information would be more than we'd got from the other murders.

Father Abraxas appeared happier at having to answer such a simple question. 'It was hard not to tell, even in the half-light. He was well over six foot tall and built like a rugby player.'

Jack exchanged looks with me and I knew we were considering the same thing. We should have put a tail on Kyle Swift when he was released.

'It was definitely a man, not a woman?'

'I'm sure,' the priest replied.

'Thank you, Father. Are you okay to give a statement to one of our officers?'

He nodded and rose from the bed. 'If I can have two minutes to collect my thoughts.'

I took one last look from the window. To be burnt alive in a dirty alley. It was some way to go. We stepped downstairs and out of the church. The night was cold, but something else sent a shiver down my spine.

Jack removed his phone. 'We better bring Swift in and check if he has an alibi, though I don't understand why he'd do this. He got what he wanted with Ripley's death.'

I checked my mobile for any messages from Abigail. It was empty. 'Maybe he got a taste for it and can't help himself.' I headed back to the car. There was nothing I could do, and I needed rest.

'Did you see Vasquez's latest piece online?' Jack said.

'Her brilliant insight into what happened in the pub this morning? Yeah, I read it before going to the school.'

'You never told me how that went.' He searched on his phone for something as he spoke.

Should I tell him everything or nothing? Or a lie? If he knew I was struggling to control my temper again, it would only worry him. And he might suggest I take time off work, away from this case; spend some quality time with my daughter. That's exactly what I should do.

So why couldn't I?

'I'll tell you about it later.' Abigail came into the fore-front of my mind again. I still didn't know how I would sort the homeschooling out. And what if Giles reported my behaviour? What would I do about those fucking kids?

Jack offered me his phone.

'Vasquez published another piece today. You need to read it.'

I took the phone and scanned the first few lines. I forced out a half-hearted laugh.

'I guess I'm Rose. Do you get a mention?'

'No, but that isn't the issue. Keep reading.'

I ploughed through the words, depressed at how Ruby Vasquez had fostered and benefited from the upsurge in the popularity of vigilante justice; despairing at how many people supported this. And it would only get worse once the public knew of Father Maxwell's murder. As I consid-ered that, the boxes containing what was left of Maxwell were dropped into a police van.

'She's got it wrong about the majority supporting our killer. It may look like a lot when you see the posts and tweets all together, but it's only a tiny minority in a nation of seventy million.' That's what I told myself, but it was still worrying.

'Keep reading,' he said.

It didn't take long to find the most interesting part.

A man commits himself to God, but preys on the weak and the vulnerable. Whose justice is that?

I scrolled back to the top of the page to check the time of publication.

'She posted this online six hours before Maxwell's death.'

'Some coincidence,' Jack said.

'Let's bring her in again, formally this time.' I handed him his phone while checking my watch. 'Make sure Cyber-crime get all her electronic equipment. I've no doubt she'll dodge all our questions again. Her internet trail may be the only chance we'll have of getting some truth from her. Let her stew for an hour and I'll meet you there.'

'Do you want to leave it to me? You look tired.'

My bones ached and my mind wanted to crawl into unconsciousness for a good eight hours, but there were too many things to be done before I could sleep.

'No, I'll be fine. There's something I need to do, but I'll see you at the station. You can warm her up for me.' I smiled at him as I crawled into the car. 'Let me know when she's there. And ask her why she didn't mention you in that piece.'

He shook his head and grinned as I drove away.

Ruby Vasquez and the flaming death of the priest could wait a bit. I had to sort Abigail's problem out first.

20   THE SEVENTH CIRCLE OF HELL

The next one had to be brazen, so why not fire? It was justice for not only the sixty-seven, but the countless others who didn't or couldn't come forward. A blazing success, you might say. The media attention would increase, adding to the danger of what I was doing. The question now was how long to wait before continuing; should it be low key or something more spectacular? The short gain wouldn't last long; the lead detective on the investigation was too smart for that. The priority had to be the long gain.

I needed the eager public to help me along. That was why I continued my communication with them. Many of them wanted to open a dialogue with me, desired to peer into my mind and discover what made me tick. But my confessions were only for the ears of Johnnie and Jim, my tastes alternating between Walker and Beam.

When it was over, I had the urge to have a cigar, even though I'd never smoked in my life. I was in the comfort of my home and needed something to settle the euphoria, to calm those shaking fingers. The bourbon tasted sweet as it trickled down my throat. I settled back into the comfiest chair in the house, one eye on the TV, the other on my phone, trawling through Twitter, waiting for the responses to my latest work.

The laptop hummed in the corner of the room: the machine I used to connect to those places across the globe which would never be described as legitimate. Money made the world go around, but it was nothing without digital fingers and feet spreading the love to every part of the planet. No matter how unwelcoming most of these countries were to the advocates of liberty and democracy in the flesh, they never refused a financial contribution which flickered through the information superhighway.

My latest payment, rerouted through more than a dozen nations, had just gone through. This would give me enough time to complete my plan. I had a choice of two prospective victims.

Decisions, decisions. Both targets were equally obnoxious. But who would create the most media frenzy?

The house phone rang. I stared at it as if it was the Batphone and I was Bruce Wayne engaged in one of my many libidinous assignations with Gotham City's finest debutantes. As I removed the vibrating harpy from its cradle, I pondered how the Dark Knight would deal with a criminal like me. The Hashtag Killer, as much as I liked the name, wasn't comic-book enough for the Caped Crusader. I could hardly run around the streets bashing people's heads in with sharpened metallic hashtags.

I was so busy thinking about such a preposterous thing, I didn't hear what the caller said down the line.

'Can you repeat that please?' I used the poshest tone I could muster. Over on the TV, the news had cut to the flaming death of the pervert priest. The Twitter display on my mobile went into a posting frenzy.

The voice wasn't on the line for long, another request I couldn't refuse. I dropped the receiver back into its place and peered at the images dancing on the screen. I moved across the room and turned the sound up on the television.

Dr Mal was a colossal disappointment. I had expected nothing revelatory from the meeting, but had hoped to tempt his intellectual gravitas with my prompting on all things religious. A discussion on hell was what I searched for, especially when I knew what awaited Father Maxwell.

I recognised what justice is and, because of my present project, believed most of the public would follow my lead sooner rather than later. But even that felt somewhat unsatisfactory. His death would never expunge Evan Ripley's crimes; the same with Bobby Thomas. As for what Father Maxwell did, a lifetime of pain and torture inflicted on his sorry frame still wouldn't suffice.

No, I had to believe those three were suffering somewhere else beyond this realm. And that place had to be hell. According to Dante; Ripley, Thomas, and Maxwell would be in the Seventh Circle of Hell. They would be plunged into a river of boiling blood and fire, assaulted by Centaurs firing arrows into them every time they shoved their heads above the inferno. It would be a punishment to last an eternity. That gave me solace as I poured out a large glass of red wine, though I wondered what terrible crimes the Centaurs must have committed to serve in hell. I guessed it must have been the male part which was guilty of something. Horses were such gentle creatures.

A pair of owls hooted outside my window. They sounded angry, like bagpipes incorrectly tuned. Do you tune a bagpipe as you do a guitar? I stared at the half-full bottle of wine – never half empty, I'm always positive regardless of the negativity I encounter – recognising the things we humans put into our bodies or fixate our minds on, are our way of retuning the psyche. Not the flesh; more often than not, we're wearing the body down, but attempting to fine-tune those problematic thoughts the Numbskulls unpack inside our heads. I'd considered a life of heroin, sex and gambling as an attempt at coping, but had dismissed the idea out of hand for two crucial reasons: first, I'd seen those three demons on their own, never mind collectively, fry people a lot better than me. And secondly, I could never forget that I wasn't doing this for myself.

I was risking my life for purely unselfish motives. I should get a medal for it.

The internet gave me the latest news on Father Maxwell. None of my plans would have come to fruition without the rise of the internet and the popularity of social media. The responses on Twitter to the priest's fiery demise made me feel warm all over. I'd never expected to receive such support. I'd dreamed of such a thing, of course, but dreams and reality were two different things.

Copycat vigilante violence was on the increase.

It was good to witness. It was perfect to see.

But nobody can be exactly like me. Even I have trouble doing it.

21 RUBY'S ARRESTED DEVELOPMENT

The shouting started in the back of my nut, snowballing until it possessed all of my skull. It was a constant rant, but it kept on changing. Imagine the worst music you've ever heard in your life, possibly Guns and Roses mixed in with the Bay City Rollers, turned up past eleven and on an endless loop inside your head.

At first, it came before I was even born. Perhaps it was a false memory, but the screaming was there as I slumbered in the womb. I had this impossible reminiscence of before I existed, of the sounds of fury shrieking through the space which would become me.

Then I was a small baby, shaking a rattle to drown out that human anger. Then rapidly through all my early years: trembling inside my pram; crying during the journey to the nursery; a dark shadow and sweaty palm on the way home from primary school. I would have sworn it was a male voice until she shrieked in my ear and pushed me off the bed. My shoulder cracked into the thick carpet, sleep falling away from my eyes and harsh reality thundering in.

'Fucking hell! What are you doing, Mother?' Dirt and

dust bounced into my mouth and nostrils, my throat like sandpaper as foreign elements invaded my system. If I didn't move out soon, I would get a lock on my bedroom door. 'One day I'll lash out and wring your neck if you keep doing this, sneaking into my fucking room.'

'You blacked out, Ruby, so I'm waking you up. Your fella's on the loose again.'

I pushed my fingers into the carpet, flinching at the grease and grime living there, and dragged my body up. Mother stood in the doorway like Norman Bates in drag.

'What are you talking about?' I spat dust into the air.

'Your fella; he's killed someone else, murdered some pervert priest. Good riddance, I say. They should give him a medal when they find him.'

I ignored my mother's twisted grin and reached for the laptop and phone together.

'Fuck fucking fuck!' I'd missed the story. Had he tweeted again? I checked the alert I'd set up through Twitter. Yep, I'd missed that. I howled and beat my fists against the bed. I'd struggled to come up with something original to write about Bobby Thomas, and now I lagged behind the rest of the media. If that wasn't bad enough, I knew her eyes were burning into the back of my head.

'See, you're exactly like him. Losing your temper at the drop of a hat and beating anything in range.' Excitement dripped off her every word. I wanted to throw up.

'I swear to God, Mother, your only pleasure in life is making me miserable.' I contemplated for the thousandth time where I'd bury her body once I finally snapped. If I got in touch with the vigilante, perhaps I could get them to do it? Electric pain galloped through the front of my head.

'Nah, Rubes, you forget I've got the fags and booze, not to mention my favourite place down the Bookies. You're just a distraction, love. It's the least you can do considering what a disappointment you've been as a daughter for all your life.'

She sat on the end of the bed as I pulled my legs up into my chest. I looked for the pills. The box had disappered. The screaming returned; only this time, it was me doing it.

'Get out of my fucking room, Mother!' I didn't need any drugs, didn't want anyone else to do my dirty work. I thrust my feet out, catching her hard on her hips. She hit the floor with a thump.

'Ruby, you cow!'

I jumped from the bed and towered over her.

'I've had enough, Mother. Now leave me alone.' Venom oozed from me. She lay there, looking up and grinning. She wasn't scared of me. It didn't matter what I did here; she would never change.

Mother's legs creaked as she got up.

'Sure, Rubes, whatever you say.'

She gave me her usual crooked grin and slithered from the room. I threw the TV remote at the door as she closed it. As the device clanked onto the floor, it must have bounced onto the power button as the TV sprang to life to show me what that horrible old woman was talking about. There was no sound, so I slipped off the bed and retrieved the remote.

'... appears to be another murder committed by the Hashtag Killer.'

Damn. I'd hoped my new term would have caught on by now. I flicked through the news shows and saw the same thing. Even the foreign language channels focused on it. I closed my eyes and started counting in my head, trying to calm my nerves. Maybe I should have taken one of those job offers.

The sound bites from the television washed over me.

Disgraced priest set in flames.

Pervert burns in hell, his victims thankful for justice.

Police silent on the investigation.

The Hashtag Vigilante strikes again.

My eyes flipped into life, my mind running through the words again: they'd said the Hashtag Vigilante. I reached for the laptop and my website; there were loads of replies to my post. I picked up the phone and checked my Twitter account: hundreds upon hundreds of people had tweeted me.

How did you know?

You're the only one we trust.

Are you working with the vigilante?

And a new hashtag was trending across social media.

#rubyv&hashtagv

'Oh my.' I had to reread the last tweet.

Are you working with the vigilante?

Sweat trickled down my cheek. I went to wipe it away, stopping when I smelt my arm. Smoke. Burning. I stank of smoke. I ignored it and scanned the rest of the posts.

I could write anything I wanted now. I had an audience; a massive audience. There were thousands of them, and the number was growing all the time. Now I had to make sure I kept them.

I grabbed the laptop, found the hacking software, and did a deep search on Father Joseph Maxwell. There was no point in repeating what the rest of the media had written about the priest. I needed something new and unique.

'He had to have secrets nobody knew about, a man as corrupt as that.' There might be links to others, connections which ran deeper into the broader church community. There would be something and I knew I'd find it.

Somebody banged at the front door and Mother told

them to fuck off. For once, I was glad of her abrasive personality, although I was unsure if you could class what she had
inside of her as a personality. I ran my nose across my shirt,
from the wrist up to the top of my shoulder, finding that
stink of smoke. The banging got louder and Mother swore
again as she stumbled to the door, with the unmistakable
sound of bottles rattling around on the floor.

Then I realised what the smell was on me. It was the
stench of Mother's cigarettes. God knows how long she was
in here while I slept. I had to ensure I kept all my stuff
locked up and away from her grubby hands.

She shouted again from downstairs. The banging had
stopped, but I couldn't make out her words. She screamed
my name. I leapt from the bed and dragged the door open.

'What do you want, Mother?'

'The pigs are here for you, girl. What've you done now?'
She continued to shout as the boots rumbled up the stairs. I
threw my shirt onto the floor as the copper burst into the
room. I glared at him as he froze in the doorway, shocked to
see a half-naked woman scowling at him. He seemed young,
but I would have thought he'd have seen worse things than
me in my bra.

I glowered at him. 'Do you mind?' He sniffed the air
and I remembered the aroma of smoke on my clothes again.
Or perhaps it was my body odour. I hadn't showered in
days.

He turned to shout for a female colleague to come up
the stairs. It gave me time to reach down and shove the
clothes under the bed. For some unknown reason, I felt
uneasy about the stink on me. This whole place stank of piss
and shit, so I wasn't sure what was worrying me.

I slipped on a new shirt as a policewoman entered the
room. She was pretty and I smiled at her. All I got in return

was frost. And then they read me my rights. I didn't move. Let them take me forcibly from the house. That would add another angle to the next blog post I'd write: postcards from inside the Hashtag Vigilante investigation.

'What's this about, Officers?' I could guess, but I wanted to see how communicative they'd be. The answer was not very. Still, the girl's grip on my arm wasn't too harsh. And even though I had a pungent aroma of barbecue over me, the female copper had a sweet scent of strawberries on her. It was always my favourite fruit.

We bounced down the stairs with only a mild protest from me. I could fight back, start a bit of argy-bargy and put that in the piece. Get a few bruises, post some photos of police brutality. I would turn all of this into a positive experience.

At the bottom, Mother gleefully blew a swirling trail of smoke into the air. It drifted towards me, grey fingers clutching at my throat. I coughed all over the pretty copper.

'See, Rubes, what did I tell you? You're just like your father, always being dragged off by the pigs. You're only a different type of criminal to him.' The dirty brown of what remained of her teeth sparkled at me as we got to the door. My mother's scrawny frame stood in the way, between the police and the exit. It was enough of a distraction for me to pull away from the girl and fall into the living room.

I slammed the door shut behind me as the shouting started, forcing my back into the wood as they hammered on the other side. They barked at me to come out as my mother howled like a drunken banshee, which she most likely was. I slipped the phone from my pocket and hit my Twitter account, practised enough to type with only one hand. And people say millennials are unskilled. I had to make it dramatic.

The police have kicked in my door. Male copper is staring at me in my underwear. They have me...

I got the post away as they burst through and pushed me down onto the floor. The handcuffs were cold on my wrists as they snatched the phone from my fingers. They rolled me onto my back and I peered into the eyes of hell.

'Don't look too happy, Mother.'

She grinned as they dragged me from the house.

My next blog post would be a doozy.

22 ALICE

It took me thirty minutes to get across the river, checking for messages from Abigail as I drove. I hadn't been to this side of the city in a long time. It had grown prosperous and affluent since then. The abandoned buildings, derelict communities and junkyards had all gone. The church as well.

Property prices must have skyrocketed considering how large the houses were. There wasn't a bit of rubbish anywhere, no dogs running around, and no kids loitering in the streets. I found the address I wanted at the end of a leafy road, turning into an immaculate drive and pulling up to a gothic building straight out of the Addams Family.

It towered over the rest of the street like King Kong.

It wasn't what I'd expected. I locked the car and climbed up the steps, expecting to find a sizeable weather-beaten bell attached to the wood which would summon an equally ancient butler to the door. Instead, there was an electronic buzzer, which I pressed once. Nothing happened for a minute and I wondered if I should have phoned ahead. This might all have been a waste of time.

I was deliberating on leaving or ringing the bell again when the door opened with a creak. I thought someone would shout Trick or Treat at me. That or Uncle Fester would offer me some boiled finger soup.

'DI Flowers,' Alice Voss said through sleepy eyes. If she'd just got out of bed, her black bob appeared styled to perfection. It was shiny and it tempted me to run my fingers through it. She wore a dark shirt with the words '*I promise not to exploit you*' printed on it. Cybercrime's best operative stifled a yawn and picked something from her teeth.

'No formalities here, Alice. You can call me Jen.' I didn't wait to be invited in, striding into a corridor big enough to fit my kitchen inside. It made me think of food and the last time I'd eaten. I thrust my hand into my jacket pocket, searching for the thing I'd brought. There was a slight shudder in my heart and I forgot why I'd come. This wouldn't help me catch a killer.

Her voice shook me from my mild amnesia. 'The living room is on the left. Make yourself comfortable, Jen.'

I walked inside and held my breath. The room was as big as the whole of the bottom floor of my house, and a curious mixture of the old and the new: well-worn furniture and a carpet which had seen better days and lost most of its pattern, surrounded by a dozen pieces of electrical equipment and a giant TV screen on the wall which wouldn't have looked out of place in a cinema. The sound was off, but I recognised what peered out of it: cameras pointed at the crime scene I'd just left. A small photo of Father Joseph Maxwell appeared on the screen. I waited for it to burst into flames and spread through the room, but it didn't.

'I was watching it on the news when you rang the bell. Is that why you're here? Do you need me to come to work?' Alice sighed and wiped the sleep from her face. Her skin

glistened with good health and I wondered which mois-
turiser she used. She was young enough not to have bags
under her eyes yet, but it looked like she hadn't slept prop-
erly in a long time.

'This isn't about the force, Alice. Haven't you just
finished a twelve-hour shift?' I felt guilty for disturbing
Alice in her home, away from work. My eyes darted across
the room. There were at least four laptops, three tablets and
two mobile phones lying around as if abandoned in an electrical dump. Too much stuff to fit into a small house with a
kid who had more clothes than a department store, that was
for sure. I knew the Cybercrime unit worked long hours and
multiple cases at once, but I'd need to do some serious over-
time to afford a place like this. It was far too big for one
person on their own. There was something about it which
seemed familiar, but I couldn't think what it was. I'd have
hated living there; the excessive space would have messed
with my head.

'Yeah, it's been a hectic few days.' She noticed me scan-
ning the room. 'Don't worry; I never bring work home.'

I laughed. Taking data out of the building unauthorised
was not only a sackable offence, but might end up with you
sharing a cell with the criminals you investigated.

'I find it impossible to throw old tech away. A process of
my upbringing. My parents were hoarders, so, luckily, we
had such a big house.' Alice held her arms above her head
and peered at the ceiling. She ran her hand across her face.

I stared at the impressive chandelier. 'This is your
parents' home?'

'It was. They returned to Australia a few years ago; it
was left to me when they died.'

'You're an Aussie?'

'No; but don't sound so shocked, Jen. My parents were

British, but working in Sydney when I was born. They came back here when I was younger, but returned to Oz when they retired.'

'And you stayed behind?'

'What can I say? I love the bad weather and the grumpy people. Would you like a drink?'

I wasn't sure if she was offering me tea or coffee or something stronger, but I refused.

'No, thanks. I'm sorry to turn up unannounced and disturb you.' The phone vibrated in my pocket. I hoped it was Abs; I took it out and read the message from Jack. They'd brought Ruby Vasquez into the station.

'Don't worry, I couldn't sleep.' As she spoke, Alice yawned again. For someone ruffled and half-awake, her ocean-blue eyes sparkled with life. I felt like crap, but I had to get this over with.

'I wanted to thank you again for spending some time with Abigail this afternoon. She enjoyed it so much she wants your job.' I'd never imagined Abs following me into this line of work. I wasn't sure if I'd like her dealing with the same shit I had to.

Alice grabbed a bottle of water from the table, grinning as she had a drink. 'That's great, Jen. Let me know if I can help at any time.'

I took a deep breath and reached into my pocket for the piece of paper I'd scribbled on before getting out of the car in front of this imposing house.

'That's why I'm here. I need a personal favour.'

Alice's face sparked awake. 'Really? What can I do for you?'

I noticed Father Maxwell's photo on the screen. Then it changed to one of Bobby Thomas, then Evan Ripley and the tweets by Justice For All and the hashtags connected to them. I sighed when I saw the name had altered from the Hashtag Killer to the Hashtag Vigilante. The case was rapidly turning into a nightmare. The news channel switched to Maxwell's crimes against children and someone representing the church. Even with the sound muted, I could guess what the excuses were for covering up the dead priest's behaviour. If the public didn't want the murderer caught, why should I bother? Abigail should be my priority.

Abigail was my priority. I offered Alice the paper.

'These are Abigail's social media accounts and her password. Could you trace who's harassing her from those?'

Alice took the paper without looking at it. 'Things didn't go well at the school, then?'

'I probably made it worse.'

Alice still didn't look at what I'd written on the paper. 'You know we could both lose our jobs over this? And a lot more.'

I noticed the words on the TV screen moving along the bottom like ticker tape.

STILL NO OFFICIAL WORD FROM THE POLICE IF THIS IS THE WORK OF THE HASHTAG VIGILANTE. THE ANONYMOUS INTERNET POSTER CLAIMS TO HAVE KILLED THREE PEOPLE. SERIAL KILLER ON THE LOOSE. REPORTS OF AN INCREASE IN COPYCAT VIOLENCE LINKED TO THE CASE.

Then it cut to snapshots of the public and their opinions on the murders. The sound was still muted, but I deduced what the consensus would be. No one would cry over a dead pervert priest, just like they wouldn't over a fascist paedo and a rapist. I couldn't blame them.

If nobody cared about catching this killer, then why should I? Right now, I didn't. All that concerned me was making sure Abigail stayed safe. And here I was, potentially getting a colleague into trouble. This had been a mistake. My selfishness was putting others at risk again.

I held my hand out to Alice.

'I'm sorry; I shouldn't have asked this of you. Please forget I came here.' I turned to walk away, stopped by Alice's fingers in mine. Outside of Abigail and Jack, I couldn't remember the last time somebody else touched my skin.

'Don't be silly, of course I'll do it. I've seen the long-term consequences of cyberbullying and harassment; we've got to protect young girls any way we can.' Alice gave me a faint smile and opened the paper. She peered at the text. 'How did you get these?'

My cheeks sank, the breath leaving my lungs in short bursts as the dagger slipped into my heart. Guilt is a terrible thing, and this was the guiltiest I'd felt in a long time.

'I searched through her stuff and found them weeks ago. I hoped I wouldn't need to use them.' And now, after we'd formed a bond of trust again, I'd betrayed Abigail once more.

'Does Abigail have the same password for all these accounts?'

'Yeah. I've told her not to, but she never listens.'

Alice put the paper on the table. 'What kid ever listens to their parents?' She checked the time on the TV; the news continued to focus on the Hashtag Killer. 'Listen, Jen, if I don't get called in for this,' she pointed at the screen, 'I'm not due in for two days so I can work on Abigail's problem then. Is that okay?'

Relief flooded through me. If this was fixed by the end of the week, I could sort out Abigail's schooling and concentrate on this Hashtag case.

We were still holding hands, and it felt like the most natural thing in the world. Formality overcame me and I grasped Alice's hand before letting go.

'I owe you double big time for this.'

'Think nothing of it.' She turned her head to the TV. 'You've got bigger fish to fry, right?'

'It's a weight off my mind to know you'll be dealing with it.'

'Does Abigail know about this?' Alice pointed at the paper.

I shook my head. 'No. And I'd like to keep it that way if possible.'

'No problem, Jen. Discretion is my middle name.'

'I didn't know who else to trust.'

'Once I've discovered who it is, what do you want to do?'

Her question threw me; I'd been relying on the school to fix this. What Alice was about to do was illegal, so we couldn't make it official police business. If it was those same kids, the ones I'd encountered in McDonald's, it was obvious no one could intimidate or threaten them.

'One problem at a time, Alice.'

She nodded. 'Are you sure you don't want a drink?'

I noticed the open bottle of wine on the table behind her. 'Why not? One for the road won't hurt.'

She smiled and retrieved two glasses from a cupboard. The wine was red, never my favourite, but I wasn't going to complain. She ushered me to a sofa and sat in the one opposite. The TV continued to show images of Father Maxwell and clips of the alley where he met his fiery end.

Alice sipped at her drink and glanced at the screen. 'Three murders with different MOs; are we sure it's the same killer?'

'We are if we believe the internet posts from the person claiming to be the killer; plus they've posted photos of the murder scenes only the perpetrator would have. So, it appears we have a serial killer on our hands.'

'Serial killers are rare in the UK.' She placed her glass on the table. 'Do you think they're a product of nature or nurture; are they born or made?'

I racked my mind, remembering a course I'd attended three years ago.

'People have argued about that regarding criminals for more than a century. I went to a lecture where an expert on the subject - he came from America where they have more of these - theorised it's intrinsic to the human survival mechanism that we have this capacity to kill repeatedly. Killers are anachronisms whose primal instincts are not being moderated by the more intellectual parts of our brain.'

Her eyes lit up; it was the police investigator part in us which made this fascinating.

'To kill is a primal instinct in us all, I get that, Jen, but when you say it's the more intellectual parts of our brain preventing this in most people, it makes me think you're claiming all killers will have limited intelligence; are you saying those with high intellects don't turn into murderers?'

'No, Alice; that's not what I mean. Perhaps it's not that serial killers are made, but that most of us are unmade, removed from our primal instincts by good parenting and socialisation. As kids, we need a healthy emotional and physical upbringing to guide us into how to behave correctly in a civilised society. There's that old saying about someone going off the rails and, in our line of work, we see it all the time where negative influences in a child's life can take them down dark and difficult paths. It doesn't mean they all end up as serial killers or even criminals, but

I guess it's more likely to put them on the wrong side of what's right and what isn't. This is what might happen if they don't get the correct guidance at the most critical time.

'In extreme cases, what remains behind is these un-fully socialised beings with this capacity to attack and kill. And often that capacity is grafted onto a sexual impulse – aggression sexualised at puberty.'

She rested her hand on her chin. 'Sex appears to play a part in most serial killings, at least the ones I've read about; but not with our Hashtag Killer.'

'Many serial killers are survivors of childhood trauma – physical or sexual abuse; family dysfunction; emotionally distant or absent parents. Trauma is the single recurring theme in the biographies of most killers. There's trauma in our killer's early life, sexual or otherwise; we just haven't figured it out yet.'

Alice's eyes peered into mine. 'I guess you'd need to have suffered something terrible to do what this Hashtag Killer is doing.' She picked up her glass. 'But why the different victim types and the variation in the murders?'

My shoulders shrank into the sofa; the wine had an immediate effect on me. I let my hand drift over the side, touching a stack of newspapers. I glanced at them and saw they were copies of the *Australian Times*. The headline of the top issue was about the latest spate of fires crossing the country.

'I've got a hunch, but I'm keeping it to myself.'

'Is this how you normally work?'

I pushed the wine aside and got up; alcohol wouldn't make my brain function better. I stared at her.

'It changes depending upon who I'm trying to catch.' I looked at the time on the TV. My night wasn't over yet.

'Thanks again for your help, Alice; and the drink. I hope you enjoy the rest of your time off.'

I smiled and said goodbye. As I left, I glanced around Alice's house and realised what was familiar to me: there were no photos of family or friends anywhere; no sign this young woman interacted with anyone else. It reminded me of Abigail's room. I grinned at the thought of the two of them at the station today, remembering how excited Abs was when she came out of the training programme. I think if I'd gone home and told her she might grow up to be like Alice Voss, she'd feel good about herself. Maybe that's what my daughter needed: an adult role model who wasn't me.

Outside, I pushed all thoughts of Abs from my head. I had one more visit to make before returning to the station. Jack could keep Ruby Vasquez entertained for a little while longer.

23 FOOD FOR THOUGHT

I picked up a copy of the free paper on the underground. The headlines of murder and sorrow told not of tomorrow, but of yesterday; of last night, to be exact. My number-one fan had written another excellent piece online, renaming me the Hashtag Vigilante. I rolled the words around on my tongue, enjoying the tang of the new syllables. Ruby deserved a reward for her sterling work.

The pages rippled in my hands as I turned beyond the first few and the details of the priest's fiery demise. I didn't want to appear to be too ghoulish and focusing on it, but I was glad my fellow commuters were deeply engrossed in the story. I resisted the temptation to take a quick straw poll to see who condoned or condemned my work. I remembered the shirts from the pub, enjoying the corners of my mouth crawling upwards.

My eyes drifted towards the other articles. Oh, what a weird and beautiful place the modern world was: a group of drunken birds had flown into windows and cars after bingeing on fermented berries. In my mind, I hummed an old Dead Kennedys song, but with new lyrics. In the next article, someone returned an overdue library book after eighty-four years. I'd hoped it might have been an original Aleister Crowley manuscript, but unfortunately, it was only a poetry anthology by the Lanarkshire Women's Institute. A robot brothel was not welcome in Houston, according to its mayor; customers were paying up to sixty dollars for an unspecified time with the love dolls. A photo of a corset-wearing redheaded doll staring vacuously into the camera accompanied the story. The figurine looked more alive than all the contestants of the last series of Love Island.

I dropped the paper into the bin as I returned to the world above. I went to a new café for lunch, a special treat; a holy bonus, you might say. It was a hipster joint, far too bohemian for my usual tastes, but I was celebrating. I slipped into a wooden seat covered with a cushion shaped like a moon and trawled through my Twitter account: my real account, not the one hibernating in the Crimea. I wondered if the powers of the Western hemisphere ever contemplated how the authorities beyond what was once the Iron Curtain were now far more dangerous to them compared to Khrushchev banging his shoe or Stalin's ape army. Hundreds of troll factories dominated the Siberian wasteland, chock full of cyber warriors spending twenty-four hours a day attacking the institutions of the West. I imagined it was like working in a call centre, only with worse pay and better clothes.

The café's staff appeared to have been recruited from a failed production of Les Miserables, dressed as they were in puffy shirts, beaded waistcoats and skirts wide enough to cover a freight train. A waitress bearing a scary resemblance to a young Margaret Thatcher took my order of green tea with a slice of lime, plus a ham and cheese panini. I expected *her to tell me there was no such thing as society as she headed to the purple-haired coffin dodgers at the next table.*

Twitter throbbed with the wonders of the Hashtag Vigilante, the sympathy for the victims in short supply. It added a smile to my face as the music in the café suddenly jumped a couple of levels. A woman's voice was strangled through a synthesiser stolen straight from the cabinet of Dr Caligari. It was a peculiar noise for such an environment designed, I assumed, to drive customers to purchase more refreshments and not to the asylum.

I wondered if it was possible to use sound as an apparatus of death. Then I remembered the Aztec death whistle. In the hands of an accomplished manipulator, the device created the hair-raising yowl of a thousand tortured souls. It's shaped like a small skull, with a ring of even smaller heads running around the middle of it. Some experts believe the pre-Columbian instruments were used to send the human brain into a dream state and, from there, treat specific illnesses.

'Surely it would be better than this torturous warbling,' I said to the waitress as she brought over my order. She stared at me with a look reminiscent of the vacuous sex doll from the newspaper. As I contemplated that and the Aztec death whistle, I decided that maybe the modern world was not much stranger than the ancient one after all.

The hot sandwich appeared to be breathing on my plate, the middle of it moving up and down. For a horrible moment, I thought the staff had imprisoned some small living creature in my food. It was only as I poked it with the fork that I realised it was a pocket of heat trapped inside which gave the bread the appearance of a thing alive. I left it to breathe and returned to the news on my phone.

Three down. How many more to go? The copycats had

already started. A rapist attacked in Glasgow. Several wife beaters given a taste of their own medicine in Reading, Plymouth and Sunderland. A child-abusing teacher only just escaped the towering inferno an angry mob had turned his house into. A shame he got away. A paediatric practice torched in Newquay was unfortunate and embarrassing for all involved but, as a sage once said, you can't make an omelette without breaking a few eggs.

Still, the people's justice was increasing, and I had to ensure it continued at pace. But what should I do next? I flicked through my alternative phone and checked the files of the hundreds of people who'd escaped justice. A taste of the ordinary wouldn't work now; I'd leave that to the converts. It had to be something big and bloody, a Grand Guignol of escalation. I opened the folder with the smallest amount of names in it, moved the details around and pondered which to pick. This would probably be the final one, so it had to be special.

My hot sandwich took its last breath. I picked it up and felt the fire against my flesh. I'd selected my next project, and now I knew how I'd deal with them. I stared across the café and wondered if I didn't exist, would anyone notice my absence?

24 FAMILY TIES

A group of dogs barked somewhere in the distance as I approached the building. The place stank of shit, and I dodged the empty beer bottles and Pot Noodle tubs. I rattled on the door, trying not to compare where I was to the gothic splendour I'd left at Alice's house. Somebody in the house swore before coughing loud enough to spew out their lungs. When the door opened, I peered into the face of a woman who looked like she'd died years ago.

'What eva yer selling, I'm not buying. That's unless you got some cheap ciggies hidden inside that shabby coat of yours.' Isabel Vasquez looked nothing like her daughter. I removed my warrant card and held it up to the woman's yellow eyes. She was probably not much older than me. Ruby was twenty-two, so her mother was likely in her early forties. This is what the ravages of nicotine and alcohol do to you.

'Yer too late, copper. The piggies in their uniforms dragged Ruby away. I always told her she took after her father.'

'Actually, it's you I'm here to talk to, Mrs Vasquez.'

A cigarette dangled from her lips as worry sailed across the crease lines in her skin.

'Can I come into the house, please?' I had a foot in the door. If it slammed shut now, it'd be painful.

Mrs Vasquez nodded and stood to the side. 'Go into the living room on your right.'

I stepped over a pile of shoes and into the room. It was a museum of things which had never been thrown away: papers piled up everywhere, stacked next to plates and cups and cutlery encrusted with grime. Beer bottles and cans engulfed most of the furniture like an infestation. The smell reminded me of the first time I'd gone to an autopsy and the pathologist had opened up the body right under my nose.

'Grab a seat where you can, copper.' Isabel Vasquez blew cigarette smoke across the room. I didn't want to touch anything in the expectation I'd have to disinfect my clothes before going home, or maybe burn them.

'It's okay, Mrs Vasquez, this won't take long.' Ruby's mother glared at me as if I was a piece of steak, unable to tell if I was overcooked or underdone.

'You're the one in charge of the serial killer case. Ruby described you to me.'

'I'm concerned about your daughter, Mrs Vasquez.' It was a truth wrapped in deception. Isabel Vasquez spat out a laugh as she sank into the sofa covered in magazines. Two piles of them split either side of her before flowing onto the floor. I stared at a photograph of an obese woman wearing a bikini. It reminded me to lose weight for the beach holiday I'd never have time for.

'Don't worry about that girl, Mrs Detective; she's bred from sterner stuff than you or I.'

'Do you know what Ruby's been doing online?'

She sucked in enough poison to lay waste to a small town. 'Perhaps you should educate me, copper.'

Fifteen years on the job and I'd encountered many parents who didn't care if their kids lived or died. I wasn't the perfect parent, recent events had taught me that, but I'd never understood how people could be so harsh to their children; and then I recalled those thoughts stored away inside my head, images of a father who was never that. The woman sitting opposite me fluctuated between dismissive and downright hostile. A low groan escaped her lungs like a wolf was waiting to pounce. The bruise on my throat itched.

'I think a killer is grooming her.'

Mother Vasquez nearly choked on her fag, coughing so much she spat nicotine-stained phlegm all over the floor. It missed my shoes by inches.

'I thought grooming was what perverts did to kids?' She reached down the side of the sofa and brought up a can of super-strength lager. It was already open and she wiped a dead spider from the top before draining the whole thing. She threw it in the air and behind the furniture. Something resembling an upturned can of worms crawled around inside my stomach.

'Any vulnerable person can be groomed by a predator, even an adult.'

'I told you before, copper, Ruby is tougher than nails.'

I peered into her eyes, knowing there were secrets hidden away in there about her daughter. Skeletons corrupted her soul. I'd seen it before; the mirror could be a harsh mistress.

'Can you tell me why she has a sealed juvenile file?'

She laughed again as she pulled out another cigarette.

'You're the detective; isn't it your job to find out these

things?' She moved her withered body to the side, sending a whole year of TV magazines sliding onto the carpet.

'We're not allowed to access it without good reason.'

'And do you have one?'

I paused. 'Not yet.'

'Well, fuck off, then.'

'What happened to Ruby's father? There's a file on him as long as your arm at the station.' Mother Vasquez's eyes turned from yellow to black at the mention of her former husband. I searched the room for family photos and found none: no images of Father Vasquez; no memories of Ruby's childhood; no framed treasures of mother and daughter together.

'That maggot slithered away before Ruby was born. What do you want him for?'

I tried to lift my foot from the carpet, but it got stuck to something wet. That meant my shoes were going straight in the bin when I got home.

'I checked the reports from his last stint in prison five years ago.' I waited for a reaction from the other woman, but none was forthcoming. 'It appears the other prisoners didn't get on with him. He suffered many beatings and broken bones before his release. Do you know why?'

Vasquez stared into space before coughing up more thick phlegm like a cat with a furball.

'He's a horrible man. They should've killed him in there.'

I wrenched my foot free and turned to leave. 'And you don't know where he is now?'

Life was sucked through her cheeks as she spoke. 'I hope he's rotting in a grave somewhere.'

'Thanks for your time.' I wasn't sure what I'd been looking for at the Vasquez house, but five minutes inside it was too much. I could only imagine what it was like for Ruby Vasquez growing up there. I glanced up the stairs as I opened the front door. Something terrible and unknown gripped my heart, and I was glad to get out of that place.

I headed to the station and the next meeting with Ruby Vasquez. I should have been angry at the way she'd interfered with our investigation, but all I felt was sadness for the poor woman I was about to interrogate.

———

MY NOTEPAD and pen lay on the table, ready for the detectives to appear. They were giving me plenty of great material, so I could hardly complain about their tactics. They'd kept me waiting for over an hour, but I understood why. They wanted to make me nervous for when they arrived, but it was all pointless since I had nothing new to tell them.

The door opened and Jack what's his name walked in. He pointed at my notebook.

'You can put that away, Ruby. This is a formal interview tonight.' He placed a recording device on the table and sat opposite me. 'Would you like legal representation?'

'Nope. Is your girlfriend not here?'

'DI Flowers will join us later.' He turned the device on.

He stated our names, the date and time. I did my best not to look bored. I had a déjà vu as he pushed a printed page towards me.

'Can you explain that to me?'

'Are you upset I didn't mention you?'

'I'm more concerned about this bit.' He read the section from memory.

'*A man commits himself to God, but preys on the weak and the vulnerable. Whose justice is that?*

'You published that six hours before the murder of Father Maxwell. Six hours before he was burnt alive by your friend the Hashtag Killer. We'd like you to explain how you knew it would happen.'

I shook my head at him. If the woman appeared, it would be more of a challenge. At least it would give me something new to write about.

'Maxwell was a convicted paedophile, so I think he forgoes the privilege of being addressed as Father. The Hashtag Vigilante isn't my friend. And it's a pure coincidence I mentioned a perverted priest in my blog; it might easily have been about a politician, celebrity or footballer. Haven't your people gone through my computer and phone yet? You'll find nothing on there to connect me to any of the murders. All you're doing here is wasting all our time.'

That could be the theme of my next article: how the police were wasting time and resources on things like this. Link it to the reduction in police numbers and the increase in crime. I leant into the chair and felt better. Perhaps this wouldn't be a waste after all.

The door opened and DI Flowers walked in. She appeared equally weary and harassed, slipping into the seat next to her partner and whispering into his ear. He muttered something to her.

Flowers fixed her tired eyes on me. 'You deny any connection between your article and the murder of Father Maxwell?'

'Of course.' I wanted to leave now. Something in Flowers's face worried me; an aroma about her I didn't like. It made me think about the smell stuck to me. I wished I'd grabbed my perfume before the coppers had taken me away; something to remove the stink of smoke still on me.

'Can you tell me where you were between six and ten o'clock tonight?'

'I was at home with my mother.'

'Your mother is your alibi for the murder of Father Maxwell?' Flowers didn't mince her words. I laughed in her face.

'Wow, you're struggling if you think I killed that perv.' I glared at her as the detective whispered to her partner again. My arm ached. I wanted to scratch the smoke from my skin.

'I spoke to your mother tonight, Ruby. She told me you weren't home when she left the house at six, and when she returned at ten you were - and these are her exact words - spaced out on the bed. She said you'd had another one of your blackouts.'

The sound of thunder rumbled inside my head. My chest threatened to burst; I wanted to crawl up and die on the floor.

'I...I... I was asleep.'

Flowers didn't let up. 'How old were you when you had your first blackout?'

'I was twelve.' I dug my nails into my legs. The pain was a slight relief. 'What's this got to do with anything?'

'If there have been more of these blackouts, then it's possible you've done things you're not aware of. Perhaps you're even in contact with the person you call the Hashtag Vigilante. It's conceivable you're being manipulated without knowing it.'

Flowers appeared convinced by the possibility of it, but I shook my head. But what about the smoke I smelt on my body? Could I remember what I was doing in Adams Park that morning? Had I gone to Bobby Thomas's flat?

'Why me? Why would anybody do this to me?' My hands trembled. The temperature in the room dropped and a chill stabbed at the front of my skull.

'When was the last time you saw your father?' Flowers said.

The mention of him shocked me back into normality.

'My father? He left before I was born.' The pain and confusion drifted away from me. 'You think he's been manipulating me and I can't remember any of it; that he killed Ripley and Thomas and Maxwell?' It was too ridiculous for me even to contemplate. Typical of the police to get this desperate.

'Did you know your father was a serial sex offender?' Flowers said.

The noise returned to my head, a sonic cacophony vibrating around my skull before splitting into a thousand pieces and scattering through the whole of my body. Gravity pressed down on me and I was a child again. Something at the periphery of my mind crawled towards me. My mother's voice replaced the shrieking in my brain.

'My mother told me he was a criminal; that's all I know.'

'He has convictions against his name for sexual assault. And that's only the ones we're aware of. I imagine some friends and relatives of his victims would like him to face justice for his crimes.'

'You said yourself he'd served time for his behaviour. I thought that was your definition of justice?'

'But your Hashtag Killer feels differently. Perhaps their idea of justice is to make you suffer.'

' But I'm not suffering because of this. My blackouts are the response of a brain wired up differently to yours. It's a reaction to stress. It happens to many people, but I'm in control of my life. Nobody is manipulating me. Not my missing father, not the Hashtag Vigilante, and not you. I want to leave now.'

'You're free to go, Ms Vasquez,' Flowers said. 'You can retrieve your items from the front desk on the way out.'

I exited the interview room, accompanied by a uniformed officer. I had to have a long conversation with my mother about my father.

And I needed to return to a past I'd sworn I'd left behind.

25 SECRETS AND LIES

I woke the next morning to find my phone bombarded with messages; I focused on the ones from work. Forensics had double-checked and located some fibres on a branch of the tree in Adams Park, strands of cloth which might have come from a pair of jeans. The Thomas crime scene overflowed with material, just like Athena Temple had said it would, but none of it appeared useful, and nothing there connected to the other two murders. As for Father Maxwell, Forensics continued to sift through his remains. The alley had been a cornucopia of human detritus, all of it likely to be useless for the investigation.

And then there were the texts from my partner. Jack wanted to know why I hadn't told him what I'd learnt about the Vasquez parents. I'd left the station immediately after the interview, too tired to say anything to him; I'd needed to make sure Abigail was okay. We didn't talk much when I got home. She retreated into her Stephen King book, and I trawled the internet before the litany of support for our killer put me in a bad mood. That continued to infest my brain as I gripped the phone.

Below Jack's message, there were two from Alice Voss. The first said:

I need to see you ASAP

The second was sent thirty seconds after that.

Can you pick me up on the way to work?

And that's why I was driving back to one of the plushest parts of the city. I'd left Abs looking over YouTube videos about writing computer code, amazed she'd dived in head-first to educating herself at home. The Voss mansion seemed no less imposing in the daylight. I was more aware of the vast swathes of trees guarding either side of the house. The door opened as I reached the top of the steps.

'Come in, Jen. I need a few minutes to get my stuff ready.' Alice's hair was pulled back tightly on her head. Dressed in a white shirt with a blue jacket and trousers, she looked like she was going to a meeting with her bank manager.

'I thought you had a day off from work?'

Alice had disappeared into another room where her voice floated from.

'They've called everybody in because of the caseload.' She strode back in, carrying nothing, so I didn't know which stuff she'd sorted. 'As well as your Hashtag Killer, we're dealing with material from a grooming gang, some dodgy dealings from a prominent bank, and numerous online links to possible terrorists. But I wanted to give you this first.'

She handed me a data stick.

'If you follow me, I'll explain what I found.'

I stepped into the room, with digital devices still scattered all over the place. I peered at the data disk in my hand.

'This looks important.'

'It's probably best if we sit down.' Alice pointed at the sofa and we sat next to each other.

'You've got the information already?' I was impressed.

'The people harassing Abigail didn't try to cover their tracks. They're either incompetent or unworried if they're found. Or...'

'Or what?'

'Or they don't think they'll be exposed.' A heavy weight infected my heart. I turned the data stick over in my hand. 'All the fake images and nasty posts Abigail received came through one IP address. Do you know of Digby's Internet Cafe?'

The name rang a bell, but I couldn't picture where I'd heard it before. And then it hit me.

'It's close to the school, near McDonald's.' We'd driven past it only yesterday.

'The messages were sent from there, and all between four and six o'clock. They were likely posted from different machines, with users logged in under fake accounts, but if you access the café's records and cameras, they'll be easy to identify.'

'I'll need a court order for that.' Which was impossible.

'Or you could hack the system.'

I raised a wry smile. 'I can barely get into my emails half the time.'

Alice stared at her nails and frowned. She grabbed some polish from behind her and gave them a beautiful purple spruce.

'Anybody can do it these days, Jen. You can download the software for free from the internet.'

My eyes bulged. 'People do this?'

'Welcome to my world and what Cybercrime have to combat every day. The simplest thing might be to create your own fake account and message these kids back. Tell them you have their personal details and you'll report them to the police unless they stop. Or even better, you'll inform their parents. That might frighten them enough to give up harassing Abigail. They're only teenagers.'

I was more relieved than I thought I would be. It wasn't over, but I saw a way out of this mess for Abigail. If only I'd thought of this sooner. But I couldn't have done it without the woman next to me.

'Thanks, Alice. I appreciate this.'

'I'm afraid there's worse than that, Jen.'

The air seemed so brittle, it might snap, and if it didn't, I might. The whole of my professional life in the police force flashed before me. It settled on the first time I'd accompanied a senior officer to tell a husband his wife had died. The look in his eyes then was reproduced by Alice now.

'Worse?'

'I think someone has been grooming Abigail through her Facebook account.'

There was that word again, grooming, the same term I'd used in the interview with Ruby Vasquez yesterday. I sat there open-mouthed, lost for words.

'What?'

'It started six months ago, with somebody claiming to be a fourteen-year-old called Tom. He eventually convinced Abigail to send him naked pictures of her. His last few messages are putting pressure on her to meet him; otherwise, he'll post the photos online.'

My entire world slowly sank around me. The ground wanted to swallow me up and drag me down to that stark place where my parents slumbered. Then they'd wake up and point at me.

'See,' they'd say to me, 'you're no better than us.'

I held onto my chest to make sure I continued to breathe.

'How do you know it isn't a teenager doing this?' I prayed to a God who'd long since abandoned me for this to be true. Alice's eyes told me otherwise.

'Experience tells me it isn't; the patterns are clear. The use of language and vocabulary points to this being a man in his forties at least. And it's likely to be someone she already knows. All the messages were sent from machines inside her school.'

I stared long and hard at the data disk in my fingers. I dropped it onto the floor and buried my head in my hands. My whole body trembled.

'This is all my fault. I should have taken Abigail's concerns more seriously sooner.' If only I'd been someone she could confide in.

'You can't blame yourself, Jen. A lot of teenagers get caught out like this.'

'You don't understand, Alice. This is my punishment.' Words flowed from me and I didn't try to prevent them. I'd kept this bottled up inside for so long, it was an emotional release I couldn't stop even if I wanted to. I dropped my hands from my head and scratched at my leg.

'I'm sure you do the best you can, Jen. It can't be easy being a single mother and a police detective.'

I told her the thing I'd spoken to no one else.

'Abigail wasn't the first time I got pregnant.'

'You don't need to explain anything to me, Jen.' Alice took hold of my hand. 'But if you want to talk, I'm here.'

I was glad of her physical human contact, needing to unburden what I'd kept locked up for so long.

'I was sixteen; he was twenty years older, a friend of my father's from the church. I thought it was what I wanted, that I was complicit in what happened. It was only later when I realised he'd manipulated me. Groomed me, as we call it now. My father was the preacher of the local congregation and my pregnancy devastated him. It's surprising how quickly a man of God will demand the death of an unborn baby to save face.'

'He forced you into an abortion?'

'He and the father of the baby made me do it. He already had a family with his wife, so there was no room for another one.'

She squeezed my hand. 'Losing a child is never easy.'

'Two years later and I set off to university. Three years after and I was pregnant once more. I wasn't going to make the same mistake again.'

'And what happened to Abigail's father?'

'He was a boy in the same year as me at uni. I never told him about the pregnancy. A year later, I was a single parent and a police cadet.'

Alice smiled at me. 'Top of your class is what I heard.'

'The determination to prove everyone wrong is a fierce motivator.'

'It can't have been easy.'

I pulled my hand away and stood. 'I haven't been as good a mother as I should have been. I don't think I've learnt anything from my upbringing.'

This all started with my fucking parents. But could I blame them for how I'd turned out? I was supposed to have learnt from their faults.

'Do you have a better relationship with your daughter than your parents had with you?'

I considered the question. I'd made mistakes with Abigail, but nothing like what had happened to me. I'd spied on her and stolen from her. I hadn't been there for her when she needed me the most. Those were terrible actions, but I was still a good mother. I knew it.

'Absolutely.'

'Then don't beat yourself up over this. As I said earlier, the modern world has made it easier for predators to prey on vulnerable people.'

'What should I do about it?' I wanted to go home and forbid Abigail from using the internet ever again, but recognised such an action would only exacerbate the problem. Abs wouldn't listen to me no matter how I tried to explain the danger she faced.

'Meet me after work and we'll talk to her together.'

'I owe you so much, Alice. I can never thank you enough for this.' Just being with her was like a stress valve easing the pressure from me.

'Thank me when we've caught the bastard doing this.'

'That's two of them we need to catch.' I held the phone, ready to text Abbey but distracted by the hashtag symbol. Perhaps if I repeatedly pressed it, the killer would miraculously fall into our laps.

Alice placed a bag over her shoulder. 'I saw on the news they're calling him the Hashtag Vigilante now.'

Pain shot through my foot as I stood on a discarded laptop cable on the floor. I stepped away from it without alerting Alice to what I'd done.

'That's Ruby Vasquez's fault; unqualified internet journalists appear possessed of an abundance of imagination.'

'It seems to have caught on with the public.'

'And with the copycats and the fans. The sooner we catch him, the better.'

'You think Vasquez is involved?'

I shrugged my shoulders. 'She knows more than she's telling us, that's for sure. There are problems with her mother and father and, from the conversations I've had with her, I don't think she had a productive time at school.

Maybe there's a connection with that juvenile record of hers you mentioned.'

Alice ran her fingers across her mouth before looking at me sheepishly. 'Well, that's the thing, Jen; there's something suspicious going on there.'

'What do you mean?'

'I must admit I wasn't as clued up with the juvenile system in the UK as I thought I was, so I suffered from some misconceptions.'

Now I was even more intrigued by Ruby Vasquez. 'What misconceptions?'

She took a deep breath. 'In England and Wales, there is no prescribed process for "sealing" a criminal record. There is no procedure to apply to a Court to have a criminal record formally sealed, so it's not disclosed. There's also no formal process for expunging a criminal record, other than police records, namely erasing someone's criminal history. In the United States, there are laws on both sealing of documents and expungement, and the rules vary from state to state. I think some people, myself included, have been caught up with watching too many American crime dramas.'

Confusion seeped from my face. 'But you said Ruby Vasquez has a sealed juvenile file.'

'That's the suspicious part: she shouldn't have a sealed file, but she has. I'm still trying to talk to someone over at the records department, but with no luck so far.'

I tried to laugh it off. 'I'm surprised at you, Alice; I thought you'd have been in and out of juvie court when you were younger.'

She threw up her hands. 'I was always a good kid, Jen; plus I lived in Australia until I was eight.' Her shoulders slumped, a willowy image of something long gone drifting imperceptibly behind her eyes. I could imagine how I'd feel if I'd been transported from warm antipodean beaches to the chill wind of the UK when I was a youngster.

We left the house in silence. As we got into the car, I turned to her.

'This predator grooming Abigail works in her school. We need to do something about that.'

'I'll think of something,' Alice said as I drove away.

The house was empty when I got home. I was surprised Mother wasn't there to grill me about my latest trip to the police station. The pull of the bookies or the boozer must have been too strong for her. All-night pubs I might just about understand, but twenty-four-hour betting shops were only government-sponsored refuelling pits for addiction.

The cops were clutching at straws trying to connect one paragraph in my blog to the death of the pervert Maxwell. Three quick murders with no apparent connection between them, apart from the fact the victims were scumbags. Was it wrong to smile when I thought about their deaths? The priest was burnt alive. I couldn't imagine how horrible it was to die that way, but he'd likely abused hundreds of kids. Didn't the Bible say an eye for an eye? I was too tired to contemplate the philosophical and moral problems surrounding the murders of these hideous people. I needed to rejuvenate my mind.

A shower and a fresh set of clothes cleared my brain for what I had to do next. The temptation was to return online and see what responses my posts had got, but the confrontation in the police station had made me realise I couldn't go forward without going back.

The conversation I needed to have with my mother would come once the old crone staggered home. There was something I had to do first. I opened the wardrobe and stared into the darkness of my clothes, a combination of jackets, tops and dresses minus a drop of light between them. At the bottom lay a mountain of loose shoes piled on top of each other. There were high heels, boots, trainers and flats giving each other comfort in the dark, all clambering together as if trying to climb out of my life.

I crouched down and pushed my hands through them, forcing the shoes aside until I found the boxes at the bottom. My fingers searched for the one with the string tied around it. I pulled it out as odd pieces of footwear tumbled onto the bedroom floor.

Something creaked downstairs, and I waited for Mother's entrance. I sighed with relief when it never came. That confrontation would wait for later.

The box sat there unmoving, my eyes glued to it like a magnet.

'How many years since I've had you open?' It seemed strange to hear my voice speaking to this inanimate object as if it were a long-lost friend. I took it to the bed, my hands trembling as I undid the knot. I brushed aside six years of dust and removed the lid. An aroma of old paper and dried leaves drifted up from the diaries I'd placed there a lifetime ago. There were five of them, one for each year of my life from twelve to sixteen. When I sealed them away, I told myself I'd use the contents for a future novel. Now I wondered if they might be background for my current project.

I removed the volumes and sorted them to start at the earliest. I turned the first page and peered at my tiny handwriting. I read the date aloud, even though I'd always remember that initial incident by heart.

April 15th

Last thing I remember - leaving school and Janice Robinson calling me a ginger scruffbag. I told her to stick her fat head up her arse. She chased me down the street, and I ducked into the cut towards the beck. Then it all went dark.

I woke up further down the stream near the bridge over the train line. My shoes drifted in the water, and there were cuts and bruises on my wrists and hands.

I stopped reading and wiped the sweat from my head. At the time, I'd believed Janice had caught up with me, beaten me up and thrown my shoes into the beck. It was only later I realised it was my first blackout.

I had eight more that year. Not once did I tell Mother; there seemed no point. It was only in December when it happened at school that someone took it seriously. My mother promised the school she'd take her daughter to see a doctor, but she never did. It would be some years before I found the courage to seek medical advice. And the desperation to swallow the pills.

I pushed the first diary to the side. What I wanted wasn't in there. I reached for the next one, for when I turned thirteen that January.

Mother bought me a birthday cake, but she ate it all herself. She buggered off to the pub, leaving mouldy cheese and bread in the kitchen for me. Then I headed to the shops for a spree.

It amazed me how much of a buzz I got from shoplifting. I'd dreamt about becoming a pickpocket after reading *Oliver Twist*, but that seemed far too dangerous to do on my own, and I had no friends to be in a gang with. The thought of being in a posse was exciting and sort of romantic. But if you couldn't talk to others, how would you connect with them?

So I turned to nicking stuff from the shops. Nothing close to where I lived or from the little family-run businesses; I wouldn't do that to those struggling to make a living. I targeted the big chains or supermarkets. I'd read a book about the evils of capitalism in the library and pictured myself as a female Robin Hood.

Most of what I stole was for me, books or clothes or jewellery, but sometimes I nicked food and drink and gave them to the growing number of homeless people in the city. I had to be careful about who I approached because some of them were less friendly than others. On two occasions, a bloke tried to drag me into the shadows, but I was too strong for him. The recollection made me shiver as I found the diary entry I wanted.

March 13th

Woke up inside an abandoned building on the other side of the river. It stank of piss and shit, and rats scurried everywhere. I heard a voice behind me. I spun to see the man hulking in the corner. He had spooky green eyes and long hair like Jesus. It was all matted and dirty, but through the gloom, I saw it shine red like mine, and it made me smile. He thanked me for the tins of food I'd given him. I couldn't remember any of that. I ran outside and my legs hurt.

I closed the pages and took a deep breath. Did I want to trawl through my past and resurrect these memories? I asked even though I knew the answer, returning to the diary and skipping through the entries. There were two more incidents with the green-eyed man: once in the park late at night when Mother had thrown me out of the house for playing my music too loud.

The second time happened in that same building over the river again. There was more in the other diaries. I'd convinced myself they were false memories, my imagination running wild because of the blackouts. I read about conditions which affected the brain, spoke to doctors and found the medication which eased the incidents, but never removed them. The potential side effects were many, including hallucinations and personality disorders. I battled on against my body, taught myself computer coding and continued with a petty life of crime. I remembered it all, including my first encounter with the police of this fair city. The copper was a man thick of neck and intellect. His voice echoed still in my head.

'She stole tins of dog food from Tesco, Mrs Vasquez. We won't charge her, but we have to produce a report of what she's done.'

I stood sandwiched between two coppers on our doorstep, my mother looking at them as if she wanted the police to take me away and never bring me back. When the fuzz left, she screamed at me before slapping me across the face. I'd thought it was concern for me expressed in the only way she knew, as anger, but it was something much simpler than that.

'Fucking dog food, what's the point of that? Why didn't you nick some fags or booze?'

I couldn't tell her the tins were for the old bloke who slept under the bridge with a pet sicker than him. I never saw him and his dog again. I fell into the police radar numerous times after that, so many occasions I'm surprised they never carted me off to social services.

Five years later, I hacked into my criminal record to

erase it. The police's online security wasn't worth shit, but I found I couldn't delete my files without the system being informed of the removal. All because of some dog food. So I changed the folder contents to sealed instead of open and left it at that. I didn't want people poking around into my past when I became a YouTube or Twitch superstar.

I dumped the diaries on the bed and opened the laptop, finding more messages for sponsorship and advertising on my site. I looked at the numbers; added together, they were impressive. The texts on there and Twitter were mainly supportive and growing. People wanted to know more about me, desperate to find a connection to this digital presence.

'What do I write next? I can't just wait for the Hashtag Vigilante to strike again.'

I had to be proactive, but how? I peered at the diaries again. Should the world get to know the real Ruby Vasquez? Maybe it was time for me to learn something about myself.

I was pondering that as the door slammed downstairs. I left the laptop and my memories where they were. I didn't think I'd be hiding them away again. I jumped down the stairs and burst into the living room. I'd got used to the tip in there, but it appeared different now. All the papers and magazines which had covered the furniture for years were dumped on the floor. Mother sat on the end of the sofa, and she wasn't alone.

'Ruby, there's someone here to meet you.' Smoke drifted around her face like pollution hanging over a chemical factory. I peered at the man on the sofa. The red hair was shorter and cleaner, but the green eyes were still like emeralds sparkling in the dark. He stared deep into my soul.

'I've missed you, daughter.'

I put my hand to my head as everything turned black.

27 WHOEVER CONTROLS THE MEDIA

I arranged to pick Alice up after work so we'd speak to Abigail together. The conversation wasn't something I was looking forward to, having to explain how I'd trawled through her stuff to get all her social media and internet details. I was unsure what I'd say to her, hoping some inspiration would find its way into my brain while I tried to solve this vigilante case.

Jack was sitting at his desk as I strode in.

I'd spent most of the drive agonising over whether I should tell my partner about Abigail's problem and the help from Alice. I dismissed revealing anything to him at this moment. There was no point putting his liberty at risk if I had to break the law to protect Abs.

'We have a press conference in an hour.' He seemed as happy about that as I was. I opened the files on the computer.

'We better see what we can give them then. I'll put something together and face the media. There's no need for both of us to go through that. Can you get the team to go over connections again between the three murders?'

Focusing on the case might help me forget about my other problems.

'Of course, partner.' He peered at me through concern-filled eyes. 'Is everything okay? Did you get Abbey's situation sorted?'

I dredged a smile from somewhere and put on my best positive attitude. 'The school is a waste of space, so I've taken her out to study at home.' And everyone should know there's a pervert working at that school who's grooming teenage girls.

'Wow, that's a big decision.' I couldn't tell if he was impressed or worried. It was probably a bit of both.

'Yeah, the sooner we have this case wrapped up, the better, then I'll take time off and get Abs sorted.' Because finding the killer of three people is always a doddle.

'I'm with you on that, Jen, but I can't see us solving this soon; not with what we've got.'

There was an unspoken message between us regarding making progress only when the Hashtag Killer struck again; something I couldn't tell those waiting for me outside, so I had to give them something else to chew over. Even if we were no closer to finding our perp, it was my job to convince the media and the public it would happen sooner rather than later. Not that most of the public minded too much we hadn't caught the killer yet.

I checked through what we had. The forensics from the Ripley murder included the material from a pair of jeans found on the branch, a style and type available in hundreds of outlets. The pathologist was certain the murderer had sat there when they dropped the garrotte over Ripley's head. We still didn't know if it was one or two people involved in that.

'Should I tell the press Ripley's killer is good at climbing trees?'

Jack ran his fingers across the unusual stubble on his face as he considered my question. The growth was odd because I couldn't remember the last time I'd seen him unshaven. As I scrutinised his features more, I was shocked to see the dark shadows under his eyes, as if he hadn't had a decent night's sleep in a while. Even his voice seemed gruff as he spoke to me.

'It's worth a mention. There might be potential witnesses who were looking up into those trees and dismissed anything strange or unusual they might have seen. At least if we get the media to report our killer was sitting up there, it might jog a few memories.'

'Is that a pun?' I flicked a piece of paper at him across the table.

'Eh?'

'Jog a few memories about a murder next to some joggers.'

He rubbed his chin again. 'No, sorry. I'm waiting for the coffee to kick into my brain.'

'Have you read the latest report from Cybercrime?' I continued to go through it as he opened the data on his screen. Reading it made me sick.

'Now we know how the killer tracked Ripley so precisely to Adams Park.' A knot twisted in my stomach as I went through the details. 'They hacked into Ripley's computer and emails and found out he had membership of a site which stalked women and provided information, at a price, of the women's whereabouts.'

Jack let out a long sigh. 'Jesus, when you think people can't get any more depraved.'

I imagined how that would go down with the media and

the public. 'At least we've shut the website down.' Cyber-crime couldn't trace the owners because they were Russian based, but we'd arrested some of the site's users.

'Cybercrime discovered a database of over three hundred members on the site. That's many people with some serious explaining to do. Do we have anything useful on the Bobby Thomas murder?'

There was a strange tone to Jack's voice; how he pronounced the word "murder" as if it wasn't that at all. I had no sympathy for Thomas or any of the others, but I wasn't like those on social media crowing over these deaths. They were still crimes which needed solving. They might not have been my current priority, but I was determined to find this killer.

'Nope, Thomas's death is a mystery. No witnesses and no forensics of any use. All we have is the stockpile of child porn he'd stored away. Cybercrime are trying to trace the kids in the photos, but with no luck so far.' I didn't envy them that job, having to trawl through those horrific images. It made me think of Alice again and the massive debt I owed her. I also wished I was in Australia with Abs.

I scrunched up a piece of paper and threw it at Jack's head. It bounced off his nose and he gave me a fake smile.

'Did you know Alice Voss is from Australia?'

The stubble on his chin bristled. 'She's a Wizard of Oz?'

'She was born there, but her parents were British, which means she is, but I guess she is pretty mystical on the computers and everything digital.'

He pointed at the screen in front of him. 'I remember the days when cases were solved by using good old leg work out on the streets, but now this is the world we live in. We'll be replaced with police robots soon enough, mark my words.'

I reached for the sandwich on my desk and unwrapped it from the thin plastic. Abbey had made it for me this morning before slipping back into her bedroom and playing some God-awful doom metal band turned up to eleven. I had no idea why she even had twelve pairs of headphones in there.

'Don't you worry, partner; no humanoid automaton would ever replace Dapper Jack Monroe in the annals of the city's finest detectives.'

He stuck two fingers up at me as I moved across my screen to the Maxwell files. All we had was the description of the murderer which was of little help beyond telling us we were looking for a big bloke. We'd interviewed all sixty-seven of Maxwell's victims who'd testified at his trial. I wouldn't tell the media that. Adding to their suffering to find the killer of their abuser wouldn't go down well with the public in its current mood. We had nothing else of note on Maxwell's death, but we had reams of documents describing all the terrible and sick things he did.

I clicked open the folder labelled SUSPECTS. There were two documents, one for Kyle Swift, the other for Ruby Vasquez. Swift had no alibi for Ripley or Thomas, but did for Maxwell since his latest drinking buddies from the pub swore he was with them when the priest went up in flames. I scrolled down the document to find the image of him in his uniform. Just below was some new data about his military service. He might look like the typical dumb squaddie who claimed he'd killed insurgents with his bare hands, but he also spent time assigned to communications and cyber warfare.

So not only did he have the motivation to kill Ripley, he probably had the computer skills to hack into his laptop and find Ripley's membership of that stalking website. Plus, he might have had help from his pals in the military. His description fitted with what the eyewitness saw at the Maxwell murder, but so could thousands of others. Perhaps he hacked into the priest's computer and Thomas's digital collection? According to Alice, anybody could do it with the right software.

I watched Jack collating information about Maxwell's victims and had an epiphany.

'You're probably wasting your time with those.'

He glanced up from his computer. 'You got something?'

I thought I did. I hoped I did.

'What if the connection between the three of them is they were all on the internet, all looking at things they shouldn't have? Everything else is just random.'

He arched his eyebrows at me in that way which demanded more information. 'Go on, Lady Sherlock.'

'Let's say our killer searches online for a history of people he believes got away with their crimes. Then he filters them out by location and ease of access and if they're connected to the internet. And now he's working his way through the list at his convenience.'

Jack leant forward so his chin rested on his screen. 'How does the killer get into their computers?'

It was evident to me. 'The killer hacks into the computers or phones through their social media accounts, probably Facebook. It's easy to do, apparently. And I'm guessing most people don't update their internet security or change their passwords enough.' Abigail's problem might help me with this case.

'Have Cybercrime finished with our victims' digital devices?' Jack said. I sent a message to Alice as he spoke.

'I'm checking now. And also to ensure they haven't only been looking at what Ripley, Thomas and Maxwell were doing, but seeing if anyone has hacked into their machines.'

Jack let out a low laugh. 'I'm sure they'll love you telling them what to do. But if your theory is true, does it point to someone we know?'

'Well, Kyle Swift still has motivation and means.' I turned to the screen and the documents about our other suspect. 'But I guess you prefer Ruby Vasquez.'

Jack walked around to my side of the desk. 'You can't deny this has helped her fake journalism career, and she's the one who coined the names Hashtag Killer and Hashtag Vigilante. Plus, she was awful quick to appear at the scene of Ripley's murder.'

'That doesn't explain Father Abraxas's description of the person who set Maxwell on fire. Remember, the attacker is tall and built like a rugby player.'

That stumped Jack as he ran his fingers through the dimple in his chin.

'Maybe she and Ripley are working together, or she has another accomplice. You mentioned her old man yesterday. You must have had a reason for that.'

I stared at the information we had on Ruby Vasquez and her family. 'There's no trace of him after his last spell in jail two years ago?'

'He didn't keep up with his parole meetings, but to be honest, nobody bothered to find him. He's a low priority in an under-resourced and overstretched metropolitan police force.'

'You think this might all be a ploy to make money?'

Jack shrugged his shoulders. 'We both know plenty of people who've done worse for a lot less.'

I was pondering his words as a new message came through from Alice.

'Alice says it wasn't her working on the Ripley and Maxwell digital devices, so she's unsure what they checked for, but all she found from Thomas was what we already know. If she gets the chance, she said she'd look at them this afternoon.'

'You appear to have become pally with Ms Voss.'

Was that jealousy I heard in his voice?

'She helped Abigail out the other day, so I owe her a favour.' I owed her more than one.

He returned to his desk. 'So what shall we focus on?'

I stared at the photo of Ruby Vasquez on the screen. 'I've got what I need for the press. Let's see if we can trace Charles Vasquez and wait for what Alice comes back with.' I stood, headed out of the room and downstairs to the media centre. I remembered not to smile and answer only those questions which wouldn't make me look foolish. As I gazed into the flashing lights, I hoped Abigail was okay on her own.

A bigail spent all morning watching videos about computer coding and hacking. She had three personal Facebook messages waiting for her, but she left them unanswered. She took out her writing pad and looked at the notes she'd made when Alice led her through the internet security training at the police station. Her fingers flicked through the pages until she found what she wanted.

CATFISHING

Catfishing is a deceptive activity where a person creates a fake identity on a social network account for attention seeking, bullying or as a romance scam. A "catfish" is a person pretending to be someone they're not on the internet. People use fake profile pictures, names, and often genders. Catfishers create bogus profiles to trick others into thinking they're someone else. Usually, the fabricated life displayed is the one they wish was their own, making it easy to act as if it is really them.

Even with everything going on with the kids at school and the images they sent her, Abigail had never considered Sam wasn't who he claimed he was on Facebook. She'd checked his profile and his Instagram account. She believed all he told her. Then she did everything he asked, even sending those photos. It made her feel good at first, that somebody thought she was attractive. Especially when she was getting texts at the same time saying she was ugly and she should kill herself. And he loved her. He'd said it so many times it must be true. And she loved him.

She knew she couldn't tell her mother about the messages. She wouldn't understand and would only worry, telling Abigail she was too young for a boyfriend. There was nobody else to talk to about it, so she kept it all to herself. Abigail preferred it that way. The secrets made it more exciting, made it more about her. She finally had something to herself, had someone to herself.

But then Alice told her about the Catfish, and Abigail's entire world came crashing down. She'd denied it at first, wanting it all to be a terrible thing which happened to other people, not her. But the more she read over the messages, the more she recognised how he'd manipulated her into doing those things, how he'd escalated getting her to reveal more of herself both physically and emotionally. And now he didn't just want more photos; he demanded she meet him. If she wouldn't, he threatened to post them all online and send them to every kid in school and her mother. She couldn't have her mother looking at those pictures.

Abigail stared at his last message on the screen.

If you don't come to me, those photos will be everywhere. They'll follow you for the rest of your life. You must meet me. Nothing will happen, I promise.

But she didn't believe him anymore. She realised what he wanted; she knew what they all wanted, those men who harassed her on the way to school. The boys who said they hated her but still peered at her.

Abigail turned on the TV to see a repeat of a news conference her mother had given this morning. She wanted to tell her everything, but she couldn't. Her mother was strong, whereas Abigail was weak. She listened to her mother tell the country that the police, that she - Detective Inspector Flowers - would find the Hashtag Killer and they would be brought to justice. Abigail reached for her phone and logged onto Twitter, even though she'd promised she wouldn't. On there, the Hashtag Killer was the Hashtag Vigilante, and everybody said how what they were doing was true justice: justice for those who'd been wronged by others.

True justice. That's what Abigail craved. She went to her Facebook account and read his messages; this grown man pretending to be a fourteen-year-old boy. Her head was clear as she typed.

Six o'clock tonight, over the railway line, in the Old Man's Hut. I'll be there. I can't wait to meet you.

He sent a smiley face in reply. She slipped the carving knife into her bag and stared at her reflection in the mirror as she left.

I WAS SPRAWLED on the floor when I came to my senses. There was a long throbbing ache in my back and an even worse pain vomiting inside my skull. I looked up and the memories cascaded down, green eyes peering at me. His fingers were on my flesh and I shivered. I kicked out as he went to help me up. Somewhere in the room, my mother coughed out her lungs and a vile revelation.

'See, I told you it was your fault Ruby blacks out. One look at your face does it to her.'

Her laugh sliced through my soul and ate at my life. My head was stuck to the carpet and my brain hurt. I thought I was bleeding until I pushed my hand away and smelt stale jam. I dug my fingers into the filth next to me and crawled backwards and up. His head was close to me, stinking of whisky and gasoline. My hands ached and I resisted the temptation to wrap them around his neck. He was taller than I remembered, big enough to be a basketball player on steroids. His cut-off t-shirt highlighted his muscles and his tattoos, flesh covered in naked women and grinning skulls. I inched away from him and towards the door. My teeth groaned because I was grinding them so much.

'What do you want? There's nothing for you here.' I had to run from that room, but I also needed to hear him speak, wanted to know why he'd abandoned me so long ago.

He turned around, snatched the cigarette from his estranged wife's hand and slipped back into the sofa.

'You owe me a lot, daughter. You have to give me seventy per cent of everything you're making from the vigilante murders.' His grin was vampirish, the leer of a Wall Street banker.

I was struggling for a response so burst out laughing instead. It was a long snicker like the approach of thunder, ready to roar down your throat when it reached you. It gave me enough time to know what I wanted to say to him.

'Go fuck yourself, old man. Even if I had any money, why would I give it to you?'

He blew smoke into the air and grinned at my mother. For one brief second, I imagined them at the altar, happily married and planning to ruin the life of their unborn child.

'Tell her, Isabel.' The words slid from his mouth like a snake approaching its prey.

Isabel Vasquez, not my mother, never my mother,

scratched her skin and looked as nervous as I'd ever seen her.

'I've read all your messages, Ruby; I know how much cash you've got coming because of what you've been writing about the Hashtag Killer. It's only fair you give some of that to your mam and dad.' She dropped cigarette ash onto the floor and posed as if she was Mother of the Year.

The impossibility of it made me shake my head. 'How can you read my messages? There are passwords on every-thing.' My mother accessing my digital machines was as unlikely as him returning here now.

'It was easy, Ruby. I downloaded the software off the internet and it did it for me. You never turn your laptop off, and there's no password on it. All I had to do was leave a Trojan on your computer, and it recorded all your pass-words and sent them to me.'

I didn't know what was worse: the fact I'd been too lazy to secure the machine or that my Luddite mother had beaten me at my own game. How the fuck did she even know what a Trojan was, never mind how to use it? Still, it was a valuable lesson learnt, and better it happened now with these two buffoons than with someone who could hurt me. I regained control of my breathing and focused on the old man.

'How did you convince a woman who hates you to have you back?' Inside my head was a continuous cacophony of rants and tirades my mother had unleashed about him over the years.

He turned his green eyes from me and to the wife with the nicotine-stained face.

'Don't believe what she's told you, Ruby; Isabel has always loved me.' He grinned at her. 'Plus she wants your money as well.' They held hands and an invisible machine gun fired a thousand bullets into my gut.

I wanted a stiff drink and a sit-down. My heart was back to normal, but my spine ached to fuck. The weight of these two bastards standing in front of me could drag me even further into the abyss. I reached into my pocket for the medication, but it was empty. Had I used them all or left them somewhere?

'You should listen to him, Ruby.' Her voice rattled inside my head.

'We can be one big happy family again, daughter.' Those green eyes of his flickered tiny sparks of emerald light through the smoke drifting across the room.

I'll tell him what he wants to hear, then get my stuff and never return. This was the final motivation I needed to leave this dump. I'd rather sleep on the streets than stay here another night.

I moved towards the stairs.

'Sure, I'll get right on that tomorrow once I've recovered from the shock of this unexpected family reunion.'

My hand was on the door as he spoke.

'It's not that I don't believe you, daughter, but if you don't do as I ask, your new career as a journalist will be over before it's begun.'

I turned to face him, fighting off all those memories written in my diaries. Did I force his return by getting those books out of the box? Was this all my fault?

'What do you mean?'

He leered at me and took out his phone.

'Give me what I want, or there'll be no more stories for you to post. You'll go back to being a nobody in a shitty dump with no future. Take a good look at your mother because that's the life waiting for you if you don't do what I say.'

I scowled at him. 'You're talking rubbish, old man. I don't need you to write my articles.'

He laughed at me. 'Of course, you do.' He stood up and showed me his phone. He flicked through half a dozen images. With each one, my stomach churned even more. They were crime scene photos from the Ripley, Thomas and Maxwell murders.

'Where did you get those?' I knew the answer before he replied.

'Jeez, girl, you can be as dumb as your mother. I took them.'

I felt my face glaze over and I wanted to throw up.

'But that means...'

The green of his eyes stared right through me and all those memories came back in waves, crashing against my heart, including the ones I hadn't written in my diaries.

'Yes, Ruby; I'm the Hashtag Killer.'

29 ROSES IN THE HOSPITAL

O nce a month, I volunteer at the local hospital, visiting those patients who have no family or friends. It's the same scene every time I go: people complaining about having to pay for the car park, observed by a continuously changing audience of those living with cancer sucking on their cigarettes. Other visitors shake their heads and occasionally chastise the smokers, but it makes perfect sense to me: if the photos on cigarette packets of disease-blackened lungs wouldn't dissuade them, then nothing would. As long as they keep that stink away from me, they can do what they want with their organs. Of course, there's an argument to say people who deliberately poison their bodies shouldn't be allowed free medical treatment on the NHS, but that seems harsh even for me.

A guard stopped me on the way to the ward. I've been unable to work out if hospital security is to prevent nefarious types from getting in or to stop patients escaping. Whoever compared hospitals to prisons was spot on apart from the food being better inside Her Majesty's pleasure. Still, at least I was stepping into what survived of the good old NHS and not suffering the financial constraints of the American medical system, where treatment would cost you an actual arm and a leg.

'I need to see your ID card.' The security guard was new to me; I guessed he was in his late thirties, but there was the adolescent about him. It may have been the long fringe crawling out from under his cap, or the homemade dragon tattoo peeking at me from the top of his unbuttoned shirt. The level of professionalism in the workplace was unpardonably low these days. He even wore training shoes.

He followed my gaze to his feet as I showed him my badge.

'I need to wear them because of my bunions.'

I fashioned an expression of apparent sympathy and headed towards the ward. Modern hospitals have a smell all of their own: a heavy dose of antiseptic and bleach sprayed everywhere to cover the aroma of blood, sweat and tears. And the piss and shit. There's a definite whiff of that if you're unlucky enough to take a turn down the wrong corridor or meet those unable to control their internal organs.

For a long time, I was unable to control the events inside my head. The struggle and shame pressed down upon me daily. It was my fault, what happened; that's what I told myself for years. But over time, I realised it wasn't my burden, it was his, and if I couldn't punish him, then those like him would face justice. I didn't shut myself away or hide from the world. On the contrary, I mingled, I went out, but even when we're surrounded by people, it's easy to be isolated.

It was only when I started to recognise that others suffered as I did, that tormented thoughts and ideas sprinted through all human minds, I realised I wasn't unique. Our emotional challenges may well be unique, but I at least understood I wasn't alone in the struggle. All I had to do was reach out, make a connection, and deal with my problem in my way.

The trips to the hospital were the first part of the journey. I had to witness physical suffering close-up to see if I could handle the pain of others. Plus, I thought I'd be helping the public.

You can learn a lot by being around vulnerable people. It heightens your compassion and empathy to the point you have to step away sometimes for your well-being. Of course, some can fake those emotions, can forge a resemblance to life, but not me. A hospital is an excellent place to get a grounding in reality. And I enjoyed helping folks.

There were new patients on the ward as I walked in. They were gawking at a game show on the TV. A hipster dude who pumped iron in his spare time tried to guess the name of a Dostoyevsky novel.

'Crime and Persecution,' he said to the groans of the audience. The standard of cultural knowledge in the population had fallen to a shocking level.

At the far end sat a little old man on his lonesome. I made my way past the TV watchers and sidled up to his bed. Save for a tattered Ayn Rand paperback and an opened packet of Fox's glacier mints, there was nothing personal next to him. The other patients had family photos or pots of flowers, but this bloke had zilch; unless he was a relative of Ayn Rand. The thought was too horrible to contemplate.

'That book will keep you up at night, what with all the jokes.' I usually avoid physical contact with strangers, but I held my hand out to this fella. The long-haul bags under his eyes made even me sad.

'Who are you?' He glared at me. I gave a half-grin and showed him my identity badge.

'Do you have anybody come to visit you...?' I let the words linger in the germ-free air, waiting for him to speak his name. He didn't bother, so I didn't push it. He grabbed the book and crawled into bed. Behind me, the others were shouting at some ignoramus getting a question wrong on the game show.

'I disowned the family years ago. Bunch of parasites they are.' His teeth flashed yellow, and I could tell from experience he was on the cusp of either going full hermit or spilling his whole life to me; one of those blokes who enjoyed telling you how much he hated others. If he had an exciting story to tell, I was game, but you never knew with this age group.

A nurse came into the ward and turned the TV off. If you've never heard half a dozen old people coughing asthmatically and complaining at the same time, you've missed a treat. It would've made a great soundtrack to a Keystone Cops silent movie. The nurse shushed their cantankerous hand waving impressively, especially considering she looked about sixteen years old. I knew the NHS was struggling with recruitment, but I hadn't realised the government were reintroducing child labour into the British economy.

'It's time for our medication.' She said this as if she would be the one taking the pills. Maybe she wanted to. I think I would if I worked there.

I checked my phone, and I'd got my times wrong. That was unusual. The work I'd put into this project had overloaded my senses.

'I'll see you next month,' I said to the Ayn Rand acolyte. He grunted and turned away. As I left, I wondered why I'd said those words. Having looked at him, I had a three-way toss-up between him still being there, back home in his isolation or, most likely, pushing up the daisies.

As I exited the building, I analysed my motivations once

again for these regular visits. It might appear somewhat masochistic to put myself this close to death but, ultimately, the trips to the hospital were the final motivation in putting my plans into action.

My work had taught me that death might come at any time for any of us. Mortality is the lesson we ignore until it can't be unnoticed, and I couldn't overlook my responsibility anymore.

It was time for the end game.

It was time for me to repay a debt which could never be repaid.

Alice got back to me in the afternoon, confirming what I'd thought about our victims' computers. I told Jack everything over a coffee in the police cafeteria.

'Alice found multiple instances of hackers getting into their machines. Each part of their digital life was compromised. Whoever was spying on them knew every move they made.'

Jack dropped four enormous sugar cubes into his drink; I imagined all that sweetness going to work on his guts like bayonetted soldiers climbing out of the trenches and stabbing at everything they found.

'That's how they knew Ripley would be in that park, that Thomas was on his own and Maxwell would visit his church.' He placed a hand over his mouth and attempted to stifle a belch.

I nodded. 'Thomas emailed his old organisation minutes before he died. The disgraced priest mailed his brother to say he was going to the church one last time. Trying to find absolution, I expect.' I shut down the images of my father and his congregation creeping into my mind.

Jack sipped on his hot sugar rush. 'Any luck tracing the hacks to their owner?'

'Sure, all the way back to Russia.'

'Maybe this is all a Russian ploy to destabilise our way of life?'

I couldn't contain my laughter. 'You have an active imagination, Jack.'

'So, what's our next move?' he said before biting into a doughnut. If he ingested any more sugar, I'd have to roll him out of the building.

'We need a fresh lead. Did you have any luck finding Charles Vasquez?'

'It's funny you should say that. I'm reliably informed he was spotted drinking with his wife in the Crown and Anchor two days ago.' Bits of doughnut stuck to his chin.

I ransacked my mind for when I'd seen that pub. 'Isn't that around the corner from where Ruby Vasquez lives with her mother?'

'It is,' Jack replied. 'Shall we bring him in on his parole violation?'

I watched him eat the rest of the doughnut, marvelling at how he could consume so much sugar and still not get fat. I only had to walk past a bar of chocolate to gain weight. Abigail was the same and I knew it was one more thing she worried about.

'It's no wonder your guts are always playing up considering the crap you put in them.' Jack grinned at me as I answered his question. 'Sure, bring him in. We might learn something useful about his daughter.'

And with that, I was done for the day. I got up and left him to poison his body as he saw fit. I texted Alice to say I'd meet her at the car in five minutes. I messaged Abs to ask what she wanted to eat tonight and to tell her we'd have a guest with us, but there was no reply. The lack of response worried me. Abs was never without her phone.

Alice was already there when I got outside, leaning against the car and staring into her phone. She slipped it into her pocket when she saw me. I unlocked the doors.

'Thanks for what you did with those computers. I hope it didn't drag you away from something important.'

Alice laughed as she slid into the passenger seat. 'You did me a favour. My team is working on this huge corporate fraud case. It's fascinating, but not the same as a triple murder. Have you considered what you'll say to Abigail?'

Even with the Hashtag investigation, I'd thought of little else other than how I'd tell my vulnerable teenage daughter she was being groomed online. How do you recover from such betrayal?

'I hoped you'd give me some advice on that.'

Alice took a deep breath. 'It won't be easy, but she needs to hear the truth.'

I agreed and we discussed how to approach it on the journey over.

'I'll tell her I gave you the password and social media details.' I was worried Abigail wouldn't trust me after this. Alice tried to reassure me as we got out of the car.

'She'll be upset, but once we explain it to her, she'll understand.'

I hoped that Abigail liking Alice would help smooth things over. I put the key into the door.

'It's not as impressive as your place,' I said as we walked in. She followed me inside. 'Grab a seat, and I'll see if she's in her room.'

'No problem, Jen.'

I strode up the stairs. 'Are you there, Abs? I've brought you a visitor.' Abigail's bedroom was empty. I checked my phone, but there was no reply to my messages. I looked around her room, searching for a note or something to tell me where she was.

The bathroom door was closed, so I knocked on it. 'Abigail, are you in there?'

There was no reply; then a voice came from downstairs.

'You better come here, Jen.'

The concern in Alice's voice forced me to sprint downstairs and into the living room. Alice handed me a piece of paper.

'I found this next to the TV.'

I read it with a heavy heart.

I have to sort things out by myself, Mum. I'll find my justice.

'Shit. She could've gone anywhere.' My legs gave way, and I slumped into the sofa. I reread the note, the word justice burning into the front of my brain. If she'd gone to confront the kids from school, maybe it would be a good thing for her to stand up for herself like that. But it could also cause a lot more trouble. Shit. Shit. Shit.

'You could check her Facebook, see if she's added anything.'

I got my phone. 'Even better, I'll log into her account.' It meant spying on her again, but I had to find where she was. I entered Abigail's password and accessed the page. She'd posted nothing on her timeline in two days. There was one new message for her, so I opened it and stared at the fake profile picture of the supposedly teenage boy called Sam. The words crushed my spirit.

I can't wait to meet you. I'm already here. There's so much for us to talk about. But don't tell anyone else. They won't understand. This has to be our secret.

I dropped the phone and it bounced onto the carpet. It

took an age to get there, rolling in slow motion through the fibres at the same speed the air crawled from my lungs. It landed face up, the flickering screen gazing at me, those words of his cutting through my eyes and sinking deep into my heart.

'Oh my God, Alice, she's gone to see him.'

Alice picked up the mobile and read through the messages.

'Do you know where this Old Man's Hut is?'

My skull ached like the centre of a black hole. 'Yes, it's an abandoned storage unit the other side of the railway tracks, about thirty minutes' walk from here, maybe ten in a car.'

Alice grabbed my hand. 'Come on, then. Looking at the time on these messages, I guess Abigail's not there yet and we can catch up with her before she meets him.' She dragged me up as if I was a rag doll. Where had my energy gone? My daughter was in danger, and it felt like I was walking in treacle.

I glanced away from Alice, staring at the framed photo on the middle shelf of the bookcase of Abigail and me. How old was she in that photo, ten or eleven? She wore a Harry Potter t-shirt which disappeared two years later. She'd said she lost it, but I knew she burnt it in the bin at the back of the house because she thought she was too old now for, in her words, 'all that kids' stuff.' I'd let her grow up without taking proper care of her, without educating her in the dangers of the world. It was up to me to save her, regardless of the cost to me or others.

Energy rushed through me as I let go of Alice. We left the house and jumped into the car. I knew the quickest way to get to the railway lines and pulled out without bothering to fasten the seatbelt. Alice scrambled into hers and, even without looking at her, I felt the tension in her bones. Or maybe it was all coming from me and seeping into the car and turning me into a Formula One driver. I drove as fast as possible, killing no one but hitting the brakes at the traffic lights.

'I could call the station for back-up,' Alice said.

My blood boiled as I glared at the red light. 'We'll get there quicker.' I slammed into the accelerator when the lights changed. 'The two of us should be enough for one pervert.'

I spun around the corner as if I was in a dodgem car. Alice gripped onto the seat. 'I've never worked outside the office before.'

I focused on the road ahead. 'You've completed your physical training, though; you can handle yourself in a fight?'

Alice gulped and nodded slowly. 'Maybe we should call the station?'

'No time for that. What does it say on her phone?'

Her eyes were glued to Abigail's Facebook messages. 'Nothing has changed since the last one.'

I weaved past a cyclist, and then a taxi driver who beeped his horn at me. There was less traffic now and the field which ran parallel to the railway lines was just ahead. We'd made record time to get there, but it felt like I'd been in suspended animation all the time I was driving.

A stray dog ran out in front of me and I swerved to miss it, pulling the car to a stop at the edge of the field. Alice struggled with her seatbelt as I fell out of the vehicle. There was no one around apart from the dog I'd nearly killed, which stared at me through watery eyes. The field was all downhill, leading to a high fence. On the other side was the train track. I pointed towards it.

'We need to be down there, and then right. About fifty yards on is the Old Man's Hut. There used to be a hole in the fence to get through. Otherwise, we must climb over it. Are you ready?'

Alice lifted a finger to her chin and rubbed at it; her eyes were wide and nervous.

'Why don't I send him a text from Abigail's account and say she's changed her mind? He might go away then.'

'Because I want to catch this bastard so I know it's over and Abigail's safe.'

I didn't wait for her to protest and ran towards the fence. The lethargy which had possessed me back at the house was a distant memory, replaced by electricity I hadn't felt in years; it was as if some demented marionette controller was propelling me forward. Without looking at the ground, I bounded across the grass, dodging the dog shit and random bricks scattered over the field.

Was I putting Abs at risk by not calling for back-up and dismissing Alice's idea about sending a message to the pervert? Fear and anger created a volatile cocktail inside me; I wanted to crush the life from this man. My feet bounced through the grass and the mud, my heart ready to explode.

Is this what it felt like to seek justice at any cost?

Alice followed, but even though she was the younger of the two of us, she struggled to keep up. I hit the bottom of the bank and pivoted to the right.

'Can you see the opening in the fence?' I shouted as I sprinted forward. I didn't turn around. Alice gasped for breath behind me.

'I can see it, Jen.' She coughed loudly and spat phlegm onto the fence. 'But we can't just go rushing in. We might put Abigail in danger.'

I wasn't listening to her, my feet sliding through mud. Pushing the hair from my eyes, I reached the gap and stretched through it, ready to step onto the other side until something pulled me back. Shit. Shit. Shit. My jacket was caught on the fence. I pulled at it and ripped a hole in the side, leaving part of it dangling there as I paused before the tracks. The dilapidated building was fifty yards in front of me, but I'd have to cross two sets of lines to get to it.

The sound of rumbling metallic wheels vibrated through the air. I didn't wait for Alice to catch up and continued running. The steel echoed as I moved parallel to it. I glanced around but couldn't work out which way the train was coming from.

As the din grew louder, Abigail appeared ahead. She was already across the tracks and outside the building.

'Abigail!'

The word flew from my mouth. Then I repeated it, but my voice was drowned out by the noise of the oncoming train. There was a lull in the cacophony before I heard the scream.

31 TRAIN IN VAIN

The scream came again, a loud shrieking wail flashing through my ears and taking residence inside my skull. It vibrated and echoed off the insides of my head, paralysing my legs and forcing dread through my chest.

It was Abigail.

My feet left the ground as one, my limbs sprinting towards that awful sound. There was pressure on my chest as Abigail's voice filled every part of me, swimming through my blood and invading my senses; my head sank under water; my vision clouded with dust and sweat and tears and grass swirling everywhere. A cacophony blasted through the air and threatened to cut me in two.

Then an arm pulled me backwards, the wind blowing across my face as the front of the train missed me by inches. The carriages rattled along the tracks, their motion rippling my trousers against my legs. The vibrations of the train pushed air across my clothes and dropped a blanket of pressure over my face. In between the gaps, I glanced at the swirling panic in Alice's eyes. Her mouth was wide open, her lips trembling as she spoke, but it was impossible to hear her in the thunder of the train's passing.

She dragged me from the line.

'We have to wait until it passes,' Alice shouted above the roar. Metal screamed on metal, but all I heard was Abigail's tortured scream. Curious passengers peered at me from the windows; a small child pressed a SpongeBob toy against the glass; a horse-faced woman pushed thick glasses up her thin nose; a gammon-faced man mouthed something I couldn't hear. They flashed across my vision like cartoon frames in an animation.

The passing lasted for an eternity, the carriages speeding by as the dreadful parts of my life resurfaced at the front of my mind. My father's voice replaced the roar of the train. All the faces in the windows became his as he told me I had to give up the baby, as he forced me down the terrible path I never wanted to take.

But I wouldn't lose another child.

The train vanished into the distance, the pulse of the track matching the rhythm of my heart. The image and sound of my father disappeared with the last carriage, and I leapt onto the rail. Two arms held me back.

'Let me go, Alice.'

'We can't rush in, Jen. We could force his hand. We need to use caution.' Her eyes were wide, her words rushing at me at a thousand miles an hour.

I jerked away from her, all my police training disappearing down the black hole at the pit of my stomach.

'Fuck caution.'

I jumped over the tracks, running faster than before, pushing through the weeds and rubbish discarded there. A broken sink lay to the side, while crushed cans and dirty clothes were scattered in front of me, a trail of garbage laying the way into the disused edifice holding Abigail. Sweat dribbled on my head and everywhere stank of shit.

I reached the building and paused. My heart thumped like a jackhammer, my fingers creeping into fists. I pushed the door open and peered into the gloom.

There was nothing to see but more debris across the floor and thick grass peering from the concrete at my feet. The place stank of human faeces and vomit. Blood pumped through my ears and all I heard was the sound of my fear.

'Abigail?' Dread dripped from me.

A light flickered through the broken window, bouncing off something in the far corner. Then I saw the knife. Somebody pushed Abigail forward and the blade nipped at her throat.

'Mum.' Her voice trembled. 'Mum, he says if you leave now, he'll let me go.'

He was hiding in the shadows, whispering in Abigail's ear.

'Shit!' Alice stumbled through the door.

The whisper came again, the weapon cutting into Abigail's flesh as she spoke his words.

'Turn around and leave. Go across the tracks and up the field. Then I'll let her go.' It was her voice, but not her voice. A trickle of blood crept down Abigail's neck. The blade was caressing her throat, but it pierced my heart.

Alice grabbed my arm. 'We must do as he says, Jen.' I didn't take my eyes off my daughter. Alice leant into me. 'We can call for more officers outside. He won't get away. There's no way out apart from this door.'

I ignored her and stared straight ahead. I stopped being a mother and became a copper again.

'Have you seen his face, Abigail? Do you know who he is?' Abigail never moved, but the answers were in her eyes.

His whispering became more frenzied as the knife inched closer to her chin. 'Because if you know who he is, he'll never let you leave here alive.' My mind raged, but I forced myself to reach for my negotiating skills. I'd done this before with hostages. I could talk him down. 'If you let Abigail go now, you'll likely only be charged with grooming a minor. You might not even get any jail time.'

Silence engulfed everything. Time stood still for me, my gaze on Abigail, trying not to stare at the blade at her neck. What if I'd got this all wrong and all I'd done by coming here, by barging into this place, was make a desperate man even more desperate? What if I'd left him with no choice but to kill her?

'I'll slit her throat.' He spoke with his voice now, a guttural snarl which betrayed no fear. 'Both of you back against the wall. I'm not messing around here.'

Alice tugged on my arm, doing what he said, but my feet were rooted between the weeds. Blood trickled down Abigail's neck and stuck to her top. She didn't cry or whimper, but there were terrible things in her eyes, and I knew she expected me to save her.

I let go of my anger, allowing Alice to pull me with her to the wall. I stepped onto broken glass, and the sound echoed around the dark space. The floor vibrated under my feet, signalling another train on its way.

As we moved to the side, he pushed Abigail forward, the light creeping in through the broken window and settling on her face. She was deathly pale and I wanted to reach out and snatch her to safety. I needed to look her in the eyes, to tell her not to worry, that everything would be okay, but I couldn't take my gaze away from the knife nipping at her flesh. If he stumbled over the ground, he'd slice her throat in one go.

As that terrible thought stabbed at my brain, he pushed Abigail at me. The surprise of it knocked me sideways, Abigail falling into me, the two of us tumbling into Alice and then the wall.

The three of us ended up on the floor, squirming through grass and crap as he loomed over us, nothing but a shadow with a large knife in his hand. I put myself between Abigail and him, holding my arm up as he brought the blade down in one swift movement; it sliced into my jacket, ripping through the material and taking a chunk of it away as he pulled up.

Another train screamed outside as he attacked again. This time, he caught the side of my hand, the blunt part of the blade bouncing off my skin but knocking me back into Alice. Abigail was defenceless now, crouched and frozen before him. I was ready to howl as he jumped to the side and fled out the door before I could respond.

I pulled Alice and Abigail up with me, turning to Alice as I did so.

'Look after Abs.'

There was no time to console my daughter; I was sure she was all right, physically at least. I had to catch this bastard. I stumbled out of the door and went after him. The train had gone and he staggered not far ahead of me. He didn't have much of a start, his legs moving as if made of lead. There were maybe twenty seconds between us.

As I ran, the tracks rattled next to me. Another train was on the way, coming towards us this time. I saw it on the horizon as I edged towards him. He lurched onwards, his feet struggling with the small stones underfoot. My hand clasped his shoulder before he moved any further, my fingers digging into his flesh, transferring my pain into him.

He spun around and thrust the blade at my face,

missing me by inches. I let go of his arm, staring at a face I recognised. Tension seeped out of me and I shook my head.

'Why am I not surprised?'

His laugh was vile and insidious. 'I guess I'll never work in a school again.' Giles's teeth were brighter than the sun.

'They might give you a teaching job in prison. I'm sure you'll be popular. Your kind always is.'

I expected him to lunge at me again, but he had other ideas, spinning on his heels and trying to flee. But the grass grew longer where he was and his feet struggled with the constraints of nature. The train was nearly upon us, speeding down the track towards me. There was no chance he'd escape, and even if he did, I knew him now. But what if he wriggled his way out of this, got himself a decent lawyer and escaped a prison sentence? He'd be free to do this again, to groom some other innocent kid and do God knows what. Was I prepared to let that happen? It would be easy for him to slip while attempting to flee. I'd try to catch him, but wouldn't be strong enough. He'd be on the lines before I could do anything about it. There would be justice. I would have my justice.

Both Abigail and Alice shouted somewhere behind me. The train rushed forward, drowning out their words. Giles struggled to move, making it easy for me to step near him and grab his arm; the one holding the knife so he couldn't swing it at me. I dug my fingers into his flesh and he dropped the blade onto the track, the metal clanging onto metal. I didn't see where it went. Death appeared so close to us now. Many noises were inside my head: the shriek of the train; Alice telling me to stop; Abigail calling my name and, worst of all, my father's voice, calling me every name under the sun. It's funny how things you thought you'd buried into the deepest parts of you could return at the worst of times.

Giles pleaded with me to let him go, but I dug further into his flesh, feeling the blood seeping onto his clothes. He wriggled in my grasp like a worm on a hook; the fear in his face excited me. The train howled at us as my arm twitched and he slipped from my grip. I watched the carriages fly past me. None of the faces in the windows were my father's.

Abigail would be safe now. Giles lay on the ground, motionless.

'Fuck me.' Alice was out of breath as she caught up. Abigail came behind her. 'I thought you'd throw him onto the tracks in front of the train.'

I bent down and pulled Giles's arms around his back. I put the cuffs on him and read him his rights. I spoke to Alice.

'Can you call this in?'

She nodded and I turned to Abigail, happy to see my daughter smiling. We hugged each other as Alice got on the phone. I looked for the blade, but it had disappeared. It would have been difficult to explain to my colleagues what my kitchen knife was doing here.

'I saw all of that,' Abigail said. How traumatic would this be for her? 'It was like the climax of my favourite movie.'

I racked my brain to remember what that was. '*Aliens*?'

Abigail burst out laughing. It was good to see.

'No, silly. *Night of the Demon*, the Jacques Tourneur classic from 1957.'

I grinned at Abs. 'Didn't the monster eat the villain at the end of that film?'

Abigail grabbed my hand. 'Well, it was that, or the bad man fell in front of the train.'

I smiled at her as blue lights and sirens drifted our way.

I locked myself in the room until they left, watching them from the window as they giggled hand in hand as if they were teenagers again. Pain surged through my stomach as I shoved the diaries back into their hiding place. I couldn't stay in the house, knowing they'd return at some point. I picked up the phone and went to my Twitter account, finding Justice For All in my list of who I followed. The six direct messages I'd sent had no responses. I sent another one.

I need to talk to you. Can we meet?

I dumped the mobile onto the bed, expecting nothing from the digital screen and getting just that. I shut my eyes and saw the image again. Ripley's face turning blue, his eyes open and bulging and staring upwards. Not dead yet, on the cusp, his head still attached to his shoulders. The photo was taken from above.

How could someone strangle him and take those photos?

And there was Thomas with the statue of Big Ben inserted into his skull. Then the image of Maxwell smiling into the lens as the match floats towards him. Then he's ablaze, and his face is melting.

Photographs only a killer could have taken.

But you couldn't throw the match and take the photos at the same moment unless there was more than one of you; one to kill and one to record it.

I grabbed the phone from the bed and sent another message.

I've seen the photographs only the killer has. Are you working alone?

I unlocked the door and ran from the house. It was time to talk to the witness in the Maxwell murder. The police and the media hadn't mentioned the name, but it had to be someone inside the church, and I had the material my hacking had uncovered. I headed for the underground. I hated using the Tube, but at least it wouldn't be busy now. I rechecked my phone before going below, unsurprised to see no replies.

My cheeks were aflame as I swiped the card at the barrier. It was only two minutes' wait before I stepped into the carriage and the first empty seat. I'd always avoid eye contact on the Tube, but needed a distraction from what had transpired at the house. There was a middle-aged couple opposite who I assumed were American tourists. She wore a shirt with the Stars and Stripes on it, while on his head sat a cap emblazoned with the phrase Make America Great Again. I wanted to ask him if it had happened yet, but his apparent nervousness made me uneasy. His hands kept slipping to his waist as if looking for something to protect him.

It may have been the teenagers to his right listening to some rap music who put him on edge. They seemed harmless enough, and I hummed along to the lyrics. The only other person in the carriage was a woman reading a book. The heat was stifling, inflaming my head and making me scratch my scalp.

I took out the phone and stared at the no signal sign. What would I do about the man claiming to be my father? The train juddered to a halt at the next stop. I concentrated on the screen as the doors opened, then closed again. I'd once seen a bloke nearly lose his head between the doors when he didn't get inside quick enough. It made me think of Evan Ripley; and I wondered if anyone had told his mother about his death.

A barrage of shouting distracted me; there were half a dozen men in the next carriage yelling at each other. As they jostled around, I saw the scarves they wore and realised they were football fans. The American man got even twitchier while the woman bowed her head. I hoped the group would get off at the next stop, cursing as they twisted around to stare at me. They yelled something obscene as they strode towards our carriage. I slipped my phone in my pocket.

'England for the English,' they shouted. The leader spun to one side to laugh with his moronic mates, showing off the foreign name on the back of his favourite football shirt. He turned to me.

'No immigrants allowed on here.' He pointed at me and wagged his finger at me. 'Where you from?'

The American hung his head to the floor. I stared at the caveman breathing on me. Warm German lager and cold curry washed out of him.

'I'm British.'

He scrunched his face at me, his friends egging him on. These weren't kids; they were men in their thirties.

'Nah, where you really from?'

'My parents were born in this city. My grandparents were Irish and Mexican.'

He hooted as if he'd just won the lottery. 'You're a double mongrel.' They howled as a group. He grabbed hold of my hair and pulled hard. I ignored the pain.

'But I guess you're sort of pretty.' He glanced at his mates. 'What do you think, lads?'

A few days ago, I might have put up with this shit, but not now. While his gaze drifted away from me, I reached up and seized his wrist. I pushed it to one side at an unnatural angle. The snap his bone made echoed around the carriage; so did his screams. His mates hesitated. The next stop approached, so I stood, pushing harder on his hand, and he fell to the ground. His friends stood frozen to the spot as the train slowed to a halt.

'You better get off before I break your fingers.'

They stared at me in amazement. The doors opened and his tears sank to the floor. The others muttered something before scowling and trooping past me. I twisted him around and waited for the right moment as I edged him towards the exit, kicking him out before the doors slid shut.

The train departed as I sat down. Everybody in the carriage stood and clapped. I stared at them, my heart threatening to leap from my chest. I placed my hands on my legs to stop everything from shaking.

Fifteen minutes later and I was off the Tube and sprinting. My pulse had slowed a little, but it was as if my feet were about to lift from the ground and float away.

'Where did that come from?'

The wind caressed my skin and I turned towards the church. I'd been drunk before, I'd been stoned before, but nothing had ever felt this glorious. I stopped running and caught my breath. I'd panicked when the weirdo approached me the other day, but now I was magnificent.

'I have no fear.' My words shocked me.

I touched my cheeks. It was early evening, but my skin was warm. All around me lingered the aroma of freshly cooked food, the scent of pizza mixed in with strong coffee as doughnuts joined with fried meat. I hadn't eaten for a while, but wasn't hungry. I strode towards the church and up to its open doors; a sign outside said *Everybody Welcome,* so I walked in.

I peered at the stained glass windows, hoping to feel something spiritual, but nothing came. It was the second time I'd been inside a House of God. The first was when I was fourteen and searching for answers to my blackouts. I'd left that day unfulfilled. I hoped this time it would be better.

The church stood empty apart from an old man sitting in a pew at the back. I moved forward, the smell of incense and faded wood drifting in the air. I wondered if all churches were this open. Many people wouldn't hesitate to steal some of the stuff in here.

I stood beneath the statue of Christ on the Cross and addressed its stony visage. 'How do you find the person in charge?'

'He is always around you.'

The words came from above. I snapped my head back, stumbling into the pew, my hand jerking into the seat. I pulled it away and grimaced at the splinter sticking from the middle of my palm. I drew it out and dropped it onto the floor while searching for the owner of that voice.

He stepped down a set of stairs hidden in the corner.

'I'm sorry; that was rather dramatic, wasn't it?' He held out his hand. 'Forgive me. I'm Father Abraxas.'

I shook his hand. His skin was cold and wet.

'My name is Ruby Vasquez. I'm a journalist researching a story about Father Maxwell's murder.' I waited for him to ask for some credentials, busy thinking up a convenient deception, but he didn't appear to care.

'I'm sorry, Miss Vasquez, I've said all I will say about Joseph's time with the church. I'm sure you can find everything you require online.' He turned to go back up the stairs.

'Father Abraxas, it's you I'm interested in.'

He froze on the spot, staring into the shadows.

'What do you mean?' He tried to control it, but he couldn't disguise the tremor in his voice.

'I need a different angle to this story, Father. Otherwise, it'll be the same as every other piece written about your friend turning into toast.'

He twisted around to face me, peering down from the gloom of the stairs.

'Father Maxwell was not my friend.'

I stared past him and into the religious icons dotted throughout the place. I was proud of my ability to deceive even the best, wondering if I could outfox the all-seeing.

'That's not what some of his victims have told me, Father. They say you were well aware of what Maxwell did.'

He pressed his fingers into the railing on the stairs, unable to hide the strain on his face.

'None of that is true.' He took two steps towards me. I was galvanised by what had happened on the Tube, stepping near him and showing no fear.

'You could be right, Father. I'd rather explore a different angle to this story.' His shoulders relaxed as I watched the relief slip over him.

'In what way?'

'I'm more concerned with the person who murdered Maxwell. I'm interested in what you saw.'

He moved closer to me, the tension vanishing from his face.

'I gave my statement to the police. They issued the description through the media.'

'Yes, I read it.' I quoted it from memory. 'A tall man, well built like a rugby player, especially his head.'

The priest gazed at me. 'So what more do you want?'

'I'm curious about the last bit, your comments about his head. What did you mean by that?'

Father Abraxas was completely relaxed now, his body slumping forward as he placed his hands on the pew between us.

'You know how some rugby players, and boxers, have those heads bent out of shape because they've been hit so many times? It was like that, as if he had a small lump at the top of his skull.'

I considered his words, but I already had my theory.

'Could he have been wearing something on his head?'

The priest pondered the question and scratched at his chin. 'Like a hat?'

He laughed loudly. 'No, I think I would have noticed that, even in the dark.' He stared at me as if I was demented.

'What if it was a helmet, one of those that cyclists wear?'

He arched his eyebrows at me.

'Maybe, I suppose. It must have been damaged, though, for that lump to stick out.'

I turned to leave, satisfied with what I'd heard.

'No, Father. I believe that was a camera.'

33 THE GAME

Ben Bailey stared at the building again. It was a right dump in one of the dodgiest parts of the city, but he understood why the meeting was taking place here. He rechecked the last message.

I'll be there at eight. If you can get there fifteen minutes before, my secretary will meet you. To ensure the media haven't got wind of this, you understand. We need to take things slow, pave the way with the fans, and then I'm sure you'll be back at the top of the game in no time.

George.

When the initial message arrived a month ago, Ben assumed it was a stitch-up, thought one of his former team-mates was taking the piss. Why would the Chairman of a Premier League club offer him the chance of resurrecting a career dead in the water? The second jury might have found him innocent and all the charges had been dropped, but the public had long memories. And football supporters were ruthless with disgraced stars; especially one who'd been on the cusp of his first call-up with the national team when that woman accused him of something he didn't do.

But he'd put the past behind him and was focusing on the future.

He read all the messages from the last month from George. The Chairman was right; secrecy was of the utmost importance now, which was why he allowed himself a smile as he entered the shabbiest looking hotel he'd ever seen.

'What a stink.' Damp and grime covered the walls, with rat droppings in the corners. He held his nose and walked up the stairs for the emergency exit and headed for the fourth floor, searching for room forty-two. He found it at the end of the corridor. He hesitated; did he want to get back into the game like this? Would the fans forgive him? His girlfriend and parents had, so why couldn't a load of strangers?

He knocked tentatively on the door. The paint was peeling from the walls, and he had a sudden memory flash from that night and that girl in a hotel similar to this one. His resurrected doubts evaporated as it opened and he saw the young woman standing there. She was pretty with red hair, ushering him in without a word. He peered at his watch, nerves and excitement rippling through him. He'd kept himself fit, even when he was locked up, and exercised daily. He was ready for this.

'Will George be here soon?' His anxiety returned. What if this was a wind-up?

She smiled and handed him a drink, the glass cold against his fingers. There was a chill in the room, but sweat dribbled from his forehead. He wiped it away with his arm and raised the alcohol to his lips.

'I shouldn't, really.' He grinned. 'This is what got me into trouble in the first place.' He could laugh about it now but at the time it was devastating. She said nothing, but took a large gulp from her glass. The ruby shine in her hair was magnetic, pulling him closer to her.

'Okay, I might as well join you.' He sipped at the drink before downing it in one go. 'I'd forgotten how nice champagne is.' He noticed her eyes drifting towards the bed. Maybe this was an extra incentive for joining the club. He'd always had a thing for redheads. He moved forward, the woman suddenly looking more attractive than when he'd entered the room; a warm fuzz exploded in his guts and rushed up through his lungs.

'I'd also forgotten how strong champagne is.' His head buzzed and the place began to spin. He thought he'd spew, clutching onto his stomach before stumbling into the bed. It was agony inside him, a knife sticking into his stomach. The door opened and a man entered. Ben's vision was so blurred, he couldn't make out who it was, but it must have been the Chairman.

'Hello, George,' he said as he collapsed onto the bed. The pain increased as he lost consciousness.

WHEN HE WOKE, the clock on the wall said ten past eight. His head throbbed like a bastard, but at least his eyesight had returned. The redhead stood over him, but George was nowhere. He stretched his back to get off the bed, but found it impossible. His hands and feet were handcuffed to it, and he was naked. A cold shiver swept through him.

'This is kinky,' he said to her. 'Is George into threesomes?' He laughed even though he wanted to throw up. Every bone in his body ached. She stood over him with a bottle of something, the liquid a luminous green colour. Maybe it was absinthe?

'You must let me go if you want me to drink that. Or are you going to pour it into my mouth?'

He pulled against his restraints as she held the bottle over his stomach.

'Don't waste it,' he said as she poured it onto his flesh.

Ben Bailey didn't think it was possible to hurt that much. Before he could scream his lungs out, she clamped his jaw shut with her free hand. She wore gloves and the harsh leather pressed into him.

It felt as if he was inside an oven. The liquid ate into him as she stuffed a sock into his mouth. He struggled to breathe as he smoked, writhing and squirming on the bed as she moved up to his head. She dripped the liquid into his eyes, the light flickering from his orbs as they swam in the fire, emptying the rest of the bottle all over his groin.

The room was awash with the smell of burnt human flesh as the redheaded woman dimmed the lights and left the hotel.

In the gloom, Ben Bailey shrieked in silence.

34 AFTERBURN

The three of us gave our statements to the police as they carted Giles away. These were our colleagues from across the city: good people who I could trust to make sure nothing went wrong in dealing with Giles, as long as they didn't find the knife. I still couldn't see it. Abigail's fingerprints were on it, and his.

'Do you need a lift home, Alice?' I was indebted to my new friend for everything she'd done for us. There was no way I could repay her, but this would be a start.

'No thanks, Jen. I'll go back with the uniforms. I'll see you tomorrow.' She leant over to Abigail and hugged her as if they'd been friends for years. One of the other PCs took us home.

When we got there, Abigail ran to the kitchen and grabbed a can of coke from the fridge. 'I don't think I'll get any sleep tonight, Mum.'

I frowned at her. 'You won't by drinking that.' I shook my head and turned the coffee machine on. Abigail spat laughter and fizzy pop all over her arm.

'You can't talk, Mum.'

We grinned at each other and sat at the kitchen table. Was this relief for surviving the attack? There were still the school bullies to deal with. And I had to get Abbey to talk about this, about what happened; if not with me, then with a professional.

'What were you planning to do out there with the knife, Abs?'

The mood changed in an instant.

'I had to defend myself, Mum. I had to be strong like you.'

'Like me?'

'Yes, Mum. You're my hero.'

The coffee pot came to the boil. I gazed at Abigail and wondered how I could have brought up such a wonderful human being. I reached out and took her hand.

'And you're my hero, too, love.' We held onto each other until Abigail's stomach groaned. We laughed together and I got up. We could put the emotions on the back burner for a little while, but it was clear our physical needs demanded immediate attention.

'Okay, I'll cook a meal for once.'

Abigail shrieked in mock horror and threw her hands into the air. 'I love you, Mum, but I can't eat your cooking. Can't we get a takeaway?'

She was right. I nodded and reached for the phone.

'Shall we have Indian or Chinese?' I rifled through my purse for some money.

Abigail pursed her lips and thought about it for a second.

'I fancy something spicy.'

'Indian it is then.' I dialled the number and dreamt of sitting outside the Taj Mahal as the sun went down.

Two hours later, we were finishing our food when my

phone vibrated on the table. I let it ring and took a bite from the garlic naan. Whatever it was could wait until tomorrow.

'Aren't you going to answer it, Mum?' Abigail wiped curry from her chin. She looked like the shy teenager she usually was and not the knife-wielding girl who'd gone down to the train line to take control of her life. I couldn't have been any prouder of her at that moment.

'No. For one night I'm off duty and spending it with you. It'll stop soon enough.'

When it hadn't after five minutes, I groaned and picked it up.

'This better be important, Jack.'

His voice was cold. 'There's been a new Hashtag incident.'

I should have known my luck was too good to last. He gave me directions and then hung up. I peered at the phone and considered calling him back. There was always another murder. Even when we solved this case, there'd be another one. But I'd never get this time with Abigail again.

'Don't worry, Mum. I can take care of myself.'

Curry sauce ran down Abs's chin and I beamed at her. Taking the knife and heading out after the man who'd been grooming her may have been foolish and reckless, but I didn't doubt my daughter could look after herself. And I felt great. Maybe this victory would help me with the Hashtag case.

I resisted the urge to wipe Abigail's face and kissed her on the forehead instead.

I drove across town to the rundown buildings which made up Market Square. About five years ago, the whole area was gentrified and redesigned for hipsters and affluent thirty-somethings. Then the recession set in and the few places left operating as businesses had to cater to the seedier side of life to stay profitable. And that included the hotel I entered. To call it seedy would be a compliment; damp dripped off the walls and everything stank of decay.

One of the constables gave me directions to where Jack was.

'But it's not another killing?' The PC looked like he was seasick as he nodded.

So how bad could it be? I strode up the stairs and pushed back on the annoyance nibbling behind my ears. The paramedics were still in the room when I got there. Somebody spewed in the corridor while everybody else had green faces, including Jack who was holding onto his guts as if they were about to explode.

'This isn't doing my condition any good.' He tried to smile at me, but it came out as a grimace. 'Are you sure you want to see this?'

'You're the one who called me here, remember?' I arched my eyes and walked past him. Nobody looked like they wanted to be there, especially the bloke lying on the bed. Jack was right: it wasn't a pretty sight. And the place reeked to high heaven of overcooked meat.

The paramedics had removed the handcuffs from the victim's feet and hands and were busy dealing with his injuries, and those were considerable. My fingers went to the bruise on my throat, pressing against my skin to stop myself from throwing up.

Jack offered me a tissue, but I refused. 'I should have warned you, Jen.'

'Is he awake?' I hoped he wasn't, wished they'd drugged him to the gills.

Jack sidled up to me. 'No. The medics put him under as soon as they got here. He'd nearly chewed through that sock when they gave him the sedative.' He pointed to the evidence bag containing the item of clothing. I leant forward to stare at his burns. There wasn't much left of his face apart from half a nose and some of his mouth. The eyes had melted into a single black mass. Below his waist was one large pool of nothing; his genitals were gone, burnt away. Above that on his stomach, the perpetrator had used the acid to write out three words.

Justice For All.

I turned to Jack. 'And he tweeted again?' He held up his phone so I could read the text.

#justiceforall

#benbailey

#rapist

#thehashtagvigilante

'This is the footballer, Ben Bailey?' I knew nothing about football, but I recollected the case, remembered what he'd gone to court for.

'What's left of him. One jury convicted him, another let him go on appeal.'

I gazed at the mass of burnt flesh. 'I remember it. Apparently being drunk and drugged is an alternative way of providing consent. If you're not awake to say no, it obviously means yes.' I stared at the lump on the bed and felt nothing for him.

Jack put his hand on my arm and took me to one side.

'I heard what happened on the railway lines. Are you and Abigail okay?'

Hearing my daughter's name wiped away the anger in my heart. 'I've never been better, but thanks for asking.' I appreciated his concern, but I didn't want to talk about it now. 'Do we have any idea who did this? Do we know who booked the room? Why was Bailey here?'

'The guy on reception said it was reserved through the

website. Cybercrime is looking at that, and also at Bailey's phone and computer. The greasy receptionist says they have video footage of the entrance so we can view it.' As we left, I witnessed the paramedics peel what was left of Ben Bailey from the bed.

'What's the response been like online?' We walked down four floors.

'Same as the others,' Jack replied. 'There's not much sympathy for Bailey and lots of cheering for our Hashtag Vigilante; thankfully, they didn't post the worst photos, only ones of him tied up before it started.' We reached the bottom to find the receptionist waiting for us. He was a morose-looking fella with bad teeth and an even worse wig.

'If you come into the back, I'll play tonight's footage for you.' We followed him through.

I made sure I touched nothing. 'You didn't see anybody arrive?'

'No, everything is done online now. They make the booking, pay for it, and then the code for their room is texted or messaged to them. I'm only here in case anything goes wrong.'

'Well something went wrong tonight.' I stared at him and he shrugged his shoulders.

'But there's more than one way of getting into the building apart from using the reception?' Jack said.

The receptionist nodded. 'We have a fire exit for security reasons, but you can't get in that way from the outside.'

'Unless somebody lets you in or leaves it unlocked?' I said.

'I guess so.' He ran the video footage.

Jack grimaced and held onto his stomach. 'I'm surprised you have it in colour.'

'It's only because the equipment was left behind from the previous owners.'

I peered into the emptiness of the screen. 'What type of business was it?'

'It used to be a trendy cocktail bar until people stopped coming.' The receptionist skipped through the footage, pausing when the woman appeared. She wore dark glasses and a large hat, tilting her head to one side and obscuring her face, but there was no mistaking that shock of red hair.

I ended the clip and removed the tape.

'Thanks, but we'll need this.'

We strode from the building as the paramedics wheeled Ben Bailey into the back of an ambulance.

'Are you thinking what I'm thinking?' Jack said as we walked to the car.

All I could think about was one specific redhead.

'Bring her in. And let's see what she thinks of that clip.'

The smell of burnt flesh lingered on me.

35 RIVERS OF JUSTICE

I left the church and headed home, a spring in my step which wasn't there before. Now I knew how the spiritually devout felt when receiving something profoundly illuminating. The shock of my father's return, including his claims and demands, seemed a distant memory. The incident on the underground and the discovery of information I was sure the police didn't have made me happier than I'd been in a long time.

'Someone is wearing a camera to take photos of the crimes.'

Should I inform the cops? But it would make such a good revelation in my next blog. It was something to consider as I strode through the city.

And I still didn't know if my Hashtag Vigilante was a loner or had a partner. It would be easier with two of them, but also riskier. How could you trust the other person? I'd trusted nobody my whole life, even with silly trivial things. Putting your freedom in the hands of another was too scary to contemplate.

I needed to contact the Vigilante. But maybe I already had.

The thought froze my steps on the road. I couldn't head home; I didn't want to see him again. Then I remembered the camera and the photos he'd shown me. How would he have got those images on his phone if he hadn't been at each of the murders? And why turn up in my life now, at this precise moment?

'I can't return there.' My words drifted in the wind as I considered where I'd spend the night if it weren't in the Vasquez family castle. But if I wanted to meet the Hashtag Vigilante and he was my father, as he claimed, then I should go home and confront him. I should ask him why he'd done these terrible things. There were so many questions to ask.

My legs were on automatic, heading down to the river and the spot under the bridge where I'd slept before. It had been a while, but there was a warm space down there that only I knew about. I'd be safe for tonight and I'd regroup in the morning. But I needed to get something to eat as well.

Thirty minutes later, I was wrapped up and nibbling on a sandwich I'd picked up on the way over. The stars glittered in the sky like diamonds and, contrary to all appearances, I felt lucky. I was in control of my life now. My father wouldn't ruin things again.

The phone vibrated in my pocket and I grabbed it like a kid opening a bag of sweets. I froze when I saw who'd sent the message.

I've been following your posts online, Ruby. You're very impressive. I'm glad you're the one recording my deeds for posterity. I just wanted to say thank you directly. I'll be back in touch soon. I'm busy tonight.

PS: I love the new name you gave me.

The Hashtag Vigilante.

A storm of butterflies nibbled at my heart. I struggled to breathe. The Vigilante had followed me on Twitter and this was a direct message into my account from the user known as Justice For All.

Fuck. Fuck. Fuck.

I read the text again and again until I fell into a deep sleep. It was the sweetest slumber of my life.

I GAZED across the river and watched the sunrise. Drops of yellow and red danced over the dark water as I stretched my limbs and yawned. I didn't know how much rest I'd had, but I felt better for it. I couldn't remember dropping off and worried for a second it wasn't sleep which had overcome me, but another blackout. It didn't matter. The important thing was I hadn't gone home, plus I'd received a new message.

Oh, what joy it was to make a connection in life. I couldn't imagine what it must be like for those people who bond on a physical level, in the flesh. Not in a sexual way, I'd done that before, but in a spiritual way which wasn't religious. To have that unbridled pleasure when another person mentions your name; when they praise you, encourage you; when they brush against you and an electric surge ripples through your heart. A large boat belching steam passed down the river and something fluttered inside my head.

My stomach rumbled and my mouth tasted like sandpaper. I reached into my bag for the bottle of water and the remains of last night's sandwich. An aroma of salt and the city lifted off the river and floated towards me.

I reread the last message.

I'll be in touch soon. I couldn't have completed this without you.

I considered what he meant by that as I examined his work from last night. He said he'd be busy, and he wasn't wrong. A flock of birds dived at the river, threatening to plunge below the water before skimming the top and flying over my head as I gazed at the photo of the Vigilante's latest project.

Ben Bailey, of all people.

Bailey was only two years older than me. When I was fifteen he was the darling of the media with the world at his feet. I'd believed his story at first until the truth came out. His supporters blamed the girl; of course they did. I scanned through the comments on Twitter: there wasn't a lot of support for him now.

Bailey deserved it.

A drop of Bailey's to warm the heart.

I hope his flesh burns forever.

He won't be playing football again.

He wouldn't be doing much of anything again, according to the media reports. There were no photos, but the descriptions were graphic. The messages to my site had exploded overnight, so many of them I'd hardly scratched the surface, but the questions were consistent.

What do you know about Ben Bailey's attack?

I knew nothing about it. Not that I'd tell any of them that. But I knew someone who claimed to know about these attacks. I could wait for the Vigilante to get back in touch, or I could be proactive. I decided to text my mother.

Is he with you?

I didn't expect an immediate answer. I'd made my mind up to find somewhere else to live, God knows where, but there was stuff at the house I needed, and I wasn't going to return if he was there. I wasn't afraid of him, but I wanted control over when and where I saw him again.

Mother was more than likely sleeping off last night's bender, but I sent her another text.

Tell him to meet me across the river. He'll know where.

I needed to know where he'd got those photos from. And maybe I wanted to ask him why he'd left all those years ago.

I finished the drink and dropped the bottle into the bin, getting rid of the trash. My phone pinged as a message arrived. It wasn't a text, but to my Twitter account.

Sorry to keep you waiting. It looks like we were both busy last night.

My heart fluttered, finger hovering above the screen. Was this the Hashtag Vigilante and did I want to get into a conversation with him?

I replied.

What do you mean?

The birds came back and landed at my feet. I assumed they were searching for food, but I had nothing to give them.

There was another message from my new friend.

You're an internet sensation. Look at this: Ruby Vasquez Kicks Ass.

I clicked on the link and it went to a YouTube video. The sound wasn't great, but I recognised myself sitting in the carriage on the underground. After all the videos I'd made for my vlog, I'd watched myself on the screen hundreds of times, but it's always weird staring at your imperfections magnified a thousandfold by digital technology. Someone else had seen my old YouTube account and had identified me from that. And there was a link to my blog.

My heart jumped as the football thugs came into the carriage, but on the screen, my face appeared a picture of resilience. I didn't think I'd ever seen that look before when peering into the mirror. For one second, it was like gazing at an alternative version of me. I gasped as the other me dealt with the hooligan yammering at me, and then faced down his mates. When the other passengers stood and clapped, pride surged through me.

I watched it again and again. My audience of birds still cluttered around my feet, so I showed the clip to them. After saturating my eyes with last night's exploits, I turned to the comments on the video. Apprehension gripped my heart. I understood from experience how horrible some could be on these things.

I was surprised to see most posts were positive towards me. And they all contained a familiar word.

JUSTICE

I couldn't help it, so watched it again. The rush of adrenalin reappeared as I snapped his fingers back on the video. Even with the low sound, the crack of broken bones was obvious. I still tasted his fear and saw the confusion in his eyes. There was a euphoric flash through my blood and release in my brain. I wanted to experience that again and again.

Another message arrived.

I'm proud of you, Ruby. You're a shining light to all of them. You're the only one I trust.

The sun washed over my face as a warm glow spread through the whole of me. I typed as fast as possible.

What do you want me to do?

I waited for the reply, my heart about to catch fire. People drifted past me, pursuing their daily routines. My life was once as ordinary as theirs; now it would be something special. I'd gone viral. I was famous. I was fierce. I was respected. There was no going back; I had to continue. I couldn't lose this momentum.

It's time we met.

My heart thumped against my chest. Could I do this; go and meet a killer? I stared at the message for what seemed an eternity, the whole of my life crawling past my eyes and leaving me unsatisfied. There was no turning back now. I typed a reply of one word, with so much riding on five letters.

Where?

It was hard to breathe as I waited and waited.

You know where.

36 HAPPY HOUSE

I was coming out of the shower when the bell rang. I scowled and looked at the time. Having someone at your door at seven in the morning is never a good thing. I threw a top on and struggled into a pair of trousers.

'Shit.'

I banged my elbow into the railing as I staggered downstairs. I wiped the water from my eyes, shocked at the sight awaiting me.

Abigail was already up and dressed, talking to two women I'd never seen before. They were smartly attired and looked like social workers. My heart sank. I had a nightmare vision of them taking Abigail away from me because of everything which had happened on the train line with Giles.

The taller one with the tied-back blonde hair held her hand out to me. There'd been so much work done on her face, I expected to see the remains of some scaffolding hanging off her nose.

'We're sorry to turn up unannounced, Ms Flowers. I'm

Cara Edwards and this is Sue Duran.' Her voice sounded as if she'd swallowed a plum.

I shook both their hands a bit too vigorously and waited for the bad news to drop. Abs was swigging orange juice from the bottle, indifferent to what was happening. I steeled my body, determined I wouldn't lose my daughter to a bunch of faceless bureaucrats after saving her from a dangerous predator. Water dripped into my eyes as I spoke.

'Look, I'm sorry for what happened, but...'

Cara Edwards didn't let me get any further.

'No, Ms Flowers; it's us who should apologise to you.'

I was confused.

Sue Duran spoke up.

'We're from the Board of Governors of Abigail's school. We were going to contact you last night, but thought you'd need some rest after your ordeal.' She glanced at Abigail who'd taken a cursory interest in what was happening now she'd found out it involved her. I was still waiting for the bad news.

'Both of you have the apologies of the whole school and the Board,' Edwards continued. 'As soon as the police informed us what had happened with Mr Giles, of what that man had done on school property, we checked all the records of his dealings with you and Abigail.' She smiled at Abs. It was an unusual look, all shiny and watery eyes. 'We'd like to offer Abigail the opportunity to come back to school with our full support and the guarantee to her, and to you, Ms Flowers, there will be an investigation into the bullying and harassment Abigail has received.'

I grabbed a tea towel from the side and ran it through my damp hair. When I pulled it away, there was a stale bit of naan bread clinging to my forehead. I picked it off and addressed the Governors.

'Thanks for the apology, but I must speak to Abigail first before we make any...'

'I'll go back today,' Abigail said.

I was gobsmacked. The two women smiled at each other. Water slid down my cheek and I was too shocked to wipe it away.

'That's great,' Edwards said. She shook hands with an excited Abigail, and then turned to me. 'I'll ensure Abigail gets a warm welcome when she returns this morning.' They went to leave, with Edwards having one last piece of advice for Abigail Flowers. 'Just make sure you're not late, young lady.'

They closed the door behind them as I slumped into a kitchen chair and dripped more water onto the floor. There was a slight curve on either side of Abigail's mouth as if she was trying to hold in the happiness inside her.

'Abs, I'm happy you're going back to school, but we still have those girls to deal with. I know the Governors said they'd sort it out, but that's not the same as you having to see those kids.'

Abigail whipped out her mobile and shoved the screen in my face. 'It's all been sorted, Mum. I'm the hero of the school now.'

I took the phone and scrolled through the posts. My police colleagues had released no names from last night's incident, especially Abigail's and Giles's, but when social media was buzzing with talk about a local girl catching a perverted school welfare officer, it didn't take long for the rumours to grow. Then somebody put two and two together, and Abigail became the toast of the town.

There was no bullying, trolling or nastiness now. The fake images of Abigail were her as Katniss Everdeen, Wonder Woman, Daenerys Targaryen, Hit-Girl, Shuri and many others. And all of them were kicking ass. I guessed they were posted as compliments, but I didn't enjoy seeing her face transplanted onto someone else's body, especially those of women a lot older than her. Still, I suppose it was better than the previous ones sent to Abs.

'Are some of these posts from the girls in McDonald's?'

Abigail beamed and nodded.

'Not just that, Mum. They've been confiding in me with some things which have happened to them.' She lost the grin and turned serious. 'You know, from men who've harassed them and stuff. They think I'm an inspiration.' The pride in her voice was unmistakable. Her confidence made me happy.

I took hold of Abigail's hands. 'You are, love. You're an inspiration for us all, including me.' Our smiles reflected off each other. 'But you still have to be careful with whom you deal with, both online and in the real world.' I sounded like the stern mother I didn't want to be. The scowl on Abs's face cut into my heart. 'But, yes, it's great how things have changed. And I'm glad you can help other kids. You're a star.' We hugged and it was wonderful. When we separated, she was grinning again. Maybe I wasn't such a bad parent. 'Now I suppose you better get ready for school while I go back to work.'

Abigail sprang from the table. 'Isn't it early for that? You could do with a break, Mum.'

'There's stuff I need to catch up on from yesterday, and we have a briefing this morning.' I continued to scan the rest of the messages, happy to see my daughter so popular with her peers, but concerned about the number of times they mentioned the word justice. The memory of holding onto Giles as the train approached rumbled through my mind.

How close had I been to letting go of him? I scrubbed the image from my head.

I returned the phone to Abigail.

'There's one thing I still don't understand, Mum.'

'What's that, love?' I stood and shook the rest of me dry. I could have an hour on my own at work to sort everything into order. With four crimes to investigate, we would need a bigger team. I was already getting angry messages from DCI Merson about the lack of progress in the case. One benefit of the public support for our Hashtag Killer was the minimum amount of anger from the population against the police.

'Why didn't Giles sort out the bullying before you got involved? He knows you're a detective. Surely he was only putting himself at risk?'

I squeezed the last drop of water from my hair.

'It's hard to understand how the criminal mind works, love, but most of them believe they're cleverer than the police. Some of them like to insert themselves into an investigation, to challenge their skills and taunt the authorities. It's a game to them.' I didn't want to say the next bit, but I'd promised nothing but the truth with Abigail from now. 'With those school bullies, I think he wanted you to be vulnerable and weak, so you'd rely on the first person to offer you support.' Guilt swam through me at the realisation the support and understanding hadn't come from me. How close had my failures been to getting Abs murdered? It didn't bear thinking about.

'What a sneaky bastard,' Abigail said as she turned to go to her room.

I'd never heard Abs swear before.

'Abigail,' I shouted.

'It's okay, Mum. I meant how sneaky he was to get other

people to do his work for him without them knowing it.'
Abigail whistled as she slipped up the stairs, unaware of the
blood draining from my face.

'Fuck me.' Not only did the lightbulb go off over my
head, it also shattered into a thousand tiny pieces, every one
of which pricked at my skin for me being so blind.

I drove on the edge of the speed limit all the way to the
station, getting there dead on eight o'clock. The Chief had
already replied to the message I'd sent her before leaving
home. At least that was one job done. I was going through
the shared files on the computer, still kicking myself for
being so stupid, when Jack arrived.

'Is Abbey okay?'

I nodded and told him about Abs going back to school.

'That's great, Jen. I don't think either of you would
survive homeschooling.' We laughed together, the strain in
my throat making my bruise throb.

Jack leant into his computer screen. 'Who would have
thought a school welfare officer was capable of such things?
You can never tell how close the bastards can get to you.'
The team was gathering for the briefing. I approached Alice
at the door, our shared secret a stern bond between us now.

'Alice, can I have a quick word before we go in?' She
nodded and we slipped to one side. 'Has the Chief been in
touch?'

'I nearly fell out of bed when Chief Superintendent
Cane rang. She said you'd asked for me to take the lead for
Cybercrime on this investigation?'

I didn't miss the pride in Alice's voice.

'Are you okay with that?'

Alice beamed. 'Abso-fuckin-loutely,' she whispered.
'I've never been lead before. I appreciate this, Jen.'

I put my hand on her arm.

'Think nothing of it. I wouldn't have requested you if I didn't believe you were up to it. Can you deliver the latest update when I'm ready?'

'Of course.'

'Then let's get started.' We made our way to the briefing room.

I had something important to tell the team, and it was all thanks to Abs's encounter with that pervert Giles.

I thanked everyone for coming, making sure they all had a portable digital device with them. There was a lot to get through.

'We'll start with the latest attack.' I brought up a photo of the outside of the hotel building. It still looked like a dump. 'Between seven-thirty and eight-thirty last night, Ben Bailey entered this low-end establishment, the Crown Hotel.' I waited for the whispering to stop. 'For those of you unaware of who Ben Bailey is, here's a run-down of why he was such an attractive target for our vigilante.'

I changed the image on the screen to a goofy-teethed teenager wearing a football strip with a ball at his feet.

'This was taken when he was fourteen and he had a host of famous football clubs clamouring for his signature, including some abroad. Instead, he signed for his local team, and by the time he was seventeen, he seemed on the verge of the England squad and headed for a move to one of the biggest teams in the country. Four years later, he'd lost everything and was behind bars for having sex with a fifteen-year-old girl he'd groomed online.'

'Gross.' More than one person said it.

I altered the screen to show the outcome of the first trial.

'He claimed she told him she was eighteen, and the sex was consensual. He had many people supporting him, including his girlfriend. Then the full details came out, and the public's perception changed.'

New images appeared on the display, shots of Bailey's conversations with the girl and pictures of her.

'If the photos of her in school uniform didn't give it away, then the tone of her language should have. His defence team stuck to their guns: he thought she was eighteen. The medical report said she was so full of alcohol and ketamine, the doctors were surprised she could walk, never mind speak. Then video footage emerged of him dragging her out of the club and into his hotel room. If she wasn't unconscious, she was on the verge. She wasn't of legal age to consent, but he said she did. She couldn't remember anything. He was found guilty and convicted to seven years in prison. He was out in less than two when a retrial favoured his version of events.'

I removed the images from the screen.

'His conviction was overturned, but no football club worth its salt would dare resurrect his career. A few lower-league teams were mentioned in connection with his name, but when fans and sponsors protested, it was soon scuppered. But last night, Ben Bailey believed he was on the cusp of regaining all he'd lost. I'll hand over to Alice Voss of Cybercrime to tell you what we have regarding why he was in that hotel room.'

I nodded to Alice. She got up, visibly nervous, and cleared her throat. She touched her digital device, and a list of emails appeared on the screen.

'Yesterday, Mr Bailey received an email from a person he believed was the Chairman of a Premier League football club. It was the tenth such message he'd received in the previous three months. From first to last, they are a series of conversations where the Chairman promises to help Bailey get back to the top of the game. The promises come in increments, increasing with each subsequent communication.'

'Like he was groomed,' Jack said.

'Exactly,' Alice said. 'I traced the messages, and they all came from the real email account of the Chairman.'

Raised eyebrows littered the room. 'Could it be someone from the club?' I asked.

Alice continued, 'That's possible, but I don't think so. I believe somebody from outside hacked into the club accounts and sent Bailey the emails from there. Then they deleted any evidence and waited for Bailey to respond. I haven't completed a check on Bailey's digital devices, but I expect them to contain the same Trojan the other victims' devices did.'

Alice finished and I thanked her with a smile. After last night and everything she'd done for Abigail, it felt as if we were a team now.

'Photographs and the forensic report from the crime scene are on your machines. I won't put you off your lunch by displaying them here, but acid blinded and castrated Ben Bailey.' A sharp intake of breath went around the room. 'It was also used to write the word Justice into his chest. We have a short video of the suspect.'

I pressed the play button on the tablet and the clip came onto the screen in glorious colour. I played it more than once and waited for reactions. There were murmurs and chatter, and then the words came from the back of the room.

'Isn't that...?'

'Yes, the woman in the footage looks like Ruby Vasquez.' I paused it and zoomed in to what little could be seen of the face. 'But there's nothing definitive in this clip apart from the red hair under the hat. And that could be a wig.' I changed the video on the screen, and this time there was no doubting who it was.

'This was filmed on a phone at least two hours before the attack on Ben Bailey.' The team all watched as Ruby Vasquez dealt with the football thugs on the Tube. 'It proves nothing apart from the fact she can handle herself. A unit went to her house last night and this morning, but got no answer. We're also looking for her father.'

I waited for them to make their notes.

'The Hashtag Vigilante left their usual calling card on social media. The response was more support and a rise in copycat incidences of vigilantism. Kyle Swift has an alibi for the attack on Bailey.'

Even with this attack and the video clip of a suspect, we had nothing concrete to hang on to anyone. But now I had my revelation to reveal to them, and it was all thanks to Abigail.

'We've been going about this the wrong way.' I took a deep breath. 'I've been going about this the wrong way.'

Each of them focused on me. I glanced at Jack, and then at Alice.

'It's appeared from the start as if we've possibly been looking at two suspects: someone small or light who could have murdered Evan Ripley while sitting above him in a tree in the park, and going by Father Abraxas's eyewitness testimony to the murder of Father Maxwell, a large man built like a rugby player. We also have the woman from last night's attack, who may or may not be Ruby Vasquez.'

I remembered my conversation with Abigail this morning.

How sneaky he was to get other people to do his work for him without them knowing it.

'What we have here is Charles Manson crossed with *Strangers on a Train.*'

As eyebrows arched and mouths pursed around the room, I saw some flickers of recognition, especially from Jack. They should all have got the Manson reference, but the Hitchcock movie probably confused most of them. It was only thanks to Abigail's love of old films that I knew what it was about.

'I believe our Hashtag Killer, the person posting online, is not carrying out the attacks themselves. They're directing others to do their work for them.'

Curious expressions and whispered conversations went around the room. Jack asked the obvious question.

'How so?'

'They're choosing vulnerable souls, people who've been affected by violent crime where justice wasn't served, or at least it wasn't in their eyes, and convincing them to kill or maim similar offenders. We've had four crimes claimed by the Hashtag Killer. I think they were committed by different people who probably don't know about each other.'

Did it make as much sense out loud as it did in my head?

'How is the murderer selecting these individuals and manipulating them to commit such terrible acts?' Jack said.

'I guess it's a long process, similar to what was done with Ben Bailey, but over a longer period. They'll have been carefully vetted and chosen, maybe trained in certain things, probably psychology profiled. Nothing has been left to chance. Our manipulator knows how to get into their heads, identifies the right buttons to push. Then they're used like drones to be pointed in the direction where they'll cause the most harm.'

The more I thought about it, the more it seemed obvious.

'I think people are chosen remotely, online. Our mastermind, our Manson, is trawling all the internet chat groups and forums dedicated to victims of violence, or their relatives and friends, and selecting the most vulnerable; the ones with the most anger; the ones easiest to manipulate and mould.'

'They're being groomed,' Alice said.

'It's just a theory,' I said. I suddenly doubted myself, doubted everything I'd told them. I pushed those doubts away in one swoop. 'The time and planning involved will have been considerable. The manipulator may have suffered from perceived discrimination themselves and believe this is the only way they can get justice. Or they could have a grander plan.'

Heads nodded around the room. They didn't think it was a crazy theory. The question was: how would we deal with it?

'There's a new post online from Ruby Vasquez,' Jack said. 'Go to her website. It's the first thing on there.' Fingers flashed across screens as I found the page. Everyone read it at the same time.

What is Justice?

Is it fairness in the protection of rights and punishment of wrongs? Justice needs to be in the light of the democratic principle of the 'rule of law'. The rule of law is a concept that denotes all decisions need to be made in accordance with the law. Nobody is exempt from the law.

And yet the law is letting us all down.

Corporations steal billions, yet no justice comes to them. The politicians allow millions to suffer, yet no justice comes to them. Our legal system is constructed in such a way it's become another high-end business. Our law enforcement officers have their hands tied in every way.

But we are finding our voice now. Justice is rising from the people and striking down those who thought they were untouchable.

Evan Ripley. Joseph Maxwell. Bobby Thomas. Ben Bailey.

These four were not chosen randomly.

A banker. A priest. An extremist. A footballer.

Those who abuse their positions in society while the common men, women and children are forced to accept the perversions forced upon them by the elite and the privileged.

We need

Justice for all.

The room sat silent as everyone finished reading.

'What a load of bollocks,' Jack said.

I didn't disagree with him. 'We have to find Ruby Vasquez.'

'You're in luck,' Alice said. 'She's been seen going into the old abandoned jeans factory over the river.'

'Get someone over to her house and search it,' I said to the closest PC. 'And a couple of you come with Jack and me to that factory. She'll tell us what her real relationship with the Hashtag Killer is.'

My nerves were shot. I'd posted a hasty editorial on the website to calm myself, but I wasn't sure if it was working. I waited over an hour for reactions before trying to find a way into the factory.

Nature had covered most of the entrance from the last time I'd visited, as weeds and overgrown trees flourished everywhere. That and the fact somebody had bricked over most of the front meant it wouldn't be as easy to get inside as I'd expected. A pungent chemical whiff floated off the river as I dodged the scraps of metal littering the floor and headed around the back.

Rusted skips and bins obscured the rear of the building. I remembered when the factory closed down, and these containers were full of abandoned bits of material and half-constructed garments which would never fit on any human shape. They were dumped on the scrapheap like the people who'd made them. I stood on my tiptoes to peer into the first one. I didn't flinch at the sight of rats fighting over a dead bird. Even the smell didn't bother me. It was as if I'd discovered an inner strength which had been hidden for a long time.

I moved past it and the others, seeking a way inside. I found what I wanted at the end: a yellowed metal door which had once been locked. The lock lay snapped in two on the floor. The hinges creaked as I opened it and went in. A pungent aroma of rotten food hit me in the face.

I strode down the corridor, beyond what was once a row of offices and into the vast space which made up most of the factory. Tattered calendars hung from the walls, telling the tale of times long past. I stared at the rows and rows of dead metal. Hundreds of abandoned sewing machines greeted me like the motionless, foreboding eggs from the movie *Alien*. As I stepped between them, I expected a gasp of mist to drift from the floor and surround me. It was cold and I pulled my jacket tight against my chest.

I was carrying my phone to check the messages, but got no signal inside the building. I peered into the blank screen, flinching at the reflection staring at me. Sunlight sputtered in from the cracked windows in the ceiling; a low murmuring noise vibrated in the distance. I drifted towards it, my feet crunching over dirt and rubble. As I got closer, I recognised what it was: whimpering. I left the machines behind and gazed ahead. The moaning turned into sobbing as I made out a human shape tied to a chair. A noose rested over the distressed woman's head. My legs gave way and I stumbled forward.

'Mother?'

'You know she's to blame for all this.'

I saw the green eyes first, glinting towards me as he stepped from the gloom. One hand held onto the rope while the other pointed the gun at my face.

'You're not the Hashtag Vigilante.' Did I want him to be

or not? My mind swirled and twisted with conflicted emotions.

He laughed, then slipped the pistol into his pocket. 'Don't worry; I wouldn't shoot my only daughter.'

That word annoyed me more than the weapon. I glared at him. 'What are you doing, old man?'

He pulled on the noose so it tightened around my mother's neck. A tiny startled gasp escaped her throat. The veins popped in her face and a slither of blood invaded her eyeballs.

'Do you like this, Ruby? I thought it would be less messy than fire or acid or a bashed-in skull. Does it meet your idea of justice?'

I stared at Mother, with contradictory feelings surging through me. I didn't like the woman, but this was horrible and barbaric.

'What justice would this be? It's you who should pay for what you did to us.' I controlled the anger, contemplating how I could get the rope away from him. He was older than me. I wasn't as strong, but quicker in the body and mind. Maybe I could wrestle him to the ground, take him by surprise, and snatch the gun from him? My actions with the hooligans on the underground had filled me with confidence.

'I never hurt you, Ruby.' The conviction vanished from his face, released by despair and regret. 'Not directly. I should never have left you with her. I did exactly what my father did and abandoned my child.' A deep guttural gasp flowed from his chest as his fingers dug into the rope; Mother whimpered again. 'I guess it's true what they say about the sins of the fathers.'

I stared at the cord around my mother's neck. 'You're

not making any sense.' Was he the Hashtag Vigilante? 'You abandoned us; you abandoned me.'

He pulled the noose tighter and sneered at his estranged wife. 'As soon as she fell pregnant, she said it was twins. The doctors told her otherwise, but she wouldn't believe it. She was a twin sister, as was her mother and grandmother. It ran in the family, you see. She even picked out their names: Ruby and Annie.'

A dark shiver from the edge of my skull stabbed at me. That name, Annie, whispered in my head.

'What?'

'She was devastated when only you arrived. I think that's when her mind slipped.' He gazed at me and loosened the rope. 'You were only a few days old when she started addressing you as two people. One minute you were Ruby, the next you were Annie. Nothing I said could change her behaviour.'

I clutched at my chest. The memories hovered some-where inside of me, struggling to get out. But did I want them to?

'You could have got help for her.'

He shook his head.

'I tried, Ruby. I promise you I did. But I was weak. I wasn't strong like you are now. I couldn't give her what she needed. I failed as a husband and as a father. But I'll make amends for what happened. She was broken, and she broke you, but you can be fixed.'

'I don't need fixing. I'm not broken; I have medication for the blackouts and it's all under control.' I reached for my pocket, looking for the pills, but there was nothing there.

'They're not blackouts, Ruby. Not like you think they are. That's what I've been trying to tell you.'

My mother stopped sobbing. She gazed at me, but it wasn't her daughter she saw.

'Annie,' she said. 'I'm glad you returned, glad you came back to me.'

The trembling started in my legs before moving up the rest of my body. A thousand tiny jackhammers pounded at my head. I dropped to my knees, the concrete biting through my clothes and into my flesh. A gulf of mist descended over my eyes, one blanket covering my senses while another peeled away

'Sometimes she was possessed by clarity and she saw you for who you are, but other times the confusion engulfed her. I left when you were five, returning sporadically over the years when the guilt got the better of me. Your strength came to you early; you refused to be the other person she wanted you to be. But often you slipped out of yourself, and I tried to help you. I thought you had it all under control once you finished school, but it's been happening again, hasn't it?'

His words pierced my body and soul as I stared into the grey stone. I found that strength again, fingers pressed into the cold ground as I pushed upwards. My vision became clear as I studied him.

'What happened in my past isn't important; only my future counts now.' I peered into the furthest parts of his corruption. 'Are you the Hashtag Vigilante?'

His eyes were a bottomless pool of darkness. 'I showed you the images, what do you think?'

'That means nothing.'

'Maybe Annie sent you the messages. Maybe she gave me the photos. Maybe I've been helping Annie in the hope of getting my daughter back.' There appeared a brief glimmer of optimism on his face before it evaporated and he glared at my mother.

'You're full of shit.' I spat the words at him, ready to leave that place and both my parents to their fates.

'What if I realised neither of us would be normal again until she pays for her crimes?' Anger flared from his nostrils. 'She lied about me. I admit I made mistakes, but I never did the things she claimed. I never hurt you, and I never hurt her. I touched nobody else. But they never believed that in prison, so I suffered like you couldn't believe.' He pulled the rope tighter. 'She ruined both our lives and we'll never be whole again while she's alive. We need our justice.'

He turned his back on me, putting both hands around the cord and pulling on it. I didn't hesitate. My legs sprang forward, covering the gap in great strides. I leapt on him as Mother gasped for air. The three of us went down like dominoes. He let go of the noose as he struggled to push me off him.

'This is the only way, Ruby; you must see that?'

I rolled over as Mother crawled through the dirt.

'Everything you've said is a lie,' I screamed at him. He seemed stunned, frozen into that dark spot. I jumped to the side and removed the rope from my mother's neck.

He coughed and wiped the mud from his face. 'If you don't believe me, ask her.'

Her eyes were red raw, her lips trembling as she tried to speak. I stared at her, waiting for the first time in my life for her to act like my mother, to refute all the lies he'd just sprouted. That's what lies do: they start off small or inconsequential, but over time, over years, they crawl and twist their way through many lives until they drag you down into their world of duplicity and pain. I'd had enough of them; of all the times people had mocked and ridiculed me; of the times they'd lied to me and lied about me. I wouldn't put up with it anymore, and certainly not from the man who'd abandoned me. My eyes were like my mother's, in shape and colour, and now they fixed on hers with an intensity I'd never felt before.

'Tell me the truth, Mother.'

She wiped mud from her mouth. 'He's always hated you, Ruby, always hated the both of us. Don't believe a word that comes out of his dirty mouth.' I never took my gaze from her, watching her lips shiver as she dragged herself across the ground towards me. 'You know I've always loved you.'

The shock of her words, of the sincerity I heard in them, left me weak. It was enough of a distraction for him to have the gun in his hand before I knew it. I moved at the same time he fired. The noise in my ears sounded like a thousand waterfalls washing over me. My fingers trembled. There was blood on my hands, but I didn't know whose.

The last thing I saw before the veil dropped over my face was darts of green coming towards me.

'How are we going to find out which internet forums our Vigilante has used?' Jack pushed the car past the speed limit as he spoke.

'You believe my manipulation theory then?'

'It makes sense to me, Jen. We know there's more than one person involved in these attacks and the Justice For All Twitter account has access to crime scene photos only the attackers could have taken; there has to be at least two people committing these crimes. But how do we discover where Hashtag found these individuals?'

'I'm not sure we will, not without catching them; I'm guessing it's worse than a needle in a haystack. Maybe Ruby Vasquez can illuminate us on that.' We approached the bridge over the river, blue light rattling in the air like a demented Tardis. His comment about the photos irritated the back of my mind, a nudge telling me something was wrong with my thinking.

'Vasquez has to know more than she's saying.' The car screeched over the ground and onto the bridge. Two regular police cars followed behind. 'Do you think she planned this whole thing for attention?'

I twisted my face into an uncomfortable shape. 'She's clever and capable, so I wouldn't put anything past her.' We sped over the river and took a sharp left. What was it about Vasquez I was missing, something connected to those photos?

'Have you heard from Abigail today?' Jack drove the car into the industrial estate. What was once a thriving hub in the city was now a place empty of most human endeavour; crumbling, dilapidated buildings were dotted around like grey concrete dinosaurs dead for a thousand years. Or maybe they were only hibernating and waiting to return and greet those who'd abandoned them.

'She hasn't replied to any of my messages, so I'm assuming she's busy studying.' For once, I didn't worry about the lack of replies from Abs.

Plastic ghosts whistled around outside, bits of paper and debris lifting off the ground in the wind and swimming across my vision. He parked the car near the factory.

'I nearly ended up working here.' I stepped out of the vehicle. Jack scrunched his eyes in surprise.

'I couldn't imagine you as a factory girl.'

'This was when I was deciding about university or getting a job. My father wanted me to work, said it was perfect for eradicating sins.' I peered at the front of the building: it was vegetation gone wild. 'I don't think there's a way in here.'

'I've never heard you talk about your parents before.'

'That's with good reason.' I headed around the side. 'How do we know she's in here?' Icy wind grasped at my throat as I turned the corner, groups of leaves climbing into the sky and clawing at the clouds in the distance.

'One of her admirers posted online, said she was seen crossing the river and heading towards this place.'

We reached the back. A group of pigeons scattered from the ground and darted above us as I searched for an entrance.

'I'm surprised we aren't swamped with her fan club.'

Jack nodded at the factory. 'Maybe they're all inside.'

I pointed to the end of the building. 'That must be the only way in.' I stepped forward, and he followed. We both noticed the broken lock. 'This could be her villainous head-quarters.'

I had my fingers on the door when Jack put his hand on me. 'Shouldn't we wait for the others? There could be anybody inside here.' I knew from the tone of his voice he was thinking about Kyle Swift and the pub again. I let go of the handle, touching the bruise on my throat.

'We can't hang around outside doing nothing, Jack.' I pushed inside, ignoring the stink and heading down the corridor.

Jack trailed behind. 'Okay, but let's not throw all caution to the wind.'

The sun filtered in through the rafters, breaking through the gloom for me to see shadows moving up ahead.

'Someone else is in here with us,' I said as Jack stood next to me. Voices came from the spot further down the corridor, but I couldn't make out what they said. We were at the end of the sewing machines, waiting for the shades to turn into recognisable human beings.

'Don't rush in,' Jack whispered into my ear.

It was hard for me to hang back. I was turning to speak to him when the gun went off. I didn't wait, was sprinting through the gaps in the equipment when bullets sang again. I pushed ahead, kicking rubbish out of the way and banging

THE HASHTAG KILLER 265

my shin on a piece of metal sticking out of the wall. My eyes adjusted to the dark. A tussle of red hair fell to the ground; it was sprawled over the top of another body. Discarded mannequins were everywhere, prostrate on the floor as if suffering an apocalypse of showroom dummies. Two human shapes groaned in the gloom.

I recognised Charles Vasquez from his mug shot as he towered over the bodies below him, pointing the pistol at his estranged wife and daughter. He stepped towards them, and as his finger tightened around the trigger, I lunged forward, grabbing a plastic torso next to me and tossing it with all my strength at Ruby's father. It bounced off his arm as the weapon fired again. The momentum knocked him sideways, but he held onto the gun. I hurled my body at Vasquez, striking him in the chest, the two of us plummeting onto the cold concrete and landing in the middle of those unsmiling dummies.

The mannequins scattered everywhere like human-shaped plastic balls in one of those activity rooms for young kids. My arm was under his chin as he thrust the weapon up. I pushed down hard into his neck, dragging my leg around and forcing my knee into his chest; we rolled over into the corner, his free hand clawing at my face. His nails dug into my flesh, the blood warm as it flowed over my cheeks. The gun moved towards my head. My hand was on his and forced it down, the barrel pointing at my guts as his finger grasped for the trigger.

An explosion echoed around the factory, smoke and searing skin invading my senses. My throat throbbed like plutonium, ready to explode, the ringing in my ears as if a thousand church bells had been transplanted there and it was a Sunday morning. I stared at the shock of ruby hair on the floor; another pool of red trickled towards my feet as I stared at the bodies next to me. Agonising fire engulfed my stomach; my fingers were covered in blood as I pulled them away. I was thankful the black veil fell over my face before the pain became too much.

VOICES HUMMED inside my ears when I regained consciousness. The light hurt my eyes as the blurred shapes in the room shimmered into recognisable figures: Abbey was sitting next to me while Jack whispered to Alice in the corner.

'Mum's awake.' Abbey grabbed my hand as the throbbing settled down into a low hum.

'How are you doing, partner?' Jack was at my side. Alice Voss was gone; maybe she'd never been there and I'd dreamt the whole thing. I got up, stretched out my legs, and realised I was still wearing the same clothes.

'Am I in the hospital?'

'Yes, you are, Jen.' He smiled at me. 'The Vasquez women are down the corridor, but they're okay. The doctor told me you'd have a bit of bruising on your ribs and your ears may ring for a few days, but you'll be fine.' He leant close to me. 'I'd use this to get some time off work if I were you.'

'What happened?'

Jack sighed heavily. 'Charles Vasquez shot himself in his struggle with you.' He glanced at Abbey, but she was engrossed with something on her phone. 'He didn't make it, Jen.'

I slumped into the bed, letting that information seep between the noises in my skull. I tried to sit up and a sharp stab of pain vibrated through my guts.

'Have you questioned Ruby Vasquez?'

'Not yet. We can do it together when you're feeling better tomorrow.'

'We need to ask her about the Hashtag crimes, see if she has an alibi for the attack on the footballer.'

He shook his head. 'We needn't worry about that anymore, Jen.' His teeth sparkled as he grinned at me. 'We found enough incriminating evidence on Charles Vasquez's phone and on a laptop at his digs to tie him to all the crimes.'

The ringing increased inside my skull. 'But we know more than one person is involved.'

Jack put his hand on my arm. 'You were right, Jen, we have the proof now. On Vazquez's computer, there's a database of potential victims, plus the ones from our four crimes, and of people to commit them. Alice and Cybercrime are going through everything as we speak, including a shed load of photographs.'

'Photographs?' That nagging pointing finger at the rear of my head was jabbing me again. Photographs and computers and revenge and something else were in a cocktail I just couldn't quite taste.

Jack patted my hand. 'I'll get you a coffee and a sandwich, and then we'll go back to the station and see what they've uncovered so far. Unless you need to get some rest.' He glanced at Abbey. 'Yeah, have some refreshments, go home, and we'll continue with this tomorrow.'

He was whistling as he left the room, with Abbey taking his place at the bed. She thrust her phone at me.

'We have to buy Alice something to thank her for what she did for me. You can look through her Facebook and see what she likes.'

'Alice's Facebook?'

'Yeah. I sent her a friend's request and she accepted. If

you hurry, we can get it and give it to her tomorrow.' She stared at me and suddenly seemed to realise I'd nearly been shot. 'Once you've rested.'

I took the phone and did as she wanted, but all I could think about was photographs and computers and revenge.

I was in the living room before I revealed the bottle of Bollinger to Alice. My ribs were hurting as I walked in; Abbey had tried to talk me into going home from the hospital, but I had to come here first. She'd wanted to join me, but I packed her off with Jack once I'd given him special instructions. Then I stopped off to collect Alice's surprise. I waved the booze at her.

'I thought we should celebrate.'

'It's always great to close a case, and I never say no to free champagne.' She indicated for me to sit down while she got the glasses. I glanced around the place; it was far neater than the last time I visited. All the surplus computers and laptops had disappeared. Now there was only a digital tablet resting on the coffee table. There were no more loose cables or cords anywhere, and the stack of Australian newspapers had vanished apart from one on the floor next to me. A glance at it showed the date from three days ago.

Alice returned and handed me a glass as she sat opposite.

'Thanks,' I said. The bubbles jumped out and infected

my senses, surging into my brain and reawakening the worn parts of me. My fingers shook as I held the drink.

'It must have been traumatic, what happened with you and Vasquez in that factory.'

I ran my finger around the top of the glass, the tip of it dipping into the champagne. I licked it away before speaking.

'We stopped him from killing his wife and daughter, which was the main thing.'

She raised her glass to me. 'And you caught the Hashtag Killer. Congratulations!'

I put my drink on the table, untouched, and grimaced. 'I'm not too sure.'

Her eyes narrowed. 'What do you mean? I thought his phone and laptop were full of incriminating photos from the murder scenes and other evidence?'

'They are, but there are other things which have bothered me about this case from the beginning.'

'Such as?'

'Well, for starters, what's the connection between our four victims?'

She didn't hesitate with her reply. 'They're all perverts: rapist, child pornographer, paedophile and another rapist. The Hashtag Killer wanted to punish them.'

'But why those specific people?'

Alice shrugged her shoulders. 'Random choices?'

'Serial killers don't make random choices, especially not this one. I spent all my time searching for the link between the four victims when, in trying to understand our killer's motivation, it wasn't the most important thing.'

'And what was that?'

'I should have realised quicker what their purpose was.'

'Didn't we have this conversation before? Isn't it

accepted that a serial killer is driven by an early childhood trauma which is sexualised?'

'Yes, but we knew those attacks weren't sexually motivated, but fuelled by revenge. That was the whole point of the Twitter tweets. What I hadn't figured out until recently was that those posts were the real reason for the murders, and it wasn't a simple case of retribution. I mean, you can see why one person might want to punish any of our victims, but why a single killer for all four victims when they were unconnected?'

She crossed her legs and appeared relaxed. 'What if the Vasquez family has a link to the victims we haven't discovered yet? Or even Kyle Swift?'

'Swift was the perfect suspect for the murder of Evan Ripley. He had the motivation and was in London when it happened. But why would he kill the others?'

Alice flicked fluff from her trousers. 'Maybe he acquired a taste for it once it started. He's ex-military; God knows what he got up to in the Middle East.'

'It's possible, plus he's experienced enough on the computer side of things to have tricked Ripley into joining that fake website which targeted women, but I don't buy it. His hate was for the man who hurt his sister; I can't see him bothering with the others.'

'Since he was in the military, he may know people in that group Bobby Thomas set up, the English Martyrs. I saw a list of their members and an awful lot of them had connections to the army.'

I'd considered this myself. 'Bobby Thomas had many enemies, including those opposed to his politics and his ex-colleagues who forced him out.'

'And the victims and relatives of the children he exploited.'

'We checked all the photos from the child pornography found in his place and tracked down the kids. Thomas assaulted none of them. He got the images from other people.'

'I can still see why his former friends in the English Martyrs would want to hurt him.'

'But they already had. They'd kicked him out, and someone had leaked a story to the media about his vile interests. There was no need to kill him.'

'That's unless one of them had a personal grudge against him?'

'Surely the ruination and imprisonment heading his way would have been a greater punishment?'

Alice considered my question and moved on to the next victim.

'What about the priest? If anyone had enemies bent on murder, it would be him.'

'We interviewed all sixty-seven of his victims, and I watched every video. It was grim viewing, but I'd bet my life none of those former altar boys would have been able to burn Maxwell alive.'

She waved her free hand at me in mock supplication. 'You're the detective. I bow down to your experience.'

I nodded at her. 'And then we come to the disgraced footballer and the quashing of his rape conviction.'

A shadow crossed her face. 'You know he's guilty.'

It was true, but I wasn't going to tell her. 'That doesn't matter. What's important is he survived and he identified his attacker as female.'

'What about the woman he attacked?'

'She has a cast-iron alibi.'

'Could it have been one of her friends or relatives?'

'Possibly, but you're missing the most significant thing here.'

'That two people committed all four attacks. And that's Ruby Vasquez and her father. That's why he had the murder photos on his phone and sent them to her.'

'So, what was their motivation?'

'Killing for money and fame, they wouldn't be the first. They were in it together, but he wanted more, or she discovered remorse. So they fell out and he tried to kill her in that factory. But you stopped him, Jen.' She held her glass up to me. 'And that's why we're celebrating.'

'That's not why I brought the champagne, Alice.' I still hadn't touched mine.

She pursed her lips. 'So what are we celebrating?'

'Your transfer.'

Her fingers shook. 'How did you know? I only put it in two days ago.'

'Is that when you knew your mission had finished for now?'

She steadied her hand by finishing the drink. 'My mission?'

I left my champagne to bubble away on the table. 'It took me a while to get there, and I must admit Abbey's situation distracted me for most of this investigation, but once all the small things came together, I saw the bigger picture.'

'What small things?'

'Well, where to start? Probably at the beginning. With Ripley, we had a body and, likely, one killer. The posts on the internet and Ruby Vasquez's involvement complicated things, but were a godsend to our murderer. But I didn't realise this until later. We were so focused on finding the murderer by making the connection with the victim, we never looked at the greater meaning of the crimes.'

'Which was what?'

'It was never about the victims and the different killers, but a mission to get others to do Hashtag's work for them.'

She shook her head. 'That doesn't make sense, Jen.'

'Yes it does, Alice. Our Hashtag Killer is one person, but it's likely four different people attacked our victims. That's what I mentioned to you and the rest of the team. The thing is, Hashtag wasn't interested in the victims, but what their deaths would achieve.'

'They wanted revenge?'

'It was more than that. Their aim was to spread a disease through the rest of the population using the internet and social media. And they got lucky with Ruby Vasquez being there at the first murder to disseminate their message and to become their patsy, or at least for the father to be the fall guy.'

She poured herself another drink. 'This must be going to my head because I'm confused now.'

'Someone orchestrated the whole thing, planned it for months, maybe years in advance. They chose their victims and matched them up to a willing group of killers. It's genius when you think about it.'

'How would they do that?'

'The potential victim list would be easy to compile, especially if you had access to a relevant computer database. Gathering the right people prepared to commit murder would be far more of a challenge.'

Alice sipped at her glass. 'That sounds risky.'

I wet my lips and puffed out my cheeks. 'There would have been a huge risk involved, but our perpetrator was driven to do it. It took me an age to realise what drove them, but when I did, the rest clicked into place.'

'How would they find these people?'

'They searched for kindred spirits, individuals who'd suffered as they had. And one thing about the internet is if you look hard enough in the right places, you'll discover like-minded people. And they planned this for a long time.'

'Where would you find people willing to kill like that?'

'I'm guessing they spent time, maybe years, joining online websites dedicated to victims of violence or relatives of victims of violence and cultivated their potential killers there.'

'They groomed them?'

'That was the risky part, and probably why they're stopping now after these four attacks have achieved what they ultimately wanted.'

'You still haven't told me what that is.'

'It took me a while to figure it out. The whole point of these murders, of creating the persona of the Hashtag Killer, was to get others to do the same, to inspire an army of copycats to do what they can't.'

'Copycats?'

Now I was getting to the good part. 'Do you remember when we spoke about serial killers being formed by some early childhood trauma? This is what happened with Hashtag. But they couldn't deal with the individual responsible for their pain, so they used a group of people to punish proxies for those who caused them agony. Someone had to suffer to make them feel better.'

She appeared to be warming to my theory. 'This is what Ruby Vasquez did, with her father, at the same time as building up her reputation as an internet journalist. She has the computer skills to have done all this. And she got her old man to help with the murders. He killed Ripley, Thomas, and Maxwell, and then she attacked the footballer.'

'So what happened in the factory?'

Alice shrugged her shoulders. 'Maybe they fell out, or it was all a ploy to sell their little scheme even more to the masses.'

'Or they were set up by the real killer.'

'No offence, Jen, but that sounds like a stretch.'

'Well, you would say that, Alice, since you're the one behind all this.'

A chill seeped through the room. She held up her glass again.

'Nice joke, Jen. You nearly got me going there.'

I stared straight at her. 'You're the Hashtag Killer, Alice.'

Her smile covered the width of her face. 'This isn't making any sense, Jen.'

I picked up the Australian newspaper at my feet. The pages had been left open somewhere before the middle, and I scanned down to the story of a missing girl. I placed it near me on the sofa.

'The first thing which gave it away was when you mentioned you weren't aware juvenile records aren't sealed in the UK. Someone in your position should have known that.'

She drank half of her champagne. 'I'm not sure what you're getting at, Jen. I only moved here when I was eight. I must have missed a lot of what most Brits were used to.'

'Ah yes, your early years in Australia.' I leant forward. 'I thought we'd grown close recently, Alice, especially when you helped me with Abbey. I thought we were friends.'

'That's what I assumed, Jen.'

'So why didn't you tell me you had a twin sister?'

Her face visibly sank, her eyes shrinking into her cheeks. 'What?'

'If we were becoming such great friends, why didn't you

tell me you had a twin sister who disappeared when you lived in Australia? You were both seven years old, isn't that right?'

Alice got out of the chair and strode across the room. She'd lost the confidence and effervescence of earlier.

'How do you know this?'

I finally took a drink from the glass. The bubbles ran up my nose and down my throat.

'I knew whoever was behind this had to be a computer expert, which is why Ruby Vasquez's skills blinded me to what was right in front of me. But I couldn't figure out the trauma driving our killer. The clues were there the first time I came here, but I was too distracted to see them. I had to answer the question of who would want to create an army of vigilante copycat killers and why.'

'And you believe that's me?'

'I hoped not. I hoped the disappearance of your twin sister in Australia hadn't traumatised you enough to plan a campaign of revenge by proxy in this country. But then it all added up.'

'You're clutching at straws, Jen. The problems with Abbey may have tipped you over the edge.'

'Ironically, it's the help you gave me with Abbey which showed me how skilled you are with manipulating digital data. You had access to police files and Ruby's personal information. It was easy to drag her into your grand plan and set her father up as the fall guy.'

She came and stood opposite me. There was no fear in her eyes. 'Why would you consider something so outrageous, Jen?'

'I wanted to buy you a gift, to say thanks for what you did for Abbey and me, but I couldn't think what to get you. Abbey said we should check your Facebook page to see what you like. I didn't know she'd sent you a friend's request, and you'd accepted. That was your first mistake.

'I found out you liked Nick Cave and Kylie Minogue, read the books of Lee Child and Philip Pullman, and watched Marvel movies and film noir. There were plenty of ideas there for a present, but I didn't realise how addictive it is peering into someone else's life online. Even the simplest things can send you scurrying into corners you never thought you would.'

'You spied on me?'

'How is it spying if you willingly put parts of you out there for everyone to see?' She didn't reply. 'Do you know which post of yours set me on your trail?'

She pushed the glass into her chest. 'Always in my heart.'

'Yes, that's the one. I thought it would be a love affair gone wrong, a broken relationship you still yearned for.' Laughter slipped from my lips. 'How quickly we can become obsessed with other people's lives. But I couldn't find any more information about that on your Facebook page, so I did a general Google search on you. There wasn't much; I found your Instagram, Twitter and LinkedIn accounts, but nothing was forthcoming there. I even located some comments you made at a cybercrime conference two years ago. Ready to give up, I added the word Australia to the search criteria and pages came back containing you, your parents, and your twin sister.'

I stopped talking, waiting for a response from her. She was calmer than I expected.

'You shouldn't have done that, Jen.'

'Maybe, but once you start on these things, it's hard to stop.' I leant forward. 'I can't imagine what it must have been like for you to lose a twin sister; seven years old, and she disappears into thin air. She wasn't the only one, though, was she? Six young girls in total vanished over two years. The police suspected a serial killer, but had no clues. A year later, your parents returned to England and you came here for the first time.' Darkness consumed her face. 'Is that when it started, this plan of yours to punish others for what happened to your sister?'

The fury burnt in her eyes for a second before disappearing. 'The stress of Abbey's situation has affected your mind, Jen. You need to get professional help.'

'*Always in my heart.* You posted that on the second of May, the date of your sister's birthday. The day of Evan Ripley's murder, and the day the Hashtag Killer was born.'

She took a long drink. 'I'm worried about you, Jen.'

'Were four attacks enough for you, sufficient to spread your infection through the internet and create an army of copycats for your vengeance? Did you put in your transfer request because your work here is done, or are you running away because you knew I'd catch up with you eventually?'

Her breath came out in steady bursts. 'This isn't good for Abbey, Jen. You're becoming unhinged.'

'You got lucky with Ruby Vasquez, the fact she was at the first murder and posted about it. You latched onto her online, got lucky again with her criminal father, and let her run with your narrative. Sending him the photos was an added touch.'

Alice finished her drink and rose. 'It's time for you to leave.'

I picked up the Australian newspaper, glancing at the story of the missing girl in Adelaide. I threw it onto the table in front of her.

'You kept checking back home to see if anything had emerged about your sister's disappearance, but it never has.'

'Are you expecting a confession, Jen? Do you have a microphone underneath your jacket?' She grinned at me.

'Have you wiped everything from your computers, Alice? I don't believe you have. I think you're that arrogant you'll have kept your database of contacts, of those people you manipulated into committing your crimes so you can use it again somewhere else.'

Alice came over and leant into my face. 'I was about to do a bit of spring cleaning on all my digital devices, to prepare them for the move. It makes them lighter, you know.' She stepped away from me and smirked. 'It doesn't take long, will probably be done by the time you leave here and get back to the station. Give my best to Jack.'

I removed the paper from my jacket as the first thump came from upstairs. Alice glanced up, and then at me. I put the warrant on the table, face up so she could see it.

'You've mistaken me for someone unprepared, Alice. There are officers in the house, collecting your computers as we speak.' A look of horror crept across her face. 'I'm surprised they've stayed this quiet while I've kept you talking.' I straightened the corner of the warrant. 'Though I guess I'm the one who's done most of the talking.'

41 SWEET BIRD OF TRUTH

The white hurt my eyes when I opened them. I guessed instantly I was inside a hospital from the smell of powerful disinfectant mixed in with the pungent aroma of inedible food.

'You'll be great when the morphine kicks in, but feel terrible when they ween you off it.' I blinked and stared at Detective Inspector Flowers. 'The good news is you won't turn into a junkie. People have this strange belief one little drop of strong medicine will transform them into a character from *Trainspotting*. Plenty of folks are given hard drugs in hospitals, but they won't come out as addicts. You don't see many grannies with new hips searching for drug dealers once they've been discharged from the hospital, do you?'

Words failed me. A warm glow flowed through my veins as she continued.

'Apparently, addiction is a reaction to your environment. There have been legitimate academic studies on this. They don't even call it an addiction. They call it bonding. It's a connection.'

Flowers stopped talking and waited for my response. I was passive, enjoying the painkillers as my bloodstream gorged on them.

'They're certainly bonding with me now.'

The detective grinned as she spoke.

'Humans have a natural desire to bond, and when we're happy and healthy, we'll bond and connect, but if we can't do that, because we're distressed or isolated or frazzled, we'll bond with something else to ease the pressure on us. Now, that might be gambling, it could be pornography or cocaine, maybe a football team, it could be the oeuvre of Stephen King or the Beatles, but we'll bond and connect with something because that's our nature. That's what we want as human beings.'

My eyes felt like huge saucers trying to crawl from my skull. 'You sound like you know what you're talking about.'

'I've been trying to connect with my daughter, Abigail, for all her life. Ironically, it took the unwanted attention of an internet groomer to create that bond between mother and daughter. That struggle between child and parent is, I'm guessing, something you understand only too well.'

I tried to push up from the bed, but my hand wouldn't work correctly. I grimaced and attempted to flex my fingers, but something was wrong. Flowers took hold of my arm.

'Here, let me help you with that.' The policewoman lifted me with surprising gentleness. 'Though it's not all good news, I'm afraid.'

I raised my arm and saw the two fingers which should have been next to my thumb were now painful-looking stumps.

'His first shot ricocheted off your bones and went wide. You got lucky with that one. Not so much the second.' She handed me a mirror. I used my good hand to hold it to my face. I gasped at the space where my hair should have been and the scar on my skull.

'Your hair will grow back, but I like that style where it's long on one side and short on the other. It's very eighties. The scars from the operation might not heal, though.'

I took the remaining fingers on my damaged hand and ran them over the injury. It reminded me of a tortoise we used to have in school.

'He tried to kill me.' It was a statement, not a question.

'He tried to kill you twice. We got there as he prepared to do it for the third time.'

'You saved my life?'

Flowers shrugged. 'It's all part of the job.'

'What happened to my mother?'

'She had treatment for the rope burns on her neck, but was sent home after that. She's visited you every day since. It's been more than a week.'

Chemical-induced joy floated through me, but it wasn't the only thing making me happy.

'And what about him? What about my father?'

Flowers sucked air into her lungs and peered at me as her eyes narrowed; I think I knew what she'd say before she did.

'Your father is dead, Ruby. He shot himself in his struggle with me.'

I relaxed into the bed, a lifetime of pressure seeping out of me. 'Will you get into trouble for that?'

The detective reached up to her lips as if she was searching for a cigarette before realising there was nothing there.

'I should be okay, and you helped me with that.'

'How so?'

'Having the camera inside your jacket was clever. I'm

not sure if broadcasting it live through your YouTube channel was a good idea, though it showed everything which happened with your father, including the fatal shooting.'

'It was him all along? He was the Hashtag Vigilante?'

Flowers peered at me with a curious look on her face.

'The murderer tried to make us think that, but no, it wasn't your father.' Darkness engulfed her eyes. 'The Hashtag Killer is a police officer, though they didn't do the deeds themselves, instead manipulating others into committing the crimes.'

'How is that possible?'

'From the evidence we've gathered, she spent years infiltrating online forums for victims of crime. She charmed people, lied to them, prepared them, and convinced them they'd only move on in life if they could dish out their own type of justice, even if it were to strangers. I don't think many of them needed too much encouragement.'

'Oh God.' My damaged hand grasped at my face. 'And it was a woman?'

'Yes. One of our cybercrime officers. Her lawyers will no doubt state she can't be charged with murder since she didn't get her hands dirty and manipulated others into committing those acts, but that defence never worked for Charles Manson, so I can't see it working here. We've had no luck tracking the people she used, but we'll find them eventually.'

I settled back into the bed. 'They manipulated me.' They both did, this cybercrime officer and my father. Rage battled against the euphoria inside me and the drugs won.

Flowers leant to my side and picked up a bag. 'I wouldn't beat yourself up over it too much. You weren't the only one she deceived.' She lifted a laptop from the carrier.

'We've finished with this so I thought you might want it to pass the time while you're cooped up in here. You've got a lot of fan-mail to catch up on.'

I ran my good hand over the familiar machine. 'Fan-mail?'

'Your live video sent your existing online profile into the stratosphere. Two other things then made you the most talked about person in the country.'

'What things?'

Flowers reached back into the bag. 'I'm sorry about this, Ruby, but we did a thorough search of your house.' She handed me the diaries. 'I can only apologise to you, but...'

'They ended up online, didn't they?' I knew it to be true from the look in her eyes.

Flowers nodded. 'Parts of them have, yes. But these haven't.'

She gave me another set of notebooks, ones I didn't recognise.

'Nobody's read these but me,' Flowers said. 'We didn't take them into the investigation with the other things from your house because they weren't relevant.' She turned to leave. 'I hope you enjoy your reading.'

As she left, I turned over the page of the first book and stared at my mother's handwriting.

'WATCH OUT FOR THE GEESE. They pack a big bite if you get too close.' I smiled as Abigail threw bread-crumbs at the hungry birds. I crossed my legs as she gave up on the ducks and returned to the digital glare of the phone.

'They look friendly, but looks can be deceiving.' I

turned to observe my partner approaching. He nodded at Abs. 'How is she?'

'Since the incident on the train tracks, she's been top of all her classes and one of the most popular kids at school, but I can't help thinking there'll be emotional damage to come at some point. Something like that has to scar you emotionally, surely?'

'She's a strong kid, and she'll tell you if that happens. Plus, I'm sure the second-best detective in the city will spot anything wrong in her own home.'

I shook my head and laughed at him. 'Okay, Mister Best Detective in the City.' When he sat next to me on the grass, I was shocked he was unworried about the potential for grass stains on his expensive trousers. The crisscross of lines on his face was noticeably worse than it had been a few days ago. There was weariness about him I hadn't seen before. 'Are you okay, Jack?'

He brushed a stray leaf off his knee and stared at me. 'I can't get over what happened with Alice.'

I shrugged my shoulders. 'She's a troubled woman, and she's kicked up a load of consequences which we have no control over, and that's bugging me.'

His body slumped as he pulled his knees up to his chest. It was a curious pose, like a little boy lost in a larger world.

'What's bugging you?'

'Well, first, not everybody wanted us to catch her, so there's an ongoing online backlash. Then there are the copycats who aren't dwindling in numbers. Plus, we still haven't found all the people she manipulated into committing those crimes.'

Jack snatched a daisy from the ground and ran it through his fingers. 'Let's just be glad for what we have, partner.'

I smiled at him and looked over at Abigail as she fed the birds.

IT WAS another week before the doctors released me from the hospital. I'd stayed in isolation, refusing all requests for contact and communication. Flowers was right: I'd become the most talked-about person in the country. The offers continued to flood in: book deals, syndicated columns, TV appearances, magazine covers, movie projects, interviews; even slots on reality programmes. They could all wait. I had something more important to deal with.

I put the key in the lock and opened the door. The first thing I noticed was the smell: the place didn't stink anymore. The mouldy aroma had disappeared, replaced with fresh lemon spray. I walked into the living room to an even bigger shock: the house was cleared of all its rubbish and was cleaner than a showroom.

'I wanted to make sure everything was right for your return.'

Mother's appearance amazed me. She'd washed her hair and had it cut into a stylish bob. Her clothes were immaculate and pressed. She didn't seem ten years older than she was anymore.

'You look good, Mother.'

'It's time for a fresh start, Ruby.'

I took her arm and we sat next to each other on the magazine-free sofa.

'Okay, Mother, but we need to talk about something first.' I removed the notebook and opened it at the first page. 'Tell me about Annie.'

ABOUT THE AUTHOR

Andrew French lives amongst faded seaside glamour on the North East coast of England. He likes gin and cats but not together, new music and old movies, curry and ice cream. Slow bike rides and long walks to the pub are his usual exercise, as well as flicking through the pages of good books and the memoirs of bad people.

Find out more at www.andrewsfrench.com

Facebook:

https://www.facebook.com/A-S-French-Author-150145625006018

Twitter:

www.twitter.com/andrewfrench100

Instagram:

www.instagram.com/andrewfrench100

And replies to all his email at mail@andrewsfrench.com

If you have the time, please leave a review at Amazon or Goodreads

Thank you!

ALSO BY A. S. FRENCH

The Detective Jen Flowers series.

Go to www.andrewsfrench.com for more information on the next books in the series.

Book two - Serial Killer.

Book three - Night Killer.

ACKNOWLEDGMENTS

Many thanks to my wonderful wife for all her support and patience.

The Hashtag Killer was edited by Alison Jack.

Cover design by James, GoOnWrite.com